MURDER IN SEASON

Also by Mary Winters

The Lady of Letters mysteries

MURDER IN POSTSCRIPT
MURDER IN MASQUERADE

MURDER IN SEASON

Mary Winters

SEVERN
HOUSE

First world edition published in Great Britain and the USA in 2024
by Severn House, an imprint of Canongate Books Ltd,
14 High Street, Edinburgh EH1 1TE.

severnhouse.com

British Library Cataloguing-in-Publication Data
A CIP catalogue record for this title is available from the British Library.

ISBN-13: 978-1-4483-1404-1 (cased)
ISBN-13: 978-1-4483-1405-8 (e-book)

All Severn House titles are printed on acid-free paper.

MIX
Paper | Supporting
responsible forestry
FSC® C013056

Typeset by Palimpsest Book Production Ltd.,
Falkirk, Stirlingshire, Scotland.
Printed and bound in Great Britain by TJ Books,
Padstow, Cornwall.

Praise for the Lady of Letters mysteries

"Charming characters, a touch of romance, and an unexpected denouement"
Kirkus Reviews on *Murder in Masquerade*

"The follow-up to *Murder in Postscript* emphasizes Victorian social customs and society. Fans of Dianne Freeman's 'Countess of Harleigh' mysteries will enjoy"
Library Journal on *Murder in Masquerade*

"[A] refreshing libation of mystery, wit, and Victorian society, with a twist of romance"
Dianne Freeman, Agatha Award-winning author, on *Murder in Masquerade*

"A delightful character-driven historical mystery for fans of Katharine Schellman or Dianne Freeman"
Library Journal Starred Review of *Murder in Postscript*

"A very special and original Victorian era cozy mystery set in 1860 . . . a highly recommended and fun read for all dedicated mystery fans"
Midwest Book Review on *Murder in Postscript*

"Move over, *Bridgerton*! This delightful Regency-style romp features a spunky agony aunt and an intriguing gentleman."
Rhys Bowen, *New York Times* bestselling author, on *Murder in Postscript*

About the author

Mary Winters is the Edgar-nominated author of the Lady of Letters historical mystery series, two cozy mystery series, and several short stories. A longtime reader of historical fiction, Mary set her latest work in Victorian England after being inspired by a trip to London. Since then, she's been busily planning her next mystery – and another trip! Find out more about Mary and her writing, reading and teaching at

www.marywintersauthor.com

For my husband, Quintin, with all my love

ONE

London, England
1860

> *Dear Lady Agony,*
> *Is it ever acceptable to raise one's voice in public? I was in the park yesterday when I heard a governess yell at her charge in such a way that even the geese sought cover. What possible reason could a young lady have to talk to a child in that manner? Governesses must teach, not screech. Please inform your readers.*
> *Devotedly,*
> *Keep It Quiet*

> *Dear Keep It Quiet,*
> *What reasons could a governess have to talk to a child in such a manner? Plenty. Perhaps the child was standing too close to the pond's edge. Maybe the child wandered on to a busy footpath. The child might have thought to pull a prank on unsuspecting you, and the governess prevented action at just that precipitous moment. I could list a dozen more, but I think three is sufficient to demonstrate your insufficiencies with children. The one who might need to keep quiet about such matters is, ahem, you.*
> *Yours in Secret,*
> *Lady Agony*

The Regent's Park was beautiful on Sundays, and still more beautiful today because Amelia Amesbury had her family with her. Finished with their picnic lunch, Aunt Tabitha and Winifred stood near a towering willow tree, its long branches switching in the breeze. Amelia watched the pair with what must have been a ridiculously large smile on her face as Tabitha pointed out a gray heron to Winifred. The girl bent down, a slip of summer sunshine covering her head like a crown. Her blue eyes, the color of Amelia's favorite French china pattern, narrowed as she examined the bird – which had no idea of their proximity – more carefully.

Tabitha's eyes were the same light blue, the color of all the Amesburys' eyes – except Amelia, of course, who was an Amesbury by marriage, not birth. Her eyes were caramel brown like the streaks in her auburn hair. That wasn't the only difference, mind you. Her skin was warmer, her stature shorter, her hips fuller. And those were only the physical differences.

Amelia had met Edgar, Tabitha's nephew, during his stay at the Feathered Nest, her family's inn, in Mells. It wasn't until after she agreed to marry him that he told her he was an earl from one of the wealthiest families in London. Amelia's father assured her that Edgar's wealth would be an asset in finding a cure for the ailment that had already taken hold of him. But wealth held no power over his illness, which overcame him just two months after their marriage. Tabitha, his sole surviving relative besides Winifred, his ten-year-old niece, had comforted Amelia by telling her their marriage had allowed him to pass peacefully, and that thought brought her comfort in the darkest days.

And so did Tabitha and Winifred. All the differences in the world couldn't change their love for one another. They had weathered the tragedy together, and the difficulty had brought them as close as three people could be. With time, Amelia realized Tabitha was resolute but kind, and Winifred was young but resilient. Their family possessed a bond that couldn't be broken, and the strongest force on earth could not pull her away from this special moment.

At least, that's what she thought.

Then she heard a thump behind her, a voice cry out, and a rock sail past her ear. Reflexively, she ducked.

The rock continued past the gray heron and sent it scurrying in a new direction. Gripping her cane, Tabitha stumbled backward, and Winifred, with no such aid, fell on her rear.

'Beastly rock! I've fallen and torn my glove.'

Amelia froze. She could've sworn it was the voice of her younger sister Margaret that pierced the fine summer air. But she couldn't be in London on a Sunday afternoon. Her family rarely left Mells, especially on a busy travel day. And yet . . .

'Margaret Ann, *hush*.'

Amelia spun around to see her sister dusting off a brown traveling dress with a knotted ribbon that might have been a bow several hours before. She was a grown woman of eighteen, but Amelia would have recognized the playmate from her childhood anywhere. The freckles across the bridge of her nose were emphasized by the pinkness of her cheeks, and although her hair, more red than brown, was plaited at the nape of her neck, several strands had fallen around her shoulders. Their mother, also in a traveling dress, but much neater, stood beside her, with an admonishing look at the torn glove.

Amelia ran toward them, not knowing which one to hug first. She grabbed Margaret because she was closer. 'Madge! Mama! What are you doing here?'

'It's a long story,' Madge replied into her shoulder. 'And not a happy one.'

Amelia pulled back, searching her eyes, which were every bit as stunning as she remembered – not quite brown, not quite hazel, but a light mix of the two colors that had the power to hypnotize. They hinted at an unhappy secret, and Amelia decided she would inquire about *that* later.

She turned to her mother, who was as put together as Madge was slapdash. Veronica Scott's wide-sleeved paletot was green, and her hat was adorned with a corresponding green ribbon. A ruffle at her neck drew attention to her pretty heart-shaped face – neither young nor old but a steadfast age that, despite cheerfulness, spoke of a certain strength. 'How good to see you!' Amelia hugged her tight.

'We didn't mean to surprise you.' Veronica Scott lowered her voice. 'You know what Madge's temper is. I hope now is a good time.'

'Of course it is,' Amelia insisted. Tabitha cleared her throat, and Amelia gave her mother a final squeeze. For a moment, she'd forgotten where she was – and with whom. 'This is Lady Tabitha, Edgar's aunt, and Lady Winifred, his dear niece. May I introduce my mother, Veronica Scott, and my sister Mad— Margaret.'

'The rock-thrower, I presume.'

Her mother was startled, and Amelia understood why. Tabitha's voice was not as one expected. In her early seventies, Tabitha was tall, with a neck like a swan's and a visage as shapely as that of an Athenian statue. But her voice had a timbre and even a particular grit that did not enter most of high society's conversations. Almost everything she said could be taken as a challenge, and most times Amelia did.

'I'm sincerely sorry, Lady Tabitha,' Mrs Scott apologized.

Winifred joined the conversation with her usual enthusiasm. 'How strong you are, Miss Scott!'

Madge tipped her square chin pridefully. Whenever she was complimented on her workmanship, she donned the same look. She was a skilled builder, and if the inn required a repair and their father was occupied, the family relied on Madge's technical know-how. If she didn't know how to fix something, she would figure it out – or throw it against the wall. 'I suppose I am. Thank you, Lady Winifred.' She stuck out an ungloved hand. 'Amelia has written so much about you. I feel as if I know you already.'

'I feel the same.' Winifred took the hand and shook it emphatically, her eyes widening with interest at the young – and strong – woman before her. 'I'm glad to meet you in person.'

Madge smiled. 'The pleasure is all mine.'

'Let's continue our conversation at the house.' Tabitha pointed her cane at their carriage, which waited nearby. 'The sun is growing too warm to linger.'

Amelia gathered the picnic basket and blanket, casting a wistful glance back at the surroundings that moments ago had been peaceful and predictable. Somewhere near the boardwalk, a band played, and she strained to identify the soft refrain. If she visited the park next spring, the same band would be playing, the same nurses pushing prams with charges a year older. The knowledge brought with it comfort and tranquility. Now, however, comfort and tranquility were far from her mind.

Industrious and cheerful would better describe her family and their lives. They owned an inn in Mells, which was a popular stop for travelers on their way to London. From the time they were young, all four daughters were involved in the business. It wasn't so much a business, though, as a way of life – and a good one at that. Amelia and her sisters never felt the drudgery of the work. Their parents had the unique view that in serving others, they served each other, and as improbable as it seemed as a young girl, as an adult, Amelia understood how true the belief had been. Their days revolved around home and hearth, food and drink, music and entertainment. She wouldn't have changed her childhood for all the jewels in the queen's crown.

Now the memories were back – and so was her family. Seeing her mother and sister again was like opening a window after a long, dull winter. It was a remembrance of spring and the beauty and joy the season brought with it. The freckles on Madge's face reminded her of seeds and the promise of flowers, and her mother's hands recalled to her warm winds and the anticipation of long summer days. Being with them was like that, and Amelia basked in the feeling for a moment. Then the moment was gone, and they were walking away from the park.

'I assume you'll be able to join us for dinner?' Tabitha asked, her cane making tracks to the carriage.

'Oh, yes, Miss— Lady Tabitha.' Madge nodded. 'We'll be joining you for dinner. In fact, I'll be joining you for the entire season, if you'll have me.'

TWO

Dear Lady Agony,

I have a friend who is blind to her faults when making polite conversation, and no matter how hard I hint at them, I cannot get her to take a suggestion. I would list them here but understand the confinements of space. She is devoted to your column and will follow your instructions if you provide them.

Sincerely,

A Friend with an Ear to Bend

Dear A Friend with an Ear to Bend,

Conversation. Nothing should be easier, yet how many letters do I receive about the harm it's done to someone? Too many words, not enough words, misspoken words. It boggles the mind, but these words of advice will not.

1. Do not pummel your conversation with questions, compliments or disagreements. 2. Do not jump into a conversation only to assault a topic. 3. For the love of all that is holy, do not interrupt. 4. Be alert, and listen to what is being said. In some situations, silence is your best answer. Do not be afraid to employ it.

Yours in Secret,

Lady Agony

To say the carriage ride home was uncomfortable would be an understatement. For Amelia, anyway. Madge was as comfortable as a caterpillar in a cocoon. Despite their ten-year age difference, she and Winifred talked like long-lost sisters, jesting and giggling. Amelia's mother, who had four daughters, was impervious to any discomfort – or awkwardness. She'd heard it all before. If one paid attention to everything that Madge said, it would have been a very tiresome eighteen years indeed. Truth be told, Veronica Scott loved three things unconditionally: her work, her home and her family. Little could be done to change her estimation of them, especially a single word.

But between Amelia and Tabitha, the word *season* sat like a lighted stick of dynamite. Amelia lowered her gaze at Madge. *Whatever did she mean by it?* The London season stretched from May until August, giving young people a few precious months to find spouses at balls, concerts and soirees. Madge was the last person interested in courting, and the Scott family had never participated in a season. For one, the Feathered Nest kept them too busy. For another, they didn't know anyone in London except Grady Armstrong, Amelia's childhood friend and editor at the penny weekly. And he certainly didn't partake in the festivities.

But Amelia did live in London and was officially out of mourning now. She had written to her mother a month ago with the good news. Perhaps that was the impetus for their unexpected arrival. Still, it was hard to believe Madge would want anything to do with London this time of year. She was plain, practical and, to be honest, a bit of a tomboy. She would scorn most of the activities that went into making the season. Her favorite pastime was working alone in the shed. She was fascinated by mechanics and spent hours taking things apart.

And yet . . .

Madge seemed to be enjoying herself a good deal. She pressed her face closer to the carriage window as they arrived at the house, her eyes the color of toasted hazelnuts. Since she was little, she loved learning about new contraptions and places. It looked as if Amesbury Manor was now one of those places.

'Wait until I show you the garden.' Winifred's voice trilled with excitement. 'It has a maze.'

'A *maze*,' repeated Madge.

'Allow them time to freshen up from their travels, Winifred,' Amelia said. 'They must be exhausted.'

'Not at all.' Madge grabbed the door handle as the carriage came to a stop and the steps were placed. 'I want to see it straightaway. Come along, Winifred.'

'The footman will assist—' started Amelia, but it was too late. Madge was halfway up the path, Winifred close on her heels.

Amelia's mother followed Tabitha, politely taking the footman's hand. 'Margaret's enthusiasm could never be contained. She's been that way since the day she was born, I'm afraid. Never one to wait for anyone or anything.'

To put it mildly. As her older sister, Amelia thought Madge a wee bit spoiled, but her temperament didn't help, either. She was impetuous – acting first, regretting later. All the Scotts had a rash side, certainly, but Madge was the worst, or at least the most physical. She wasn't above throwing whatever was within her reach when she became angry. *As evidenced by the misplaced rock.*

'I, on the other hand, would welcome a rest before dinner.' Her mother's slouched shoulders indicated that she was more than tired; she was exhausted. Amelia wondered if it was travel that had her worn out or something else. 'Would you show me where, dearest?'

'I'd be happy to.' Amelia informed Mrs Tipping, their housekeeper, that they had guests, but she was privy to the fact already. Mother and Madge had arrived immediately after they left for the park and insisted on following them. Mrs Tipping, a brisk, middle-aged woman, who wasn't married but was called missus out of respect, had prepared rooms for them accordingly.

Amelia and her mother conversed easily as they climbed to the third floor, Mrs Addington, Tabitha's maid, close behind them. When they approached the room, Amelia gave her mother's hand a squeeze. It was as soft as Amelia remembered, with a few more wrinkles, smelling of the lavender soap she'd always used. 'If you need anything at all, just ask.'

'I'll tend to her, Lady Amesbury. Don't you worry yourself a bit.' The stout Patty Addington lifted her chin in challenge at Mrs Tipping. Although Mrs Addington wasn't the housekeeper, one wouldn't know it. Like her mistress, she thought it her duty to oversee all of the doings in the Amesbury household.

Mrs Tipping demurred, bobbing a goodbye, her pretty gray cap with a small twist of pink ribbon disappearing down the hallway.

Veronica Scott held Amelia at arm's length as she took her in from head to toe. 'My daughter, Lady Amesbury. How wonderful.' The pride in her voice hung in the hallway as she disappeared into the room, and Amelia smiled, allowing the warm feeling to wash over her as she descended the stairs.

The warm sensation dispersed immediately when she spotted Tabitha waiting for her at the bottom of the steps. 'A moment,' instructed Tabitha. She pointed her cane down the hall. 'In the library.'

Which is to say, she needs a drink. As do I.

The day had been overwhelming. First a surprise visit from her mother and sister, then the possibility of them staying for the season? Amelia switched decanters. *I've earned a spot of the good stuff.* Spanish sherry was what she needed to take the sting out of the pronouncement by her sister.

Amelia paused over a second cordial glass. 'Aunt?'

'Indeed.'

Amelia brought the glasses to the green leather couch, where Tabitha perched at the edge, her cane beside her. Amelia noted it was the one with the large round compass in the handle, a serious cane for serious people such as Tabitha who, like a chess player, was always at least five moves ahead of her opponent.

Amelia supposed she had to be. The last few years had brought with it events that no one could foresee. Edgar had passed over two years ago now, and his end, although quick, was expected. It followed a long, arduous battle with a disease not fully understood. Before that, a shipwreck had taken Edgar's parents and Edgar's brother and sister-in-law, leaving Winifred in Edgar's care. Hence Edgar's desire for a wife. Hence Amelia's place here with Tabitha.

Who looks surly.

Tabitha took the glass and held it to her lips. 'Your mother is a charming woman.'

'Thank you.'

'Your sister is not.' Tabitha tasted the liquor.

'You don't even know her!' Amelia's reply was automatic and defensive, despite the fact that Amelia wouldn't have described her sister as charming in a hundred years. Bullheaded, brave, smart – yes. Charming? Not exactly.

'I don't have to *know* her. I know her type. She's gotten away with too much in her lifetime and has had fun doing it. Thus she will get away with still more.'

'I resent that, Aunt—'

Tabitha held up her hand, a strong hand that had the ability to stop space and time. 'I am not saying I do not like her. I hold a certain amount of respect for women who can get away with anything in the era in which we live.'

Amelia blinked. Tabitha always found new ways to surprise her.

'I'm saying that trouble follows those women wherever they go, and I must wonder if trouble has followed her here.' Her Amesbury eyes narrowed, the gray lashes softening their brilliant blue color. 'Do you know?'

'How would I? They only just arrived.' Amelia drank her sherry, allowing the liquid to warm her from the inside out.

'You had no indication of their coming?'

'Not at all.'

Tabitha's eyes snapped wide. 'Then I am right. Your sister is in trouble, and they've come to you for help.'

Of course Tabitha was right. *She's always right.* The evidence was as clear as the dial on her compass – pointing south. Amelia's family didn't travel, her sister didn't court, and her mother did not make unexpected calls on anyone.

But for a moment, Amelia ignored all that and drank her sherry. She didn't care why they had come. They were here, and that's all that mattered. She'd missed them. She didn't know how dearly until she heard the name *Margaret Ann* resound through the Regent's Park. It reminded her of their favorite childhood game of Sardines, and suddenly she was ten years old again, Madge hiding in the halls of their home, Amelia calling out her name. 'You may be right, Aunt. Madge may be in trouble. If so, I'll help her. Like you, I've never been one to shirk my duties. But with new family members in the house and old sherry in our glasses, can we pretend we don't care?'

'I am not good at pretending.' Tabitha finished the sherry, set down the glass and stood.

How well I know that fact.

Amelia moved to help her, but Tabitha leaned heavily on her cane. 'I'll see you at dinner.'

When she had gone, Amelia went to her desk, where the latest batch of letters to Lady Agony lay in a plain parcel. The agony column was popular because of who she was – a Lady. The peerage wasn't enthused that one of their own had taken up the task of giving advice to the middle and lower classes, the primary readers of the weekly magazine. Yet they themselves were not above asking questions or posing problems when it suited them, which was increasingly more often. Still, they thought it shocking a Lady would condescend to take part in such labor.

The reason she'd taken up the task wasn't shock; it was need, plain and simple. After Edgar's passing, she had needed something to occupy her mind. Winifred kept her busy, and even more so two years before. Edgar's books and library were a pleasure, yes. But she wanted something to call her own, and when Grady approached her with the problem of a disgruntled writer quitting, she eagerly took up the work.

Now that work called, and she sifted through the myriad problems waiting for her: impossible schedules, stifling corsets, meddlesome relatives. Footsteps, probably her sister's, whizzed by the door, followed by a peal of laughter. *No wonder I can relate.* Amelia might be a countess, but she was also very much an outsider in a world where being an insider was what mattered. But here, at her desk, there were no distinctions, titles or rules. Only the work mattered, and with that thought in mind, she happily took up her quill.

Two hours later, the work was finished, and Amelia was enjoying dinner with her family – and extended family. The dining room was one of her favorite rooms in the house. With its high ceiling, warm wainscoting and colorful tapestries, it was certainly one of the most beautiful. But what Amelia liked most of all were the conversations she, Tabitha and Winifred enjoyed around the table. Tabitha appreciated good food, so much that mealtime revealed a side of her not always seen. Her stories were warm and intimate, and she shared details about people and places in the Amesburys' past that made Amelia and Winifred feel privy to the experiences.

But tonight was different. Anticipation hovered like an uninvited guest chewing loudly with his elbows on the table.

The first course was perfection: steamy soup with fresh vegetables from the kitchen garden and light conversation. The second course, however, moved from polite inquiries to real dialogue, and as the last slice of roast pheasant was served, the topic turned to the Scotts' motivation for their excursion to London.

'Of course, the weather's been lovely, and you hardly need a reason to visit your daughter,' Amelia put in as soon as Tabitha inquired. Amelia smiled at her mother across the table, noting her brown hair showed few signs of age. It was swept up in an artful chignon that was done, no doubt, with the help of Mrs Addington. The silver brooch at her neck shone as brightly as the crystal on the table, as did her eyes, which were the shade of blue that Amelia had wished for as a child. But she had taken after her father in that regard, her own eyes as brown as creamed coffee.

Veronica Scott returned the smile. 'I'd love to stay longer, but I'm afraid a week is the longest I can be away from the inn.'

Amelia heard Tabitha's breath release.

'My hope is that Margaret might stay on after I go, however.' Mrs Scott took a sip of her wine, perhaps assessing the table's reaction. 'To enjoy a season, and perhaps meet a gentleman here.'

'Oh, can she? Please?' Winifred begged. 'I'll tell her everything she needs to know.'

If it was hard to say no to Madge, it was twice as hard to say no to Winifred. A little chuckle escaped Amelia's throat. 'And what do you know about gentlemen, may I ask?'

Winifred giggled. 'I mean everything else.'

'The season is well underway.' Tabitha's somber tone cut through the tiny ripples of excitement. 'I don't know if now is the right time to introduce her.'

'Lady Applegate introduced her daughter just this week,' Amelia put in.

Veronica Scott acknowledged Tabitha's resistance with a sincere nod, then turned to Amelia. 'It needn't be formal, only something to . . . increase the quality of people she knows.'

Amelia noted a pang of desperation in her mother's voice. Her mother was tender-hearted, a dreamer who was patient to a fault. It didn't surprise Amelia that she wanted a season for Madge. From the time her daughters were young, she'd filled their heads with stories of love and adventure. But that wasn't the reason she was here. The pitch of her voice indicated another. 'Has something happened, Mama? Back home?'

'Something's happened, all right,' interrupted Madge. 'One of the scallywags in Mells tried to take advantage of me, and I retaliated. They practically ran me out of town for defending myself.'

Amelia felt her jaw tense. 'What? Who? Who hurt you?'

'She wasn't hurt, Amelia.' Veronica checked Madge's declaration with a silencing look. 'It was at the yearly Swansong Festival. She and Charlie were Beatrice and Benedick in *Much Ado About Nothing*, and the gentleman, Charles Atkinson – maybe you know him—'

'He's no gentleman,' added Madge hotly.

'Mr Atkinson became infatuated with his part, or your sister – I really cannot say which – and attempted a kiss. At that point, Madge pinned his arm behind his back, and the next thing I know, Doctor Kappen's being called and the arm's being wrapped for surgery.'

'What happened to Doctor Anderson?' asked Amelia.

'Oh, he's been replaced by a young man,' Veronica said brightly. 'Doctor Anderson doesn't get around as well as he used to. He's in his eighties now.'

'At any rate,' prompted Tabitha.

'Yes, at any rate, Madge is not the most popular young woman in town, and I thought what better place to take her for the summer than to her sister's house.' Veronica Scott smiled as if breaking people's arms was the most normal thing in the whole wide world.

'Oh, quite!' exclaimed Winifred. 'She can hide here, and no one would be the wiser.'

Amelia stifled a cringe. 'Not *hiding*, Winifred.'

'No, not hiding,' Winifred repeated. She tapped her chin, perhaps attempting to appear older and wiser. 'Meeting new people. At a ball, perhaps. A grand ball at our house.'

'What an ingenious girl you have, Amelia.' Veronica Scott beamed at Winifred.

I cannot argue with that statement. And Amelia's best friend Kitty did like to plan parties . . . Amelia glanced at Tabitha, who was clenching her fork too tightly. The wonderful thing about being Lady Amesbury was the perks that went along with the title. She decided what went on in her home and when. The house had been a veritable hermitage for two years. What better time to host a ball than now?

THREE

Dear Lady Agony,

Something dreadful occurred in Mayfair, and I hope you may be able to ferret out the trouble. A week ago, my coral brooch – Italian and expensive – went missing. I thought I misplaced it until a friend reported her diamond bracelet stolen. We live a stone's throw apart, and both occurrences happened at a party. It cannot be a coincidence, can it?

Sincerely,

Burgled by Bandits

Dear Burgled by Bandits,

Once is bad luck; twice is coincidence; thrice is most certainly a bad-addled bandit. I assume Scotland Yard has been summoned and done nothing, hence your letter to me. Rest assured that if the thief acts again, I will notice and take action. Beware, bandit. My eyes are on you.

Yours in Secret,

Lady Agony

A fortnight later, Amelia and her sister Madge were ready for the ball. Almost. *If Madge would stop jerking out hairpins, it would make preparations infinitely easier.*

'It's too tight, Amelia,' grumbled Madge. 'I'll get a headache.'

Patty Addington glowered at the disregarded hairpin on the bed quilt.

Amelia cheerfully picked it up and stuffed it back in Madge's hair, which was spun up in a beautiful fashion, a dazzling gold ribbon weaved intricately through her red tresses, reflecting the stunning color. 'It's not tight. It's snug, which is what you want. With any luck, you'll be dancing every dance tonight.'

'Listen to your sister.' Mrs Addington had lovely almond-shaped eyes and feathery gray-brown eyebrows, but one wouldn't know it by the way they were knitted in determination. If anyone could teach Madge anything, it was Mrs Addington. She'd devoted over twenty years of service to the family, most of which had centered on Tabitha until tragedy struck the family. She'd seen the home go from a seasonal retreat to a full-time household when Edgar passed away. She'd cared for him as she had her own husband, once their butler, when he was struck down by typhoid fever. Tabitha had never forgotten the kindness, and neither had Amelia. Despite Mrs Addington's penchant for tight-lacing, Amelia would make sure she had a home with the Amesburys for as long as she lived.

'Thank you, Mrs Addington. I'll help her with her slippers, and we'll be down directly.'

Mrs Addington left, and as the door shut, Madge stuck out her tongue, reaching for the resecured hairpin.

Amelia snapped her fingers. 'Do not even think about it.'

'When did you become such a stickler?'

'Since hosting a ball for you.' Amelia's voice sounded suspiciously like her eldest sister Penelope's, and she disliked the officious tone. But she had to be stern with Madge. It was the only way she listened. 'You must be on your best behavior.'

'I didn't ask for a ball.' Madge fussed with the neckline of her dress, a beautiful ivory gown with gold and pink satin ribbons at the bodice and hem. The skirt was made of silk organza, with embroidered flowers in the same gold and pink colors. 'And I'd rather have a dress like yours than all this . . .' She lifted her skirt and released it. 'Fluff.'

'That wouldn't be—'

'Appropriate,' Madge said through gritted teeth. 'I know.'

Amelia sympathized. Her own dress was simple but stunning, a deep purple frock that looked almost black. It had the tiniest bit of lace at its sleeves, which matched her gloves, and a beautiful neckline that hit between dashing and demure. Not appropriate for a young woman of Madge's age.

Amelia took up her sister's hands. 'You're going to have a wonderful time. I promise. All this business with Charles Atkinson will be forgotten, and you'll be able to enjoy yourself. Trust me. London is an extraordinary place.'

'If you say so.'

'Would you rather I put you back on the train with Mama to face the wrath of Mells?'

Madge wrinkled her freckled nose. 'Hardly. I wish Mama could have stayed, though.'

Amelia squeezed her hands before releasing them to fetch the slippers. 'I do as well, but you know how she feels about the Feathered Nest. Even with Penelope's capable assistance, she doesn't feel comfortable being away. I'm grateful she stayed as long as she did.' Which was one glorious week. Walking, talking and tea had been the object of their days. They spent their evenings playing cards and charades with Winifred and listening to her perform at the pianoforte. The Scott family loved music, and Amelia's mother fell in love with Winifred those evenings by the instrument. By the time Veronica Scott departed, Winifred thought of her as a surrogate grandmother, kissing her on the cheek before she left. Amelia promised they would visit Mells soon. Her mother promised Winifred she would be waiting – with candy.

Amelia held out the heeled satin shoes to Madge.

Madge squinted at the square toes and pink rosettes. 'I'm supposed to dance in these?'

'For hours.' Amelia grinned. 'Five at least.'

Madge playfully swatted her arm before donning the footwear.

After a final look at her sister, Amelia led the way down the stairs. Margaret Scott was ready for London; the question remained whether London was ready for Margaret Scott.

The house was certainly ready. Her dear friend Kitty – along with Tabitha – had made sure of that. *If one is going to host a ball, one had better do it right.* That was Tabitha's reasoning. She had no choice but to assist in everything from flowers to food to music, and Amesbury Manor was as regal as it had ever been, with royal red roses and ivory candles artfully placed throughout the house. Amelia spotted gold accents in the floral arrangements, dining tables and even Madge's hair. No detail had been overlooked. No expense spared. Tabitha might be upset about Margaret's extended visit, but no one would know it by the effort she had put into the evening.

The woman herself was waiting for them at the bottom of the

stairs, and in a pale mauve gown, she was elegance incarnate. Tabitha rarely wore colors of note, out of deep sympathy for Edgar, and Amelia's breath caught when she noticed the difference. She looked younger and less stern. A pink rose peeked out of her silver hair, and her swan's neck was adorned with a petite string of pearls.

But the grip on her gold-handled cane was one that men would envy. How strong she had been and for so long. She had put aside her own desires for the sake of the family. Amelia could see that now. When the Amesburys suffered back-to-back tragedies, she dismissed her own future as easily as a servant stealing silverware. A little of herself returned now, and Amelia was glad.

'Aunt, you are stunning.'

Tabitha acknowledged the compliment with a brief nod. 'I trust you got Winifred to bed.'

'Barely,' Amelia admitted. 'I had to promise her custard tomorrow.'

'You know I disagree with bribes.'

Yes, Amelia knew that, but she also knew what worked with ten-year-old children: bribes.

Tabitha circled Madge. 'You look handsome. When you're not fussing, you're quite pretty, Miss Scott.'

Madge opened her mouth, looked at Amelia and reconsidered. She dipped her head in an elegant nod. 'Thank you, Lady Tabitha.'

The knocker signaled the arrival of guests, and Amelia smiled reassuringly at her sister. Margaret straightened her shoulders as if facing an army of street thugs instead of London's elite.

Society descended in a flurry of ruffles, feathers and furs, eager to see the elusive countess's sister. They hardly knew Amelia, and they didn't know anything of her family members. Now they had a chance to plumb one of the oldest and wealthiest families in London, and some were as keen as vultures descending on prey.

Amelia was more nervous than she admitted and was relieved when Kitty Hamsted and her husband, Oliver, arrived. Kitty had been the first to welcome her when she moved to Mayfair, and they became fast friends. She was the only one who knew of Edgar's struggles at the end of his illness, which came and left quickly, like a thief in the night. She forced Amelia and Tabitha to take much-needed breaks while she watched over him. In those days, Amelia learned she could trust Kitty implicitly, and later, when Amelia took up her work at the magazine, she told Kitty about her secret pseudonym.

Kitty had covered her mouth to keep from shouting, jumping up and down until she broke the heel of a congress boot. Then she hugged Amelia tight, begging to let her help with the column. At first, Amelia didn't see how or when she'd need her assistance. But the column grew in popularity and correspondents' needs with it. Understaffed seamstresses, underpaid tailors, abhorrent working conditions in factories – all these Amelia and Kitty investigated together. Amelia had never had a friend like her, and to see her now, her cheeks matching her rose moiré silk gown, brought Amelia much encouragement.

'Breathtaking!' Kitty exclaimed, her blonde curls quivering with excitement. 'You, your sister – the house.'

'Lady Amesbury,' said Oliver, who sported regal black evening attire with a large wrinkle on his waistcoat, probably from perusing a scholarly tome while waiting on Kitty. His omnipresent glasses were gone, and Amelia was surprised to notice his eyes were the color of Belgian chocolate. Although they'd known each other over two years, she rarely saw him unoccupied or without his spectacles. His plain brown hair, too, was parted nicely, and Amelia surmised Kitty forced him to pay close attention to his appearance since it was Amelia's first ball. A bubble of appreciation swelled in her chest.

'Good evening,' Amelia returned with a smile. 'It's so good to see you both.'

Oliver helped Kitty with her wrap, and as she twirled out of it, she whispered, 'How is Margaret?'

'Fine, but it's only been half an hour.'

'Lady Tabitha is stuck to her side, it would seem,' Kitty continued. 'Thank you, dearest.'

Oliver gave her a lopsided grin before whisking away the article to the cloakroom, not waiting for the footman. He was so in love with Kitty that the simplest endearment turned him to butter. It would be revolting if it wasn't so adorable.

'Tabitha's determined to keep her out of trouble,' said Amelia. 'So far, it's worked.'

'Famous last words.' Kitty's usually wide eyes narrowed, and Amelia turned to find the reason. Kitty's mother-in-law, the viscountess, was the answer. She was a society favorite, but Kitty was currently out of favor with her after rejecting the idea of moving to Suffolk to take care of the Hamsted family estate.

Lady Hamsted was observing Margaret coolly. Her nephew, whom Amelia had invited as a kindness, appeared starstruck by Margaret's unconventional good looks, which didn't help matters. The viscountess had pegged him for Felicity Farnsworth, another guest Amelia invited as a courtesy. Miss Farnsworth had once been engaged to Simon Bainbridge, who allowed her to beg off the engagement after discovering her attraction to another man. She was the last person Amelia wanted at her party, but Kitty was her best friend. She would do anything to make her life easier, even if it meant inviting the devil himself – or *herself*, in this case.

'I'm going to douse that flame before a fire starts.' Kitty flashed Amelia a secret smile. 'Catch up later?'

'Definitely.' Amelia turned to the front door in time to see Simon Bainbridge, a marquis and heir to a dukedom, sweep back his black hair as he gave his hat and coat to a footman. A ripple of excitement coursed through her, and viscountesses and sisters and aunts were all but forgotten. This was the man who'd occupied her thoughts and season, a man she'd solved murders with, a man she'd grown close to and even kissed. Yet a divide existed that he would not bridge.

He lifted his eyes, catching hers, and for a single moment, everyone else in the room faded into the candlelight. His eyes, as green as the vales of Somerset, reminded her of home, but a home she'd never known. A home without boundaries. A home where she belonged absolutely.

He crossed the entryway in two large steps. 'Lady Amesbury.'

Amelia noted the huskiness of his voice as he bowed. She inclined her head. 'Lord Bainbridge. Thank you for coming.'

His eyes lingered over her dress. 'I would not miss a chance to see you – or that dress. Perhaps I like you in dark colors more than I remember.'

Amelia felt her cheeks grow warm. When they'd met, she was still wearing mourning for Edgar, even though it'd been over two years since his passing. Tabitha had insisted, and Amelia hadn't argued. She simply didn't care enough to suggest otherwise. Now, however, she cared a great deal.

'May I have the pleasure of a dance this evening?' Simon asked.

'People will talk.'

'Let them.'

Amelia dipped her head. 'As you wish.'

'You minx,' he said, chuckling. 'What's behind your speedy agreement?'

She nodded toward her sister, who was being introduced to Arthur Radcliffe, eventual heir to a baronetcy and very popular with the younger set. Although it was early, he was surrounded by several friends. He was not tall, but his evening attire was well tailored, and he moved with an agility that set him apart. He was energetic, notably so in the languid crowd, like a wolf twisting through a herd of distracted sheep. 'My sister will draw so much attention this evening that I – or my actions – will not be noticed.'

'Impossible.' He leaned close to her ear. 'I'm certain I speak for every man here when I say I couldn't ignore you if I tried.'

Half an hour later, Simon made good on his promise by leading her to the dance floor for the first quadrille. Mr Radcliffe accompanied Margaret, Oliver accompanied Kitty, and Lord and Lady Hamsted followed. They made pretty pairs, and Amelia was calmed by how well the evening was going. Margaret looked as if she had danced the number many times, switching partners effortlessly, touching hands lightly and trading bits of conversation politely. Amelia breathed a sigh of relief. Finally, she could stop worrying.

The air had barely left her lungs when Margaret's volume increased. Amelia checked over her shoulder to see what the matter was. Mr Radcliffe chuckled, but Madge didn't join him in the laughter. Arthur Radcliffe might not know the look on her sister's face, but Amelia did. If it had the words *danger ahead* painted on it, it could not have been clearer.

Amelia attempted to turn closer to the couple. The scent of Simon – wind, water and sea salt – wafted over her, and she temporarily forgot about the storm brewing inches away. Instead, she imagined an empty beach, rippling waves, a lone branch of cedarwood.

And Simon.

'Who's leading?' he asked. 'Me or thee?'

Amelia snapped back to the moment. 'I apologize. It's my sister. Did you see—'

'Yes. Ignore her.'

Amelia had to follow his advice because they changed partners. But when she returned to Simon's arms, another exclamation followed that had half the room looking in Margaret's direction. Simon drew Amelia into an elaborate turn, distracting the audience from her sister for a moment. *Excellent, keep it up*, thought Amelia. But no amount of twists or turns could lower the tone of Madge's voice.

In a loud, cutting tenor came the words, 'Is that a threat, Mr Radcliffe?'

'Of course not, Miss Scott.' Mr Radcliffe bowed, a cat stretching its paws. 'I merely stated a fact. My brother knows Doctor Kappen. They graduated together from Oxford. My brother was captain of the rowing team.'

Amelia wondered if it was too early for a glass of champagne.

The dance ended, but Madge did not wait for Mr Radcliffe to lead her off the floor. She marched herself out of the ballroom and down the hall, her gown a twist of ivory behind her.

'I'd better check on her,' Amelia whispered to Simon.

Simon bowed and led her off the dance floor. Tabitha attempted to catch her attention, but Simon wisely inquired about the new portrait Tabitha had commissioned of her late brother, and the confrontation was momentarily forgotten.

Amelia mouthed the words *thank you* to Simon before sneaking out of the ballroom to find her sister. *Impertinent girl!* What could Arthur Radcliffe possibly have said in less than five minutes to make her so angry? He was nicely dressed, well mannered and highly popular. Lady Hamsted, in fact, had suggested the invitation. What fault had Margaret found with him already?

Amelia spotted her in the portrait gallery, her auburn hair blazing red in the moonlight. Amelia suspected the rogue hairpin from earlier had been jerked out, for several strands were loose from her coiffure, the hair swirling about her face like Medusa's snakes. 'What happened? What are you doing in here?'

Madge's chest heaved with anger. 'That man, Mr Radcliffe, knows Charlie Atkinson – or the physician who treated him, anyway. He was threatening me, Amelia.'

'His father is a baron. He knows everybody. Everyone thinks he's first-rate.'

'A guise. "One may smile, and smile, and be a villain."'

Amelia recognized the line from *Hamlet*. The words were as true now as they were in Shakespeare's time. But was Mr Radcliffe threatening her by mentioning the incident with Charlie Atkinson? Amelia doubted it. In fact, he might have been searching for a mutual topic of conversation – a friend from Oxford now resided in Mells. Madge resided there, too. Madge, nervous about the information being found out, could have misinterpreted his intention.

'I took his meaning well enough,' Madge continued. 'He wanted me to understand that he knew my secret. He plans to lord it over me. You may be certain.'

Denial was the surest way to continue the argument, so Amelia went with a different approach. 'It might be true. He might plan to spread the rumor to others. However, hiding is not the answer. Facing trouble head-on is the only way to overcome it.' Amelia knew the wisdom would appeal to Madge, who liked nothing better than dealing with problems directly and with force.

'You're right.' Madge jerked on her skirt as if it were a pair of trousers. 'I wouldn't want it to appear as if I'm hiding from a weasel like him.' She held out her hand. 'Proceed.'

Amelia led her back into the ballroom, and it was the last she saw of her for the next several hours. Amelia was inundated with the tasks of a dutiful hostess, making introductions, conversing and ensuring one and all were having a fine time. For their part, the footmen ensured rout cakes and champagne were passed around every third or fourth dance, whetting guests' appetites until supper was served at midnight.

From all appearances, Mr Radcliffe had forgotten about the uncomfortable incident. He was surrounded by friends, enjoying not one but two cakes, pausing only long enough to tell an interesting tidbit. The throng leaned in automatically, hanging on his word. When the detail was revealed, they leaned back, sharing a hearty laugh.

If only my sister found him as funny, Amelia thought as she followed a debutante into a retiring room. The young woman had torn her dress and was devastated. Amelia assured her no one would notice the difficulty when she was finished. She was more than proficient with a needle, and despite the chaperone's protests, Amelia promised her she didn't mind repairing the damage. It was obvious to her that the chaperone, who was old and did not see well, was not up to the task.

Amelia examined the tear. 'This material is very fine, but I'll have it repaired quickly.' She asked the maid stationed in the room for a needle and thread. 'No one will be the wiser.'

'I hope my mother won't notice,' the debutante mumbled. 'She thinks I'm clumsy in the extreme.'

'You're not clumsy,' Amelia consoled as she started on the tear. 'These things are always a crush.' Amelia was not domestic in the least, but she enjoyed intricate work. She loved absorbing herself wholeheartedly in a task, especially one that took her mind off the event in progress.

For the next several minutes, she didn't think about anything except mending this young girl's dress. A relief in every sense of the word. In no time at all, the delicate ruffle was returned to its previous splendor.

The young woman held up the skirt, beaming. 'Thank you, my lady.'

'We are very grateful, Lady Amesbury,' added the chaperone.

'It was my pleasure,' Amelia smiled.

The young woman dashed out of the room, the chaperone fast on her heels, and Amelia followed, the smile still on her face. It dissipated, however, as she passed the balcony, and a whisper of voices floated through the open doors. One of the voices was raised in protest.

'It's over. I don't want to see you again.' The woman was insistent.

'But I loved you,' said a man. 'I *still* love you.'

The woman huffed a breath. 'You deserted me. Love doesn't do that.'

'Ann . . .'

'Don't. Don't touch me. If you come near me, I'll scream – or worse.'

Amelia decided to intervene, but before she could, Lady Ann appeared, and Amelia ducked into the shadows of the hallway. Lady Ann was in her second season, although Amelia wasn't certain how. She'd met her last year, and Lady Ann was just as lovely as she was then, with soft blonde hair and blue-gray eyes that were kind and intelligent. But now, her brow was knitted in anger, and her eyes were the color of an iced-over pond. Swallowing hard, she straightened her shoulders and took a deep breath. Then she stalked in the direction of the ballroom.

Although she seemed to have the situation under control, Amelia fell in step behind her to see if she required assistance. Amelia refused to have a woman harassed in her home, and if she needed to turn out a derelict, she would. Goodness knows the evening had enough problems without an overly friendly guest harassing young debutantes.

'There you are.'

Amelia jumped.

'It's half past midnight.' Aunt Tabitha tapped her cane to punctuate the hour. 'We cannot start supper without you.'

Finally, thought Amelia. She was looking forward to her first glass of champagne. *And second.*

'You'll go in with Lord Bainbridge—' Aunt Tabitha started explaining the arrangements but was interrupted by Mr Thomas Briggs, an American who had more money than manners.

'There is the hostess of the hour.' He dipped his head, which was covered by glossy hair the color of a Cuban cigar. 'I said to myself, I will meet her if it's the last thing I do.' He touched his barrel-shaped stomach. 'And if I keep eating as I do, it might very well be.' He laughed heartily. 'But I love food. Always have. And wine. I plan to grow grapes on my estate next year.'

Tabitha tutted, but a smile tickled Amelia's lips.

'It's nice to meet you, Mr Briggs.'

'You know me?' He looked pleased.

'Of course I do. You are the American who's recently relocated to Kent.' Amelia had heard he had an income of ten thousand a year, which made him an obvious catch of the season. She wasn't too proud to admit it was one of the reasons she invited him. Kitty had told her he *had* to be at the party, if not for Margaret, then for other young women. Plenty of London matches had been made for less.

He preened a little, looking older than his forty years. 'Yes, I am.' After shaking Amelia's hand, he stuck out his hand, gloved in fine kid leather, in Tabitha's direction. 'And you are, my lady?'

Tabitha sniffed. 'Quite hungry.'

Amelia attempted to mask the slight by rushing an explanation. 'We are on our way to the supper rooms, Mr Briggs. I'm sure you'll join us.' She bobbed a goodbye. 'I hope we may talk more then.'

'Impertinent man,' Tabitha grumbled, continuing with her lecture on supper arrangements. Like Mr Briggs, Tabitha loved food and had planned the meal down to a tittle. Ham, jellies, lamb, fowl, custards, savoy cakes – the list went on. And then decorations, including towering centerpieces made of sugar paste. Amelia was looking forward to sitting down and enjoying an exquisite meal.

Then she spotted Mr Radcliffe situated next to her sister. Her sister was frowning. Amelia sighed. Sitting would have to wait.

She twisted through the crush of people. Dozens were assembling in the supper rooms, where magnificent bouquets of roses adorned tables and sideboards, making the journey more of an obstacle course. The sweet scent of the roses mingled with freshly cut meat, heady wine and spicy cake. Amelia's stomach rumbled in anticipation.

When she reached Mr Radcliffe, however, she realized she wouldn't be indulging anytime soon. He was doubled over, both arms crossed over his stomach, and his face was as gray as ash in a cold fireplace.

Margaret touched his arm. 'Are you all right, Mr Radcliffe?'

Sweat pooled on his forehead. He silently gaped at his friend, Benjamin Worth. Amelia had met him and his friends earlier in the evening. She noted how they surrounded Mr Radcliffe like pupils awaiting instructions from a teacher. Polite then, Mr Worth's look had changed to one of anxious alarm.

Amelia took the wine decanter from the footman and filled Mr Radcliffe's glass. 'A drink perhaps, Mr Radcliffe. It's grown so warm in here.'

The footman coughed behind her.

Tabitha covered her brow with a hand. It was the footman's job to dispense the wine, and she was embarrassed for Amelia, but Amelia was used to doing things herself. A man was sick, for goodness' sake. Who cared who poured the wine if it relieved him?

Mr Radcliffe took a small sip, and for a moment, Amelia thought the danger had passed. Then he grasped his head in his hands, dipped his chin and fell forward. The danger had not passed. Mr Radcliffe was unconscious.

FOUR

Dear Lady Agony,

What can be done about a stuffy house? My parties have fizzled twice this season due to heat. One debutante fainted in the middle of a quadrille and another over a plate of mutton. I've tried ventilation, but it seems my house doesn't provide adequate air flow. What else can I do?

Devotedly,

Suffocating Scenario

Dear Suffocating Scenario,

A most suffocating situation, indeed! You say you've tried improving ventilation. Try these improvements as well. They might make the difference between a conscious and unconscious party guest. First, keep activities in rooms with the lightest papering and wall coverings. Second, mask fireplaces with flowering plants, and decorate the balustrade with evergreens for optimal airiness. Finally, provide a refreshment room or supper room on the same floor as the ballroom to prevent an unnecessary crush of people or dresses. As you must know, drink improves any situation.

Yours in Secret,

Lady Agony

Madge looked up at Amelia. 'Fate is a cruel mistress.'

Amelia admonished her with a glare.

'What are you saying, Miss Scott?' A brown curl shook loose from Mr Worth's smooth mound of hair in a toss of surprise or disgust. 'Mr Radcliffe deserves to be ill?'

Amelia immediately went to work repairing the comment. 'Please excuse my sister's impertinence. She meant nothing of the sort. It was a poor attempt at cleverness.' She scanned the crowd. 'Let us find a room where Mr Radcliffe can retire. He's obviously overheated.'

'He doesn't need rest. He needs a doctor.' Mr Worth signaled to a footman decisively. 'My carriage. Right away.'

The footman scurried away, and Mr Worth sought the assistance of his friend Captain Fitz. They'd served together in the Crimean War from 1853 to 1856, and after overhearing one of their conversations in the ballroom, Amelia knew there wasn't anything they wouldn't do for one another, including carrying a man out of her supper room. Arthur Radcliffe was not large, so transporting him would be easy. Mr Worth didn't want to attract unnecessary attention, and for that matter, neither did Amelia. A hostess did not want a guest dragged from supper unconscious.

Only those close to Mr Radcliffe and his friends were aware of the situation. That included Margaret, Miss Castlewood, Miss Farnsworth and Lady Ann. The rest of the attendees were situating themselves with food and drink. If they did wonder about Mr Radcliffe, it was only in passing. Supper rooms were notoriously hot, and fainting was common, although more so among women who suffered the ill effects of too-tight undergarments.

And he *had* fainted. Amelia had seen it with her own eyes. Perhaps that was the reason Mr Worth was overly concerned. Women fainted; men did not. Mr Worth might have felt it necessary to remove him from the situation to keep his friend's reputation intact. As a former solider, he might have been more apprehensive about it than others.

Arthur Radcliffe did look odd, however. Amelia squinted at him as Mr Worth and Captain Fitz hoisted the man's arms around their capable shoulders. He was unnaturally pale, his face twisted into a grimace. Only moments before, he'd gripped his stomach as if a knife was stuck in his abdomen. Had he mentioned feeling unwell or the food disagreeing with him?

'No,' answered Madge when Amelia inquired. 'He'd taken a piece of bread.'

Amelia looked to Felicity Farnsworth for an answer, and a single wrinkle appeared between her raven eyebrows. The rest of her face was as smooth as glass, except for a large beauty mark that drew attention to her mouth – though rarely did anything of consequence come out of it, at least in Amelia's experience. What people noticed was the way a room seemed to improve every time she entered it. The feeling was visceral and exciting.

One couldn't deny the energy that followed her everywhere she
went. It was probably what had driven Simon all the way to
America after she broke their engagement. For two years, he'd
stayed there to avoid her and the rumors. He had returned this
spring, however, for his sister's debut, and Amelia was glad he
had.

'He seemed perfectly fine.' Miss Farnsworth sniffed. 'I hope
he isn't ill. I danced with him.'

'As did I.' Madge selected a particularly large piece of sliced
ham. 'He was as fit as a fiddle.'

'I saw him drink several glasses of champagne,' Lady Ann
put in.

Miss Castlewood nodded. 'I did as well.'

'As if he could not quench his thirst . . .' The end of Lady
Ann's observation trailed off, and her blue-gray eyes lifted to
Amelia's. They were not only beautiful but keen and intelligent.
Amelia wondered how many times others had underestimated
her or her experience. Probably many.

Amelia gave her a quick smile of appreciation for the information. 'Maybe he had too much champagne.' Noting Mr Radcliffe's
departure, she added, 'I must see to them, but thank you.' She
followed Mr Radcliffe and his friends out of the room.

The hallways were clear, as almost everyone was in the supper
rooms, and Mr Worth and Captain Fitz quickly assisted Mr
Radcliffe into Mr Worth's carriage.

'Would you mind staying behind?' Mr Worth asked the captain.
'In case I don't return in time to take Miss Castlewood home.'

Captain Fitz dipped his chin. 'Of course not. See to it that Mr
Radcliffe gets to his house safely.'

Mr Worth gave him a brief nod and was gone.

Amelia breathed a sigh of relief, thankful to have Radcliffe
– and her worries – removed. She wished him well but was not
necessarily sorry to see him go. Her sister's dislike of him would
be one less problem she'd have to deal with this evening. She
turned to the captain. 'Shall we return to the supper room?'

'I'm not the highest-ranking man at the party, but I'd be
honored.' Captain Fitz held out an arm, lean and muscled. He
was tall with a calm, sandy-whiskered face and a good-natured
smile. The disruption hadn't rattled him, and his demeanor eased

Amelia's nerves a good deal as it probably had those of many of his fellow soldiers.

She took his arm appreciatively. 'I hardly care about that. I'm just grateful you're here. I hope Mr Radcliffe feels better.'

'Probably a bout of gastritis,' said Captain Fitz. 'He suffers from those from time to time. He will be better in the morning. Be sure of it.'

'Ah.' It made sense now why Radcliffe was gripping his stomach.

In the supper room, all were having a fine time. No hint of the previous unpleasantness remained. Amelia surveyed the room and exhaled. Tinkling glasses, shiny silverware and full plates. Everyone upright and conscious. *Excellent.*

Simon approached with a beverage. 'A glass of champagne, Lady Amesbury?'

'You read my mind,' Amelia muttered. 'Thank you.'

'What was wrong with Radcliffe?' asked Simon.

'I do not know.' She took an extended drink, allowing it to warm her from head to toe. 'Captain Fitz said it might be gastritis.'

'Are you certain your sister didn't poison him?'

Amelia stared at him. 'Do not even joke about that.'

He waggled his dark eyebrows at her, and an unwilling smile crept over her face. Anything was easier to tolerate – even gastritis attacks – with him at her side. It had been that way since the day they'd met. He hadn't solved her problems, per se, but he'd made them more bearable. It was the reason she opened up to him so easily.

If only he could open up more.

He'd been unlucky in love, and he worried about hurting her. She knew he did. But she'd been unfortunate, too. It wasn't the same, of course. He'd been hunted for his title, and she'd been sought out for her lack of one. Edgar had chosen her because she knew nothing of his name or fortune. They'd both suffered in their own way. If only he would realize they were more similar than different.

She put the thought aside as they feasted on fowl, ham, breads, jellies, tipsy cake and wine, and by the time they returned to the dance floor, Amelia had almost forgotten the trouble with Mr Radcliffe. Madge was enjoying the company of Captain

Fitz. They'd danced two times, and Tabitha was satisfied with her progress. Lady Hamsted, on the other hand, was not. Her nephew, Leo Morton, was next on Madge's dance card, and he was anticipating the start of the waltz with the giddiness of a first kiss.

The viscountess did her best to draw his attention away from Madge with an introduction to Felicity Farnsworth. Lord Morton responded politely, but his eyes didn't stray far from the dance floor. Amelia looked at her sister with a smile. She could hardly blame him. Margaret was as fresh as a daisy in springtime – a little too cheerful, a little too loud, a little too fun. Who wouldn't want a chance to spin her around the room?

Her cheeks were as red as her hair, reminding Amelia of when they were little girls, racing down the steep hill behind the inn. Amelia was not the best at watching her young sibling; more times than not, she joined in the fun. One hot July afternoon, they'd run down the hill together – directly into a small pond. Even the ducks sought cover, not to mention a guest who was enjoying a quiet read on a nearby bench. That little episode had earned them both extra dish duty and Amelia a day of cleaning the stables since she was older and supposedly wiser. But Amelia and Madge had too much fun together to obey such wisdom. Just having her near again made Amelia want to push back the chairs and dance a rowdy polka.

The orchestra began a waltz, however, and Lord Morton's wish was finally granted. Madge took his hand, turning perfectly around the room. Perhaps a little too perfectly. Amelia guessed Madge preferred the easy ways of Captain Fitz to the foppishness of Lord Morton. He was gallantly dressed in a perfectly cut black coat and wide cravat against a shirt and kid gloves of the starkest white. He was his aunt's nephew when it came to fashion, but thankfully his attitude was more amiable than hers.

Felicity Farnsworth was not amused by the dance. She appeared perturbed by the development. She and Lady Hamsted were conversing, probably about Lord Morton, and once in a while, Miss Farnsworth leveled a glare at Madge that could have melted the thickest ice.

Take care, vixen. Amelia answered the scowl with one of her own. *That's my baby sister you're glaring at.*

'It's not polite to glower at your guests, Amelia,' Kitty whispered. 'I know you're out of practice, but *really*.'

Amelia started at the sound of her friend's voice, and Kitty gave her a friendly nudge. 'I wasn't glowering. I was performing a curse.'

'Ah.' Kitty's dimples showed. 'Did it work?'

Amelia frowned. 'Not yet. She still has two legs instead of four.'

Kitty covered her mouth with a gloved hand, preventing an unladylike snort of laughter from escaping. 'You need more instruction. Perhaps you'll have to attend another one of Lady Easton's spiritual balls.'

Amelia watched as Lord Morton led Madge off the crowded dance floor. The musicians were taking a break, and he seemed disappointed that he wasn't able to extend their time together. He was a daring young man, and an unexpected detour wasn't out of the question. She kept a close eye on him as they navigated the crush of people. The last thing she needed was more controversy. 'I thought the spiritualist was extraordinary.'

Kitty wrinkled her button nose. 'She made my skin crawl.'

Amelia shrugged. 'Mine too, but that made it all the more authentic.' Lady Easton was known for her obsession with all things macabre, and seances were popular. Since Lady Easton's husband's death several years ago, she'd been trying to communicate with him. To date, she'd been unsuccessful, but Amelia suspected she had a lot of fun trying.

The couple was approaching, and Amelia said no more on the subject.

'Thank you for the dance, my lord.' Madge dipped her head politely.

Leo Morton gave her a dashing smile. His mustache was not quite filled in, and like his light-brown hair, it was hampered by too much wax. 'Thank *you*, Miss Scott. Perhaps we will have another chance later this evening?'

Madge's gaze roved over the crowd, and Amelia had the impression she was looking for a different partner. 'Perhaps.'

Amelia noted Lady Hamsted's pointed look. 'Your aunt looks as if she requires your attention, my lord.'

Leo Morton frowned in the viscountess's direction. 'That's

just her appearance, I'm afraid. I've found she always looks a bit out of sorts. Haven't you, Mrs Hamsted?'

A peal of laughter escaped Kitty's lips, but Amelia didn't catch her response. She was too focused on the subject of Madge's attention to notice. It wasn't Captain Fitz; it was Benjamin Worth, and he was trudging toward them like a man coming in from a rainstorm. His clothing was rumpled, most likely from helping Mr Radcliffe into the carriage, and his cravat was untied, hanging open to one side. His eyes, which were dark brown like his damp curly hair and side whiskers, were glazed over as if in a trance.

Amelia puzzled over his appearance. Perhaps Mr Radcliffe was better. Perhaps that was why Mr Worth returned so quickly. After all, he still had to retrieve Miss Castlewood. But if that were true, why did he wear such a face – and clothes?

'Welcome back, Mr Worth.' Amelia donned what she hoped was a welcoming hostess's smile. 'How is Mr Radcliffe?'

'I'm glad you asked, Lady Amesbury.' Benjamin Worth did not look at Amelia, however. He stared straight at Margaret. 'Mr Radcliffe is not doing well at all. In fact, Mr Radcliffe is dead.'

'Dead?' Madge repeated. 'Good God.'

'It *is* what you wanted, isn't it, Miss Scott?' Mr Worth's voice, bright and jaunty, was so different from his disposition that it was hard to reconcile the man and the words. 'The fates to strike him down?'

'I never said that.' Madge's cheeks were flushed, and her eyes were narrow bullets, boring holes into Mr Worth's claim. 'I never wished Mr Radcliffe harm. I only wished him to mind his own business.'

'About the man in Mells, another subject of your ire?' Mr Worth forced a chuckle. 'That encounter ended with a broken arm. Mr Radcliffe has not been as fortunate, I'm afraid.'

Amelia cut in before Madge had a chance to respond. 'I am so sorry about your friend, Mr Worth. You have our deepest condolences. You've obviously been through an ordeal this evening and need some time to process what's happened.'

'*I* understand what happened.' Mr Worth shook his head. 'It is you who doesn't understand. His death was not normal, not natural.' His face, gray in color, slackened. 'I've seen death in all shapes and sizes, but I've never witnessed anything like this.'

He swallowed a shudder, perhaps trying to rid himself of the memory.

Amelia wasn't sure how to answer or if she was supposed to. 'Again, I'm truly sorry for your loss.'

'Your sister will be more than that if she harmed Mr Radcliffe.' Mr Worth's statement hung in the air like fog on the Thames. Thick, dark, dirty.

Amelia frowned.

Mr Worth pointed a finger in Madge's direction. 'She'll be held accountable.'

FIVE

Dear Lady Agony,

How does one address rude behavior at a party? People are increasingly disposed to make the most curious comments, for either sport or attention. I know not which. A pointed look does not do the job it once did. How else might one end such conduct?

Sincerely,

Manners are a Must

Dear Manners are a Must,

I agree. Manners are a must, but so few subscribe to them anymore. It's striking what one will say in public. My best advice is to dismiss the behavior – and the person, if necessary. Let them act like a boor in their own homes. In your own, they should act like a prince or go.

Yours in Secret,

Lady Agony

Two years ago, Amelia might have shrunk from the implication. Two years ago, she might have fled the ballroom. Two years ago, she might have even fled the city. But two years ago, she had understood little of London society. She knew now that the best way to fight an accusation was to dismiss it. Amelia owed Mr Worth nothing, certainly not an answer. Although her heart thumped hammer-hard in her chest, she refused to react.

'You must be unwell, Mr Worth, to make such a statement.' Amelia glanced at Bailey, the footman, and that was all it took for him to join her. 'Bailey will make certain you find the way to your carriage.'

A little of the color returned to Mr Worth's face, and he looked more like the steadfast solider he was than the disheveled man who'd entered the ballroom. Perhaps he realized he might be

unwise to make such a statement to a countess and in the middle
of her ballroom, no less. He smoothed his curly brown hair, but
frizz had already started at his temples.

Captain Fitz, who was a head taller than Mr Worth, clapped
a hand on his shoulder. 'That's a good idea. It's been a long
night, friend.'

Mr Worth nodded.

Theodora Castlewood arrived in a rush of blue and silver
organza. Her skin was peach-colored and silk-smooth, except for
the two deep wrinkles between her eyebrows. Her plain blue eyes
grew round with concern as they passed over Mr Worth's
disheveled appearance.

'Oh, Benjamin!' Miss Castlewood exclaimed. 'I just heard the
unbearable news.'

Mr Worth grasped both of her hands. 'It's true.'

'I'm so sorry, dear.' Miss Castlewood's eyes searched his with
sympathy, seeing the hurt behind his anger. In that moment, he
seemed to come undone, to release something that he'd been
physically holding on to. He lowered his shoulders.

'An unfortunate turn of events to be sure.' Captain Fitz spoke
as if he might be talking of spoiled meat or a broken vase. His
face was placid, a mask revealing nothing. He, too, was familiar
with death, yet it didn't seem to affect him as it did Mr Worth.
He turned to Margaret. 'But nothing more.'

Madge released a breath, seemingly calmed by his words or
his composure. Amelia imagined his voice had that effect on
most people he encountered. The quality must have eased many
minds, and it didn't surprise her that he was a captain in the
British Army. Duty and steadfastness were two words that immediately came to mind when she thought about their brief
encounters.

Mr Worth squeezed Theodora's gloved hands, then released
them. 'I should go. You're welcome to stay.'

'Of course I won't. You shouldn't be alone.' Miss Castlewood
dipped her chin in Amelia's direction. 'Thank you, Lady
Amesbury, and good evening.'

Amelia acknowledged the remark with a nod.

Mr Worth followed Miss Castlewood out of the ballroom.

Captain Fitz watched them go. 'I hope you won't hold his

words against him, Lady Amesbury. He is in a state of shock. I've seen it before.'

'Of course not,' Amelia murmured.

'I most certainly will,' huffed Madge. 'He accused me of harming Mr Radcliffe!'

Thank you for the recapitulation, sister. As if anyone needed one.

Captain Fitz's calm face broke into a smile, his large teeth straight and white. 'Don't let an unseemly implication taint your debut, Miss Scott. It's not every day one comes out in society in such high fashion.'

Or high anxiety, added Amelia to herself. She could feel Tabitha's crystal-blue eyes on her, and if she turned around, she was certain they would petrify her in place. The night could not end this way. In fact, it could not end at all for at least another two hours; otherwise, Margaret's debut would not be deemed a success, and heaven knew it had enough hurdles already. 'A dance would certainly take her mind off the trouble, Captain.'

'And yours as well.'

Amelia was relieved to see Simon offering her his hand. Tabitha couldn't petrify her if she was moving.

'Shall we?' he prompted.

The orchestra began a waltz, and Amelia leaned into Simon, buoyed by his presence. For the moment, no one could get to her. Simon would make certain of it. From the instant they met, they'd been partners in ordeals they thought they'd have to face alone. Their relationship brought her relief and even strength.

'Stop frowning,' said Simon as he whisked her past a particularly rapt group of onlookers, flashing them a swoon-worthy smile. Amelia could have sworn she heard a few sighs.

'Excuse me for forgoing a grin. How thoughtless of me. Positively insipid really, considering a man has fainted, then died, and my sister has been accused of harming him at my first – and mostly likely *only* – ball of the season.'

Simon chuckled as if she revealed a delightful nugget of gossip. Then he leaned close to her ear, his breath tickling. 'And they are enjoying it immensely.'

She considered his statement. She'd assumed the onlookers were taken with Simon's good looks and rare attendance. Now she wondered if they were actually having fun. She hazarded a glance at the society doyennes. Lady Sutherland, an elderly matron who had gorgeous gray hair with snow-white streaks, nodded to Mrs Grover, who held up a glass appreciatively. They certainly approved of the crystal. It had been engraved with the Amesbury crest at Murano.

'Do you think you are the only one who enjoys adventure, Lady Amesbury?' Simon pulled her closer still, and her breath caught. The whiskers on his jawline brushed against her face, sending shivers down her spine. Then he released her into a twirl.

The effect was dizzying, and for a single second her only thought was of Simon. He made her feel young, attractive, alive. She was no great beauty; she had brains and a decent figure, not exactly what set one apart in a sea of lovely people. But in his arms, she felt as if she were the handsomest woman in Mayfair. Something special, unordinary – exquisite. Like the crystal admired by Tabitha's friends.

'They also enjoy the excitement,' he continued. 'You have to remember it has evaded them most of their lives.'

'Do you think so?'

'I know so.' Simon's bottle-green eyes flickered under the passing candlelight. 'A beautiful debutante, a wealthy widow and a dead would-be baron. What could be more exciting?'

She smiled. 'Two dances with a much-sought-after marquis? There will be rumors.'

He maneuvered around another couple. 'I don't mind if it improves your situation.'

Her stomach sank a little. Of course, the dance was about distraction from the obvious problem: one dead Mr Radcliffe and one troublesome Margaret Scott. She wished it was about more, but Simon had been a lifelong family friend, and if the past was any predictor, he would be nothing more.

Not that he hadn't had opportunities. It wasn't that long ago that she'd kissed him in a carriage. Yes, she'd kissed him, but he had kissed her back. She might be inexperienced in the usual ways. Edgar had been ill the two months they'd been married, and she was more friend than wife. But she knew when she was being kissed. Maybe Simon had indulged her for the sake of politeness. As he was indulging her with a dance now.

She donned what she hoped was a placid look.

Simon held her gaze. 'Tomorrow all will be forgotten, except the fowl, flowers and finger cakes. Trust me.'

She did trust him. From the moment he found her at St James's Park with a dead body, she had given up all her secrets. It was easy to do. Like a conjurer, he had a powerful influence on her, but she liked to think she had an influence on him, too. He was more controlled, certainly, but if she leaned too close – *like this* – or tilted her head – *like so* – he did come a little undone.

He inhaled the scent of her neck, and she saw him close his eyes briefly. When he opened them again, she imagined this was what he looked like at sea. Free. Brave. Reckless, even. How she wished to know *that* Simon. The Simon who instinctively grasped her waist tighter and her body closer. But a second was all he gave her. Then he composed himself, readjusting the pressure of his hand, light as a feather.

Amelia was no feather. She might be a young woman, but she felt as if she'd lived a half-dozen lives already, and he'd known some of them. She wished he didn't feel as if he had to shield her from life – from himself. She didn't regret her choices; she wouldn't choose differently even if she could.

But he had made this decision for her. He was not the right man for her. The Amesburys and Bainbridges had been family friends for years, and he had been Edgar's best friend and confidant in the Navy, the one who'd told him to find a wife who was unaware of his wealth and title. Only then, he assured Edgar, could he be certain he wasn't being utilized for his position. The past was not perfect. He was not perfect. But *life* wasn't perfect. Wasn't tonight a testament to that truth?

Lord Morton twirled by them with Felicity Farnsworth on his arm. Felicity, not one to waste an opportunity, cast a winsome glance at Simon as the couple twirled past them.

Amelia narrowed her eyes, whispering, 'Beware, Lord Morton. The cat has her claws out.'

Simon quirked a brow.

'You cannot deny it. She has set her sights on him, and she gets what she wants.'

'Not always.' A smile quivered on his lips.

'What of Lord Morton? He must be a great catch to pique her interest. What do you know of him?'

'When did you become a busybody? The work at the magazine is going to your head.' The dance finished, they bowed, and he led her off the dance floor.

'When did you start evading questions about Miss Farnsworth?' she quipped. 'That's right. Always.'

He slowed her progress with the touch of her elbow. 'You asked about Lord Morton, if I recall, not Miss Farnsworth. And I haven't evaded questions. As with most stories, you've summoned one that serves your purpose. If you think I would marry a woman for her good looks, you're sorely mistaken.'

She opened her mouth to object and then shut it.

'You of all people should realize not everyone is what they seem.' He leaned close to her ear. 'Lady Agony.'

A response escaped her, and after the pause, he kept walking. She was forced to follow him, gulping in little bits of air, trying to digest what he'd said. It had been hard with his lips so close to her ear. She shook her head. This wasn't the time or the place to delve into the mysteries of Felicity Farnsworth. A man was dead. Her sister had been accused of harming him. Revelers could drink punch, eat cake and dance, but she had work to do.

'Close your mouth, dear,' Tabitha muttered when Amelia arrived at her side. 'It's so unbecoming when you gape.'

Amelia did as she said. 'What do you know of Felicity Farnsworth?'

'Does this have anything to do with the marquis?'

'No.' Amelia attempted nonchalance.

'You're not chasing after him again, are you?' Tabitha crooked a finger at her.

'What do you mean, *again*? And no. My interest is purely concerning Lord Morton and my sister.'

'Your sister has a number of problems. Lord Morton isn't one of them. I have it on good authority that he's as poor as a pauper. He won't be pursuing your sister if he knows what's good for him.' Tabitha lowered her voice. 'However, I have fielded several inquiries about Mr Radcliffe. What attendees need from you is assurance that everything is perfectly fine. The dance with Lord Bainbridge was nice, but now you must talk – about anything but Radcliffe's untimely death.' With those precipitous words, Tabitha graciously greeted Lady Hamsted, who inquired about the flower arrangements.

'I'm glad you find them acceptable, Lady Hamsted.' Tabitha's chin took a haughty position, one the viscountess could appreciate. 'We'd be happy to recommend our florist, wouldn't we?'

'Of course.' Amelia forced a smile. 'I'll find you Miss Rainier's card.' It was a good excuse to get away from the ballroom to clear her head, if only for a moment.

On her return trip to the ballroom, Amelia once again heard a noise outdoors. She stopped. 'What the devil?'

A snap of a branch was her answer. It sounded as if someone was in the gardens below.

Could it be Lady Ann's pursuer? Had he lured her farther into the lawn for privacy? If so, he would find the attempt useless when she caught up with them.

Abandoning her task, she rushed out of the double doors and stood sentinel, waiting for another sound to signal her direction. The only noise that happened was a swift breeze tinged with the scent of English lavender ruffling the curtain behind her. Despite her distress, or perhaps because of it, she inhaled deeply, grateful to have one of the largest gardens in Mayfair. The house was nice, but the grounds were superb, luxurious even, in a city with so many inhabitants and very little space. Unfortunately, they were also the perfect place to disappear.

She walked the length of the balcony to the steps of the semi-circular balconet, the ballroom in full view behind it. The soft clinking of glasses and the hum of the orchestra's refrain ensured her everyone was having a fine time. She looked left and right. With only silence as her guide, she descended the steps and turned toward the gazebo.

The night was clear, and with the moon shining high above, she had no trouble traversing the uneven ground in her slippers. She tiptoed noiselessly over the grass, which was soft after a morning burst of rain, scanning for the culprit. Except the gazebo was empty. She glanced over her shoulder. Really, she should return to the party. Yet the garden gate was only a few more paces. A glimpse was all she needed to see if someone had passed through it.

She kept walking. The gate was unlatched, hanging open. However, no one was on the other side. She sighed. Perhaps her work at the magazine *was* starting to have an effect on her. She was seeing phantoms where there were none.

She started back toward the house, then stopped. A tortoiseshell button lay on the ground near a crimson rhododendron bush, one of two that bloomed on either side of the gate. She picked it up, rubbing a finger over the shiny object. It must have been from an overcoat, or some kind of outer covering. She guessed it was a man's, but it could have belonged to a woman just as easily.

Suddenly, she heard footsteps – heavy footsteps, moving quickly. They must be on the rose path. It was the only area with cobblestones.

She started at a half-run to see if she could spot the person, nearly tripping in the process. Off came her slippers for better traction. As she grew nearer the rose garden, she spotted someone, a tall man with broad shoulders. He was stalking around the heady-scented circle, bent forward like a caveman with a club.

'You there! Halt.' She worried he would sprint off, but he didn't. He slowly turned around and smiled.

'I understand you're new to hosting, Amelia, but really, think of what Lady Tabitha would say about accosting guests.' Simon raised a single black eyebrow. 'It is simply not done.' His eyes flicked to her slippers, still in her hand. 'And without shoes, no less.'

'What can I say?' She shrugged. 'I mistook you for a troll.' She sat on a bench. 'What are you doing here anyway?'

'What are *you* doing here?'

'I heard a noise, a twig break.' With some difficulty, she tried stuffing her foot back into her slipper. 'But it was nothing. The wind, perhaps.'

'I'm looking for my sister, Marielle.' His jaw clenched. 'I haven't seen her in an hour at least, and that Lord Traber fellow has been pursuing her all night. I do not like him.'

'I think he's nice.' It was his sister's first season, and Simon was observant to a fault. Amelia wasn't sure how Marielle was supposed to meet anyone with him scrutinizing her every move. After the recent trouble with George Davies, a deceitful suitor, however, perhaps he had the right to be watchful.

'Nice?' The word stuck harshly in his throat. 'Did you see them on the dance floor? His proximity was unconscionable.'

A chuckle escaped her lips, and she started on the other slipper, but it promptly fell to the ground. Simon retrieved it so that she didn't have to bend over in her ballgown.

'It was perfectly appropriate,' she said. 'You're being overprotective.'

'Appropriate?' He held up her slipper. 'Hardly. I've never seen such brazen behavior.'

'Says the man holding a lady's slipper in a moonlit garden.'

He opened his mouth, then shut it and proceeded to help her foot into the slipper. 'This is different. You're a widow, and I'm a . . .'

'Confirmed bachelor?' she tried.

'No . . .'

'A jaded aristocrat?'

His emerald eyes turned to narrow blades of grass.

'A lonely curmudgeon!'

At that, he started tickling her foot and wouldn't stop until she apologized. 'All right, all right! I'm sorry.' She laughed, wiping the tears from the corners of her eyes. 'I didn't mean it.'

'I might be a curmudgeon, but I'm not lonely.' He put a hand on her calf to ease her foot into the slipper. 'I have you, and you keep me quite . . .' He swallowed. 'Occupied.' The extent of the situation seemed to hit him then: she lounging on a garden bench, her foot on his thigh as he stretched on the slipper.

The shoe was on, but neither of them moved. Amelia was mesmerized by the color of his eyes in the moonlight, the amber flecks in the center burning bright, and the scent of English roses, full and heady as the summer night. 'Occupied?' she repeated.

He gently put down her foot. 'With mischief and murder.'

It might have been 'love and flowers' by how tenderly he said the words. She heard herself sigh as he touched a tendril of hair that had come loose during her hectic attempt to reach him.

'But I've had a fine time, Amelia.'

She wanted to second his words but didn't dare; she feared if she did, it would break the spell that fell over the garden. She and Simon and the roses and the moonlight. The chirping of crickets and the waters of the lily pond. Alone for an instant, yet surrounded by everyone they knew.

It was as if the moment had been made just for them. As if Venus put Amelia here on this fine night so that Simon would see her. Not Edgar's wife. Not his friend's widow. But her, Amelia Amesbury – a woman with a young heart and an old woman's love life.

If he didn't kiss her, she'd know for certain he never would. She'd know he would never be anything more than her partner and friend. And if that were true, she'd go back to the ballroom and find the first man she could to forget about him and his damnable stubbornness. Or pride. Or loyalty. Or whatever the hell it was that kept him from her.

And when he pulled her to her feet, without so much as a brush of her cheek, that's exactly what she did.

SIX

Dear Lady Agony,

Do you think it's ever acceptable to ask for an introduction to a gentleman? Granted, it would be easier if a certain man asked to be introduced to me, but since he hasn't, what would be the harm of me prompting the action? Is it not the same in reverse? I hope you think so.

Sincerely,

Impatient Patty

Dear Impatient Patty,

It's dreadful to wait for something to happen, is it not? I can think of few things worse than fate being left to a man. Why not be the hero of your own story? Take action, Impatient Patty! Find a way to be introduced to the man, and if you cannot, bump into him near the refreshment table. Accidentally, of course.

Yours in Secret,

Lady Agony

Upon entering the ballroom, Amelia walked straight to Lord Drake, the most infamous man in the room, and made his acquaintance. Not directly, of course. Ladies were always introduced – *another rule that should be thrown out with the book.* Lord Drake hadn't been expected to return from Cornwall until the following week, and Amelia was ecstatic that he should make his entrance at that fortuitous moment. She recognized him from a scar near his lips, a small flick that drew attention to his dazzling white smile and handsome jawline. It was a scar all the ladies talked about; they said he received it as a young man when a drunkard turned a cruel word to a bar wench at a tavern in Cornwall, and he defended her. His heroic reputation had only grown since then. His father was a duke, and the family estate on the rocky southwestern coast was known to be one of the most impressive entailments of all the *ton*. It was the reason women flocked to him, but Amelia only wanted a dance, and he asked for one within a quarter-hour of meeting her.

It was wonderful – in the fact that Simon watched them. Was it petulant and childish? Of course. Did it satisfy her longing for revenge? Absolutely. Besides, Tabitha said the revelers needed a distraction. *Well, Aunt, now we have one.* Half the room watched as Lord Drake twirled her around the ballroom faster than any man had ever dared. Truthfully, she was glad to have shared many late nights dancing with her mother at the Feathered Nest. She might have flown into the punch bowl – and that was in the other room – if she hadn't had the practice.

Lord Drake didn't treat her like a feather. Quite the opposite. It was as if he was testing her mettle, conversing the entire time he pushed her around the ballroom floor. By the end of the dance, she knew everything from his penchant for lemon cakes to his dislike of spiders. Before they parted, he had a question for her.

'You haven't asked me once about my Cornwall estate.' Lord Drake's brown eyes were full of light and curiosity as they searched her own for recognition. 'Do you know of it?'

'Of course I do. Doesn't everyone?' She hardly wanted him to believe her ignorant of his largest – and most famous – piece of property. 'I assume it is still standing?'

'Why, yes.' His lips twitched with something like surprise.

She wasn't certain what else there was to say. 'And I trust you enjoyed your recent visit?'

'I did.' The smile left Lord Drake's lips, and a furrow crept upon his brow. 'My father has been ill, so that is difficult. I long to find him relief, but with a disease like his, relief is hard to come by.'

The rumor was the duke had consumption. 'I am sorry, my lord. I myself know how difficult it is to see the ones you love suffer and not be able to give them peace. My husband has been gone over two years, and I still ponder ways I might have helped him. It is a hard habit to break.'

'It is never far from one's mind; it's true.'

'If your mind ever needs relief, my ear is available,' Amelia said. 'It is not a situation one should bear alone.'

'Thank you.' He stopped, hand on her arm, near the edge of the ballroom floor. 'I appreciate that.'

She smiled at him, unsure why the sentiment meant so much to him.

With a bow, he was gone, and Kitty was in his place, watching his figure disappear into the crowd. After he did, she turned to Amelia. 'Do you not know who that is?'

'Lord Drake.'

'Drake *the Rake*,' Kitty whispered. 'He's a known scoundrel.'

'Good.' Amelia took a glass of champagne from a passing footman and drank deeply. She was parched from the dance and the taxing night. 'My intention was to take everyone's minds off Mr Radcliffe's untimely exit.' She lifted her eyes toward the crush of people.

'Thank heavens,' said Kitty. 'I thought the eye-catching interlude might have been about Lord Bainbridge.'

Amelia took another drink. 'Oh, him, too.' She turned to look directly at Kitty. 'Do you know he had every opportunity to kiss me in the garden not twenty minutes ago and sat as still as a post, rooted into the ground? You're always saying I need to take more chances with my personal life. That advice should be heeded by Simon stupid Bainbridge. I wash my hands of that man.'

Kitty leaned in, her overly full dress rustling with the movement. 'Are you saying you'd prefer he ravish you in the wake of London society, who could stumble upon you at any moment? My mother-in-law? Your sister? *Lady Tabitha?*'

Amelia waved away the questions. 'One kiss, Kitty. It's hardly ravishing.'

'I feel as if a kiss from Lord Bainbridge might indeed be quite ravishing,' Kitty murmured.

Margaret came upon them as quietly as a child raiding a cookie jar, surprising them both with a 'Hello!' Her face was a pretty pink color from dancing, and the tint made her look even lovelier. The smattering of freckles across the bridge of her nose was more visible now, reminding Amelia of when she was a girl. With those freckles and that smile, Margaret could get Amelia to do just about anything, and the same could probably be said for the men in the ballroom. 'What topic has your two heads together like a couple of hens?' asked Madge.

'Ravishing,' stated Amelia.

Madge scrunched up her nose.

'Are you enjoying yourself?' asked Kitty.

'Immensely, now that Radcliffe is gone. Not just gone but dead.' Madge swallowed. 'Crikey.' She reached for a glass of champagne, and Amelia swatted her hand away from the tray. All her sister needed was alcohol to spark a new quarrel.

'Shh,' warned Kitty. 'Here comes the viscountess.'

Lady Hamsted floated closer. In the hollow of her neck was a large amethyst. The white silk dress had a purple lace bertha that matched the gemstone, making the viscountess's blue eyes a shade prettier. But even the nice color couldn't hide the peevishness of her face.

'Lady Hamsted,' Amelia said in her peppiest voice. 'And Lord Morton,' she added when the young man stepped from behind her. 'A glass of champagne?' She held up her own, noticing it was empty. She quickly relinquished it to a passing footman.

'I'm still waiting for the name of your florist, Lady Amesbury.' Lady Hamsted's voice dripped with exhaustion. 'It appears you've forgotten.'

Of course she had. Amelia removed her glove, where Miss Rainier's card was tucked safely inside. Also inside was the large tortoiseshell button. She didn't have time to glance at it now, but it served as a reminder to scour the ballroom later for guests with missing buttons. 'I apologize.' She smoothed the card the best she could. 'Here it is. I confess my attention was diverted.'

'I noticed.' Lady Hamsted arched an eyebrow. 'Lord Drake had all your devotion.'

Amelia didn't rise to the bait. 'He's a fine dancer.'

'As is your sister.' Lord Morton wasn't afraid to make bold statements. He was a daring man with a devil-may-care attitude. Too bad Lady Hamsted didn't share some of the family spirit.

'Thank you, my lord.' Madge tipped her square chin. 'I've had some practice.'

Lord Morton lifted his eyebrows. 'I thought you were new to London.'

'I mean in Mells, at the Feathered Nest.'

Lord Morton pursed his lips, an amused twinkle in his eye.

'The Scott family's *inn*,' Lady Hamsted clarified with a sniff.

After a moment of consideration, Lord Morton flourished a hand. 'Perhaps you could show me one of those country dances, Miss Scott? I'd love to try.'

'A splendid idea,' Amelia said at the same time Lady Hamsted was making excuses. The more gentlemen Madge danced with, the better it would be for her reputation, even if Lord Morton was too dandified for her tastes.

Kitty distracted Lady Hamsted with a comment on her necklace, and Amelia took the opportunity to peruse the ballroom, looking for a garment with a missing button. Her perusal led only to her appearing like a caged tiger, for she saw no such article of clothing. The button might have been attached to a man's overcoat, and if that was the case, all the searching in the world wouldn't help her find it. At least not in the ballroom.

After a full circle of the area, Amelia ducked into the cloakroom.

'May I help you, my lady?' interrupted the butler. Like most areas of the house, the cloakroom was one Mr Jones supervised. An entrance or exit wouldn't go unnoticed by the diligent man.

'No, thank you, Jones,' she said. 'I need to check on an article myself.'

Mr Jones frowned, smoothing his limp brown hair into place. It was constantly coming unparted by his hurried actions. 'If you're certain, my lady.'

'I am.' She patted his arm. 'Perhaps you could check on . . .' She glanced down the hallway. 'The card room. Someone might need assistance with a refreshment.'

Mr Jones straightened, instantly concerned about the possible breach of service. 'Right away.'

The coast clear, Amelia ducked into the cloakroom, which smelled of cigars, spice and sweet perfume. Coats, cloaks, mantles, shawls. There was no end to the fashion possibilities when it came to the London season. She started with the darker options since the button itself was brown. Fabulous frock coats accosted her eyes, but most of them were in varying shades of black or navy.

After thumbing a dozen coats, she decided she was making too much of the button. It was nothing – perhaps even a button from her own gardener or staff. She took it out of her glove and stared at it. There was something familiar about it . . .

She put the button back inside her glove. The weight felt important against her skin, but she had a ballroom to manage, and her search had come to naught. Whoever lost the button was long gone. The noise she'd heard had obviously been Simon.

Now she heard another sound and stood still. Tabitha would have Amelia's head on a platter if she was found in the cloak-room. She barely breathed as she waited for the voices, a man's and a woman's, to pass.

'I have a fine estate in Kent.'

It was the American, Mr Briggs. His accent was unmistakable, as was his pride in his newly acquired land.

'So I've heard.' A familiar woman's voice. Amelia leaned closer to the doorway.

'You must visit in August,' Mr Briggs encouraged. 'You said you long to flee the city. What better time than grouse-hunting season?'

'It could not be soon enough. Thank you for the invitation.' The woman was anxious to leave London and during the heart of the season at that. A curious decision, especially if she was unmarried.

'Is that a yes, Lady Ann?' he chuckled.

Amelia clapped a hand over her mouth. Could it have been Mr Briggs that Lady Ann had rebuffed on the balcony? If so, Amelia would reveal her location if she had to. She would not allow a man to intimidate her again.

'That is a "we shall see in August", Mr Briggs,' Lady Ann said firmly. 'Good evening.'

Silence, and then the orchestra started its final piece, 'Finishing Dance'. It sounded as if Mr Briggs and Lady Ann had departed.

Amelia hazarded a glance out of the door. To the right was no one. To the left was an old woman progressing down the hallway with a walking stick. Amelia sighed a breath of relief.

'Lady Amesbury.' Simon materialized in front of her. He must have come upon her while she was looking in the other direction.

'I beg your pardon!' Amelia was so stunned by his presence she could think of nothing to say.

'What mission now has you hiding in the coat room?' He lifted one dark eyebrow.

'I'm not hiding. I'm – investigating.' It certainly sounded better than *spying*.

Simon dropped the clever look. 'Something you require my assistance with?'

'No.' The word came out a little too forcefully, and she added, 'Thank you.'

He smiled his most gracious smile, the one that relayed he'd been unmoved by their encounter in the garden. They'd been mere inches apart an hour ago, yet the moment seemed as far away from his mind as the River Nile. 'Then, if you could be so kind as to fetch my black tweed and hat, I would be forever grateful.'

Her jaw dropped, and she clenched it shut, flinging her hand in a sweeping gesture toward the cloakroom. 'By all means, my lord. I would not know your coat from a stranger's.'

Which was a lie. She was quite fond of his black tweed and could identify it out of a hundred coats, maybe more. That bit of information, however, she kept to herself.

Instead, she turned toward the ballroom to bid her guests goodnight.

SEVEN

Dear Lady Agony,
How can you be certain you will find the thief in Mayfair?
I appreciate your advice, but really I think you take it too
far when you propose you can do what the police cannot. A
Lady should not deign to say such things – let alone do them.
Sincerely,
Stick to Suggestions, Please

Dear Stick to Suggestions, Please,
Thank you for the advice. I shan't be taking it. A Lady
should deign to say and do all the things in her heart. And
my heart is set on finding a thief. Be sure of it.
Yours in Secret,
Lady Agony

In anticipation of an afternoon full of callers, Amelia had woken hastily, walked briskly and breakfasted heartily. Later, her drawing room would be filled with well-wishers extending their congratulations on last night's ball. Therefore, she decided to tackle her Lady Agony letters immediately, taking a cup of tea with her from the breakfast room to the library.

She had only dunked her quill in the inkwell, however, when Jones delayed the task with unexpected news. A detective named Collings was here at – she checked the time – eleven o'clock in the morning.

Amelia frowned. 'Are you certain he said *Detective* Collings?'

'Quite,' said Mr Jones. 'One doesn't misunderstand the word.' He cleared his throat. 'Shall I tell him you're occupied?'

A man didn't faint in a supper room and then perish hours later without some questions being asked. It was natural a detective was here, Amelia assured herself. A formality to be dealt with. 'I'd best not put it off.' She stood from her desk. 'I'll see him right away.'

Jones nodded. 'Very well. I'll seat him in the drawing room.'

Detective Collings was not what Amelia expected. She assumed someone from Scotland Yard would be distinguished, powerful – a presence. But Collings was short with darting eyes and a weak chin. He eyed her like a cat watching a mouse. 'Mrs Amesbury?'

'Good morning, Detective.' Amelia gestured to a chair. 'Please, have a seat.'

He didn't return the greeting but did sit down, scanning the carpet, furniture and portraits as if taking inventory of the room. He stopped on a painting of the senior earl, Edgar's father, Edwin. His face had been kind, like Edgar's, with an openness rarely captured on canvas. His blue eyes sparkled with a life that would be taken too soon, and his mouth, although not smiling, might have laughed a moment before. Detective Collings moved on to Edgar's portrait, and Amelia could have sworn his lip curled slightly. 'Did you have a function last evening? A ball?'

'Yes, I did.'

His eyes landed on hers, and she noted they were steel-gray. Not brown, not blue, but the color of a beam underneath a shadowy bridge. 'Was Arthur Radcliffe in attendance?'

'Yes, he was.'

Detective Collings's thin mustache twitched at the confirmation. It was brown and nondescript, an afterthought on his face.

'I'd never met the man,' Amelia continued. 'I invited him at the request of Lady Hamsted. He was very popular in certain circles, hers in particular. I thought he would be a good addition to the party.' When he didn't reply, she added, 'You see, my sister is young and unattached. I thought to invite as many eligible men as possible.'

'Margaret Scott,' he said.

'That's correct.' Amelia was unnerved the detective knew her sister's name.

'Who lives in . . .' He unfolded a piece of paper from his coat pocket. 'Mells.'

She nodded, words sticking in her throat. Not only did he know her name but he also knew where she lived. That was interesting.

'According to Mr Radcliffe's friend, Radcliffe grew ill at supper. Tell me about that.'

Amelia relayed what she knew of the incident. 'The supper rooms were warm, and I assumed he overheated. A friend escorted him home, and that was the last I saw of him.'

'Your sister was seated next to him.'

Amelia recognized the intelligence behind his hard gray eyes. He knew more details than she supposed. 'As were other guests, who are perfectly fine, I might add.'

'You know of Mr Radcliffe's passing, then.' Detective Collings leaned back in the chair, as if he owned it – owned her. He crossed a foot over one knee, and she noticed the worn sole of his shoe, the heel impossibly thin. His covetous eye might have been due to his own penury.

'Of course I do. I assume that's why you're here. Benjamin Worth returned to the ballroom to share the dreadful news with me and my guests, which I did not appreciate. It's bad enough to be a girl of Margaret's age, with the entire world making plans for you. It's even worse when a man like Mr Worth disrupts your party in an emotional moment. In fact, something ought to be done about *him*.'

Detective Collings stared at her for a long moment. 'Such as?'

'I wouldn't know. That's your area of expertise, Detective.'

His eyes flicked to the door. 'I'd like to talk to your sister about her argument with Mr Radcliffe.'

'It was hardly an argument, and I cannot see why it matters now.'

'It matters a good deal.' Detective Collings leaned over his crossed foot. 'Arthur Radcliffe's brother is a physician. He tended to him last night. He does not believe his brother died of natural causes. I will, therefore, be investigating all possible *unnatural* causes, including your sister.'

'Absurd!'

'Not absurd.' The detective tilted his soft chin, but it only made his eyes look smaller. 'It's very likely something happened last night to cause Mr Radcliffe's death.'

Thoughts flew through Amelia's brain, and she discarded some and latched on to others. Radcliffe suffered from gastric attacks. Captain Fitz had told her last night. 'Perhaps there *was* a reason.

Captain Fitz told me Mr Radcliffe suffered with gastric attacks for years, and he was drinking – heavily.'

'Nonetheless, I'd like to speak with Miss Scott. If I may.' The statement left little room for refusal, and Amelia had Jones fetch her at once.

Madge shuffled in carrying a teacup and saucer. Her fringe of bangs, brushed away from her forehead, was no longer attractive and, if Amelia was completely honest, made her look a little bit mad. Her eyes were tired, but her smile was genuine, adding a rosy glow to her otherwise sleepy face. 'Mrs Addington practically dragged me out from under the covers. Said I had to get ready for afternoon callers. It feels as if I just went to bed.'

'Yes, well, it would feel that way, being your first ball.' Amelia cleared her throat, trying to indicate the severity of the situation. 'This is Detective Collings. He has some questions about last night.'

Seeing Amelia's glance at her hair, Madge tried and failed to smooth it down. She took the seat closest to Amelia.

'Tell me about your argument with Mr Radcliffe last evening.' Relaxing into the chair, the detective said the words as if they were *Tell me about the last great book you read.*

'It wasn't an argument,' said Madge.

Amelia beamed at her sister.

'It was *intimidation.*'

If Amelia could have gotten away with pinching her just then, she would have. As it was, she clenched her fists at her sides.

The detective was clearly interested. 'How so?'

'Mr Radcliffe said his brother had heard about my fight with Charlie Atkinson – a second-rate actor and a bit of a baby, in my opinion. He wielded the information like a loaded gun, aimed right at me.'

'You did not like Mr Radcliffe.'

'She didn't even *know* Mr Radcliffe,' Amelia put in.

'I didn't like him at all,' answered Madge. 'But that doesn't mean I hurt him – or that anyone did, for that matter. People die, Detective. That's a fact of life. I've seen calves birthed one minute, dead the next. No rhyme or reason for it.'

'True enough, Miss Scott. True enough.' The detective's voice took on the intimacy of a whisper. 'But we're not talking about

about a human being. I will investigate until
·ath – or murder.'
＼ at Madge, and she stared back. Amelia
who would blink first. Her sister was as
..ume. Amelia had seen her intimidate a feral
...s after a litter of kittens in the barn with a single word.
ɒut the detective was determined, too, perhaps hoping to make his mark with the death of a man much beloved by society. Who would blink first? Amelia was growing more nervous by the second.

Then three taps of a cane, like the waves of a fairy godmother's wand, answered her question.

Never had Amelia heard a more beautiful sound. It was strong enough to quell rumors, questions – and detectives. Amelia followed the tip of the walking stick to the hand of its owner, who gripped the black raven handle with a firm grasp. Tabitha pointed it at the detective. 'Who are you?'

Collings stood from the chair, almost falling backward. 'Detective Collings, ma'am.'

'Not *ma'am*. *Lady*. Lady Tabitha.' She emphasized all five syllables with the cane. Her nostrils flared in indignation, her alabaster face pink with anger. 'It is not even noon, Detective, and Miss Scott is our guest. How dare you accost her with a word like *murder*? And in my drawing room. How uncivil and ghoulish. I have a mind to contact your superiors.' The detective started to interrupt, and she held up her hand. 'As it is, I'll ask you to leave.'

'But . . . I . . . if I may—'

Tabitha tipped her chin, revealing flared nostrils. 'No, you may not.'

Jones entered with the detective's hat, shoving it at him with more force than Amelia thought was in him. His wispy brown hair had come unparted, and his scowl gave him a resolute appearance.

Reluctantly, the detective placed the hat on his head. 'I'll be in touch.'

Amelia, Margaret and Tabitha watched him leave. When they heard the front door shut, Tabitha turned to them. 'And that is how you deal with an uninvited guest. You should know in case

another member of the Metropolitan Police happens by ⌐
us of killing our guests.' She lowered herself onto the
'What were you thinking, Amelia?'

'I was thinking I didn't have a choice but to answer his ca.
answered Amelia. 'Rejecting him would have only made us look
more suspicious.'

Margaret finished her tea in a large gulp and replaced the cup
on the saucer. 'We'd have to deal with him sooner or later. It
might as well be sooner, in my opinion.'

'We've heard enough of your opinions, Miss Scott. It is your
opinion that put us in this predicament in the first place.' Tabitha
raised her hand before Amelia could interject. 'Your parents have
been indulgent with you. I will not be. Had you not informed
Mr Radcliffe of your *opinion*, the detective would have had no
reason to knock at our door.'

'He fell into his plate in our supper room, Aunt. Margaret did
not cause that.'

Tabitha turned her cool gaze, as brisk as a winter morning, on
Amelia. 'Do not spoil her, Amelia. You can see where that has
brought her – into trouble. I will not cover up her crimes.'

That got Madge's attention, and she sat up straight in her chair.
'You do not think I had something to do with this, do you, Lady
Tabitha?'

'No, I do not,' Tabitha answered. 'Had you killed Mr Radcliffe,
you would have taken a vase off a nearby table and cracked him
over the head with it. You wouldn't be so discreet as to slip
something into his beverage.'

Madge tapped her square chin. 'You think he was poisoned.
Not a bad supposition.'

Amelia took a deep breath, forcing herself not to pull on
Madge's slipshod braid. 'It is indeed bad if it happened at our
house! Think of it. A poisoning at Amesbury Manor!' She covered
her face with her hands if only to shield the eyes of the canvasses
on the wall, first of her father-in-law and second of her husband,
who had possessed so much confidence in her abilities. If he
could see her now, he might question his decision to leave her
with his family and fortune.

'Winifred!' scolded Tabitha. 'How long have you been standing
there?'

Amelia glanced at the doorway to see Winifred and her friend Beatrice Gray standing in the entryway. *Dash it all!*

'Not long,' said Winifred. 'I only heard "poisoning at Amesbury Manor". Has there been one?'

Bee rocked on her heels, excited for the answer.

'Of course not,' Amelia said with more conviction than she felt.

Margaret stood. 'I wonder if you could show me the new fountain in the garden. I heard it's twice my size.'

'And it's naked, too,' whispered Bee, which sent Winifred into a fit of giggles.

Margaret rushed them out of the room, chuckles following them down the hallway.

Amelia hazarded a glance at Tabitha, whose eyes were as narrow as fence slats. 'I'm sorry, Aunt. I'll fix this.'

'How?'

'I don't know, but I will.'

Tabitha stood. 'Not without my help.'

Amelia's jaw slackened.

'Our family's reputation is at stake, Amelia. You did not suppose I would allow such an accusation to stand, did you?'

Of course she didn't. This was the same woman who had given up her own pursuits for the family. The woman who revered her brother and his children above all things. The woman who avoided colors out of respect for a nephew who died more than two years ago. She wouldn't allow a rumor to affect the Amesbury reputation. This should have made Amelia feel better, but somehow it didn't. It only added to the pressure she felt to clear up the misunderstanding.

Not misunderstanding. Murder. Amelia had avoided the word until now, but no more.

'Ready yourself for the afternoon,' Tabitha continued. 'I'm going to call on Lady Sutherland. She knows a man at the Yard.'

Amelia smiled. It figured that Tabitha had a friend who knew someone at Scotland Yard. Her friends did not keep to shopping and needlework, nor did they wait for solutions. They insisted upon them. 'I will.'

'And keep that sister of yours out of trouble,' added Tabitha. 'Heaven knows it's a full-time occupation.'

EIGHT

Dear Lady Agony,

My friend and I are as close as can be, but recently we argued, and I have a mind to reproach her for her words. Should I? It would make me feel inherently better.

Sincerely,

Boiling Point

Dear Boiling Point,

Reproaching your friend might make you feel better for the moment, but in time you would regret the recrimination. How many letters I have received from correspondents who have said too much? And yet not a word from those who have not said enough. The evidence speaks for itself: let the immediate emotions pass, and retain your friendship. Your future self will thank you.

Yours in Secret,

Lady Agony

Amelia and Margaret were receiving callers in the formal drawing room, the unpleasantness of the morning visit from Detective Collings swept under the paisley rug. Margaret looked perfectly pretty. By the exquisite shade of her violet afternoon dress, one would never guess she'd just been accused of murder. The high color of the dress agreed with her skin tone, and her hazel eyes appeared more blue than brown from the reflection of the window. So lovely.

And bored.

Something outside had her attention, and Amelia went to work returning it to the drawing room. 'That's interesting, Miss Andrews. I had no idea the milliner on Regent Street sold velvet in that color. Did you, Margaret?'

Margaret pulled her eyes from the window. 'I don't even know where Regent Street is.'

Amelia chuckled, hoping it didn't come out nervously. 'My sister hasn't had time to peruse our beautiful hat shops yet.' Indeed, they had to put a rush on her ballgown and were still awaiting several dresses. Hats were lower on their list of priorities, and Amelia had several beautiful ones that Margaret could borrow.

Jones announced a new caller, Felicity Farnsworth. That got Margaret's notice.

Miss Farnsworth garnered attention as bees did honey. It was more than beauty. It was the curve of her jawline, the tilt of her head. The way she moved commanded an audience. It was impossible not to watch her, and Amelia did so as she crossed the room.

Maybe Simon had planted the idea in her head, but Miss Farnsworth looked different from last night. As she selected the ivory chair across from her, Amelia noticed a sharpness to her cheekbones, a look in her eyes akin to hunger. A void or carelessness.

Miss Andrews quickly made her excuses. She'd stayed the customary fifteen minutes to thank the hostess. She could leave without incident and seemed anxious to do so when Miss Farnsworth arrived.

Amelia understood the feeling. If she could have slipped away, she would have. 'I trust you enjoyed your evening, Miss Farnsworth?' Amelia asked as she poured out Felicity's cup of tea.

'Indeed.' Miss Farnsworth took a sip of the tea, leaving the cup at her lips. 'Although the situation with Mr Radcliffe was a dreadful business.'

'A shame,' Amelia murmured in agreement. 'Did you know Mr Radcliffe well? I only met him last evening.'

'He was popular among certain circles.'

'Your circle?' Madge pressed.

'Yes,' answered Miss Farnsworth. 'We enjoyed his company. He knew everyone and everything, all the delicious tidbits.' She leaned in conspiratorially. 'In fact, he told me an interesting fact about you, Miss Scott.'

Madge jerked her chin. 'Is that so?'

A smile twitched on Miss Farnsworth's full lips.

'One can hardly imagine Mr Radcliffe knew much of my sister. She came to London only a fortnight ago.' Amelia coolly sipped her tea. However difficult, she was going to have to be the level-headed of the two Scott sisters. Margaret looked as if she was readying herself for a dogfight, her hands clenched into fists at her sides.

'Some people are an open book.' Miss Farnsworth sipped her tea.

'And others have secrets buried deep within the pages,' added Amelia.

Miss Farnsworth fumbled her teacup on its saucer.

'You danced with Mr Radcliffe last evening,' Amelia continued. 'Did he say anything that might suggest he was ill?'

'I danced with many gentlemen.' Miss Farnsworth's eyes flicked to Margaret. 'I, like your sister, am looking to make a good match this season.'

'I am not,' countered Madge.

Amelia leveled a gaze at her sister, willing her to keep quiet. 'But when you danced with Mr Radcliffe, did he mention being ill?'

Miss Farnsworth tipped her chin, her silhouette a masterpiece of angles. 'He did not. In fact, he said his brother gave him a new tonic for gastritis attacks. He said he was feeling better than he had in a long time.'

Gastritis attacks. That was the second time Amelia had heard them mentioned in relation to Mr Radcliffe.

'She's right,' Margaret said to Amelia. 'He has a brother who's a physician. He boasted of his graduating from Oxford. He was on the rowing team.'

Amelia wondered if the new tonic was the problem. It was a question they could ask the brother. If Arthur Radcliffe had a bad reaction, it might explain his death – and clear her sister's name.

Jones's shuffle at the door announced the arrival of a new guest. 'Lady Ann.'

Felicity Farnsworth stood to leave, and the differences between the two women were stark. Felicity was tall and willowy; Lady Ann was small and slim. Felicity had thick raven hair; Lady Ann had hair the color of spun yellow silk. Their eyes made for the most noteworthy contrast, however. While Felicity's were piercing, Lady Ann's were a soft blue-gray and had the advantage of kindness. They greeted each other with civility before Miss Farnsworth made her excuses.

Lady Ann adjusted her green skirt after selecting a place on the settee. She'd paired the skirt with a pretty green-and-white Garibaldi shirt and looked as stylish as she was smart. 'Thank you for the lovely time, Lady Amesbury. You must have your cook share her raspberry compote recipe with mine. I've never tasted fruit as bright as that.'

'Of course, but I'll warn you that Cook has a raspberry bush that is the envy of the neighborhood. The shrub can do no wrong.'

'Ah.' Lady Ann smiled. 'That might explain it.' She glanced at Margaret. 'And Miss Scott, you were a vision last evening. You are just what we needed to enliven this season.'

'Thank you, but I'm afraid I've made a muddle of everything.'

Amelia was about to come to her sister's rescue when Lady Ann beat her to it.

'Nonsense.' Lady Ann's brisk response left little room for doubt. 'Everyone feels that way after their debut. I, for one, can't wait to be settled and out of this city.'

Madge sighed. 'But does everyone's debut end with someone dead?'

Amelia counted to ten. If her sister wasn't careful, *she* was going to be dead, and Amelia was going to be the one to kill her.

'That had nothing to do with you.' Lady Ann caught Madge's gaze and held it. 'Anyone with a modicum of intelligence would understand Mr Worth was overwhelmed with grief when he returned to the ballroom. I'm sure he'll apologize. His fiancée will insist on it. She's a lovely person, so he must be decent as well.'

Margaret's eyes turned hopeful, but her lips were still pouty. 'Miss Farnsworth seems to think it has plenty to do with me.'

Lady Ann waved away the idea, her confidence making her seem older than she was. She couldn't have been more than one or two years older than Madge, but her voice exuded assuredness.

'Likely, Miss Farnsworth is envious of all the attention you received. She herself is looking for the perfect match this season, or – if Mr Radcliffe is to be believed – her father is. He does not want her to go one more year. He was practically salivating at the possibility of her and Lord Morton, yet he set his sights on you.'

Margaret's brow quirked with curiosity.

'Oh, yes, don't let Miss Farnsworth fool you. She may be the most beautiful woman in the room, but she's also a bit frantic. Her history with Simon Bainbridge has done her no favors. No one begs off an engagement with a future duke without reason or fault, most likely her own.'

Madge brightened with the information. The *ton* had plenty of secrets, but this was one Amelia wouldn't mention to a single soul, not even her sister. What had transpired between Simon and Felicity Farnsworth was still unclear, but Lady Ann was right in her supposition. Miss Farnsworth had been the one at fault in the relationship.

'So chin up, Miss Scott.' Lady Ann tipped her chin, her blue eyes a bright dove-gray. 'I, for one, cannot wait to see what good things this season brings you.' She glanced at the door, where Jones stood with a guest. 'And speaking of good things, here is Miss Castlewood.'

Amelia stood, welcoming her warmly. 'Miss Castlewood, I'm glad to see you.'

The comments seemed to bolster Miss Castlewood's confidence, and she continued into the room a little more assuredly. 'Good afternoon.'

'I wish I could stay, but I have another call to make.' Lady Ann stood, lifting her eyebrows in Amelia's direction as if to say, *I told you she'd call.* 'Please give my best to Mr Worth.'

'I will.' Miss Castlewood smiled appreciatively. When Lady Ann was gone, Miss Castlewood turned to Amelia. 'I must apologize for Mr Worth's behavior last evening – to you as well, Miss Scott. He was not himself when he returned.'

'Thank you,' said Amelia. 'I understand it was a difficult night.'

Miss Castlewood's light-blue eyes flicked downward. Some might call them colorless, reflecting the hues of whatever she gazed upon. 'Still, it gave him no right, and I am truly sorry.'

'You can say that again.' Madge dug her slipper into the carpet. 'A detective was here this morning asking questions.'

Miss Castlewood's mouth opened with surprise. 'Oh dear.'

As if they needed the word to get out even faster, Madge was telling their afternoon callers about the visit from Scotland Yard. *Thank you, sister.* Amelia went to work repairing the damage. 'It was to be expected. Mr Radcliffe's death was unforeseen. It's only natural that the police would inquire about his behavior at the party.'

'He seemed fine to me,' Miss Castlewood said.

'If fine means unbearable, I suppose he was fine.' A lock shook loose from Madge's coiffure. 'I don't understand why everyone liked him so much.'

A small smile touched Miss Castlewood's lips, and it brightened her otherwise serious face. 'He *was* very popular.'

'Why?' Madge pressed.

'I could not say,' Miss Castlewood replied. 'He was Mr Worth's friend, not mine.'

Amelia was relieved to switch topics and motioned to the three-tier plate on the table. 'A piece of cake, Miss Castlewood?'

She eyed the desserts longingly. 'I really mustn't.'

'How is Mr Worth today?' continued Amelia.

'He is better.' Her shoulders lowered. 'He is with his nephew, and children have a wonderful way of putting life in perspective.' She bowed her head, revealing a pretty emerald pin in her plain brown hair. 'Since the war, he has had a hard time processing events he cannot anticipate. You must not fault him for it.'

'I don't.' Amelia knew Miss Castlewood was right. Many men who fought in the Crimean War seven years ago still struggled with its after-effects to this day. Correspondents wrote in about the problem, and after a while, she saw a familiar pattern emerge. Yet the army and even the soldiers themselves were slow to acknowledge the issue. Amelia gave Miss Castlewood what she hoped was an encouraging smile. 'I'm glad he has you, Miss Castlewood. I hear you're soon to be married.'

Miss Castlewood's face lifted, and her eyes appeared bluer in the light from the window. 'Next week, in fact. We cannot wait to embark on our new life together.'

'Congratulations,' Amelia said.

Margaret seconded the felicitations somewhat begrudgingly.

'Thank you, and thank you for your generosity.' She stood to leave, clasping Amelia's hands in a spontaneous gesture. 'You're very kind to accept my apology.' She turned to Margaret. 'I wish you the best of luck this season, Miss Scott.'

'Thank you,' Margaret demurred. When Miss Castlewood was out of earshot, Madge added, 'I'm going to need it.'

NINE

Dear Lady Agony,
What do you do with our letters after you've read them?
Do you collect them, or do you toss them into the fire? I
imagine you would be remiss if someone found them.
Sincerely,
Another Letter for Kindling

Dear Another Letter for Kindling,
Your letters are important, and I could never destroy
them. I have them in a perfectly safe place. You will excuse
me, however, if I do not share the location.
Yours in Secret,
Lady Agony

Amelia was tucking her last response into a parcel when she thought she heard Aunt Tabitha shout from her room. She paused to make certain. Hearing a second exclamation, she shot up from her desk. Obviously, another problem had arisen, and it must have been one of magnitude for Aunt Tabitha to raise her voice in such a way. Aunt Tabitha stomped her cane, but she did not yell.

'What happened?' asked Amelia as she crossed Tabitha's doorway.

'It's not here.' Tabitha tossed a handkerchief over her shoulder. She was staring into an ornate gold filigree jewelry box, fingering each piece carefully.

Amelia recognized the box. It held her special family heirlooms. Edgar's father, Edwin, was Tabitha's only sibling and her favorite person in the whole wide world. When she lost him and his eldest son, Edgar's brother, she had been devastated. When she lost Edgar, too, she became more determined than ever to honor the family's legacy. 'What's not there?' asked Amelia.

Tabitha faced her. 'The Amesbury diamond.'

Amelia swallowed. The Amesbury diamond was famous, or at least known among London's oldest families. The brooch was shaped like a flower with a considerable diamond at the center, six rose-cut diamonds surrounding it and six more diamonds surrounding those, for a total weight of ten carats. 'I'm sure it's there. Perhaps you've misplaced it.'

Tabitha tilted her head like a bird that had spotted a worm. 'It is not something one misplaces.'

'Did you ask Mrs Addington for assistance?'

'She's searching for it now.' As if to underscore Tabitha's statement, Patty Addington's heavy footsteps padded past the room. Amelia heard her mumbling, 'Lordy, lordy, lordy.'

'When was the last time you saw it?'

'Last night.' Tabitha's answer was immediate. 'If you recall, I wore my pearls. They were also in the jewelry box, but I store the brooch in here.' She pulled out a velvet-cushioned drawer. 'Nothing else goes in or out of this drawer.'

'When you returned your pearls, was it there?'

'Mrs Addington did not look. There was no reason to.' Tabitha released a haggard breath. 'What possessed me to wear jewelry last night? I should have left the box alone.'

'Do not blame yourself. We'll find it,' Amelia assured her.

'It didn't go walking off by itself. Someone has taken it.'

Amelia was about to dismiss the suggestion when she remembered the recent spate of thefts in Mayfair. One of her readers had written to her about them. Two readers, to be exact. She needed to review the contents of the letters. It was possible that the thief had acted again. It certainly made more sense than Tabitha losing an heirloom piece of jewelry.

But was there any evidence of a break-in? The room was neat and orderly. The ornaments on the mantelpiece were perfectly arranged by height. The rug was recently brushed. The bed was tucked so tightly that turning over would have been an act of defiance. 'Did you notice anything different about your room when you returned? Was anything else missing?'

'It was two o'clock in the morning.' Tabitha searched the jewelry box again. 'I was exhausted. I'm not as young as I used to be, you know.'

Tabitha looked as she always had. Tall, distinguished, slightly terrifying. But, of course, she was growing older; they all were. Was it possible age had something to do with the missing piece? Amelia found it difficult to believe.

Amelia put an arm around her shoulders and squeezed. 'I'll look, too. Aunt. Do not worry. We will find it.'

Glancing up from the jewelry box, Tabitha patted her arm with her free hand. 'Thank you, dear.'

Amelia made haste to the library. Her correspondence from the magazine was hidden behind a secret panel, and she went to it now. Two years ago, she'd discovered it out of sheer curiosity. At the time, she had noticed a low shelf of Greco-Roman art tomes with a thin layer of dust. It was an interesting subject, and she wondered why the staff neglected the area.

She reached for one of the tomes and found out. A latch behind the book was triggered to open a small compartment for secret storage. She was disappointed – but not surprised – to find it empty. Her late husband Edgar was an open book. Unlike Amelia, he didn't have secrets. Indeed, it was extraordinary to her now that he could have been so enigmatic when he'd met her. He hadn't mentioned a word of his wealth or title. He'd followed Simon Bainbridge's advice to the letter, not revealing a word of his history until she accepted his proposal. Only then, Simon assured him, could he be certain that his niece and name would be well cared for.

But now, hundreds of letters greeted her as she opened the panel. Like old friends, they came back to her in a wave of signatures: Too Good to Be True, Too Mad to be Sad, Too Dead to be Wed. They were more than names; they were turning points in her life – and if her advice was true, their lives as well.

She skipped to the most recent letter, skimming it for details. It mentioned two thefts, both in Mayfair. Both occurred during a party. Amelia leaned back on her haunches. One would think that a house full of people would deter thieves – unless they were invited.

That was an idea.

She tapped her chin, considering the partygoers. Her intrigue changed to amusement as she contemplated the possibilities. She imagined Lady Hamsted tripping over her long dress as she scurried down the stairs, the stolen jewel in hand. *No.* Amelia shook her head. It wasn't the viscountess. Had she lacked money, which she didn't, no one would be the wiser. She – like so many others at the party – would keep up the appearance of wealth as long as possible. In fact, the thief might overstate his or her position or wealth – a case of protesting too much.

Amelia replaced the letters, closed the panel and stood. The first thing to do was request the guest list from Mrs Tipping. The second was to ask Grady Armstrong about the recent thefts. He always had his ear to the street for newsworthy information. Perhaps he'd heard about an increase of crime. Quickly, she jotted a note to him, asking about the thefts as well as Arthur Radcliffe. Then she handed the note to a footman and went in search of Mrs Tipping.

The entire house was upside down looking for the Amesbury jewel. Servants scurried here and there. Voices echoed from hallways. Cook almost pushed her over on the way to the kitchen. Finally, Amelia found Mrs Tipping in the butler's pantry. Her cap was askew, the pretty pink ribbon untied, and perspiration had moistened the brown hair above her ears, curling it slightly. Mrs Tipping was calm under pressure, decidedly so, but today her movements were hurried and frazzled.

'Mrs Tipping,' Amelia said.

Mrs Tipping jumped at the sound of her voice. 'My lady! You frightened me.'

'I'm sorry. I should have called out.'

Mrs Tipping smoothed her apron, uncharacteristically wrinkled. 'How may I help?'

Amelia indicated an open drawer. 'I assume you're looking for the lost jewelry?'

'Isn't everyone?' She sighed. 'Jones is always losing the silverware. I thought I might as well try here. We've looked everywhere else.'

'No luck?'

Mrs Tipping shook her head. 'None.'

'I'd like to see the guest list for the ball,' Amelia said. 'Do you still have it?'

'Certainly.' Mrs Tipping set her chin resolutely. She seemed relieved to have a task she knew she could complete.

'Thank you, Mrs Tipping. Bring it to the morning room when

you have it.' Amelia set off in that direction. As she passed the dining room, she noticed a chair pulled out from the table. Beneath it, Bailey scanned the floor, presumably for anything sparkly. Amelia shook her head. She doubted the famed brooch would be carelessly forgotten on the rug – unless Tabitha had worn the brooch, and it came unpinned. If that was the case, Amelia had a larger problem than theft. It would mean Tabitha was struggling with her memory.

Amelia paused and took a step backward, staring at the misplaced chair. It reminded her of something. She tried to recall what. She'd been in a half-dozen rooms this morning and some of them twice. She closed her eyes, replaying the morning in her head.

Her eyes flew open, and she hurried to Tabitha's room to confirm a hunch. She was right. Tabitha's dressing-table chair was not where it was supposed to be.

Tabitha must have recognized the alarm on her face because she stopped what she was doing. 'What is it?'

Tabitha's chair was next to the window, not tucked under the dressing table. 'Did you move that chair, Aunt?'

'What chair? No!' Tabitha had a quick mind and immediately followed Amelia's train of thought. She called out to Mrs Addington, who entered with a pink face. Her feathery eyebrows were knitted in determination. 'Patty, did you move this chair when you were looking for my brooch?'

Mrs Addington blinked at the chair. 'No. Never. I'd have no reason to move it there. Who did?'

'That's what Amelia wants to know, and so do I. My guess is that the thief who burgled my jewel absconded out of the bedroom window.'

'Heavens!' Mrs Addington proclaimed. 'A thief at Amesbury Manor!'

'Inform the staff,' said Tabitha.

'Right away.' The words had barely left Mrs Addington's mouth before she was scurrying down the hallway, telling one and all the unfortunate news.

Tabitha's face fell, her high cheekbones duller and softer. Amelia attempted to comfort her, lightly touching her arm. 'We cannot know for sure, Aunt. It's only a theory.'

Tabitha sighed. 'It's the right theory. You know it as well as I do.'

'I told Mrs Tipping to bring me the guest list.' Amelia kept her tone upbeat. 'Maybe I'll note a discrepancy.'

Tabitha quirked her brow, and a little color re-entered her face. 'What do you mean by "discrepancy"?'

Amelia shrugged. 'Someone unexpected. Someone unknown. A person capable of committing the crime.'

'I know every person on that list. I made it. I cannot think of anyone who would steal the jewel. What could they possibly do with it? Most of London knows it belongs to the Amesbury family.'

Amelia worried the jewel would be dismantled and thus unrecognizable, but she didn't relay her concerns to Tabitha. 'Peruse the list with me. If nothing else, it will keep your mind off the brooch.'

Tabitha stared at the jewelry box for a few moments. Then she pointed her cane at the door, indicating for Amelia to proceed.

The thumping of the cane behind her was a good sound. An active sound. Tabitha was happiest when she was absorbed in a task. Despite the pain in her joints, she wasn't one to stand still. In fact, she had once told Amelia that movement made the pain better, which accounted for the omnipresent sound of her cane. It'd become part of Amelia's day, and she could detect the kind of mood Tabitha was in by the tap of her stick. Today, for instance, Amelia knew she was distracted by its lack of punctuation. When Tabitha was on task, she didn't allow it to drag so.

The guest list was waiting for them on her desk in the morning room, and Amelia gathered the sheets of paper. 'Let us take a look.' She brought them to the blue-and-white-striped settee, where Tabitha joined her. 'If you see someone's name you do not recognize, let me know.'

Tabitha studied the first sheet. 'As I said, I know everyone.' She flipped to the next page. 'Except a few of these young men, but I believe Mrs Hamsted recommended them.'

Amelia nodded at the names. 'Kitty thought they might be of interest to Margaret. I'll ask her for specifics, but I can't imagine her not being careful in her selection.'

'Lord Morton, Lady Hamsted's nephew. Her brother's son.'

Tabitha's long finger paused over his name. 'I did not like his face. It looked as if he was hiding something, and his father was always a bit of a spendthrift. If my memory serves, he has a terrible gambling habit. Lord Morton may be in need of money, or the next best thing – jewelry.'

'Certainly, he is a bit of a dandy,' Amelia said. 'But he was quite affable, twice as kind as his aunt.'

Tabitha glanced up. 'That is easily accomplished.'

If Tabitha could suspect Lord Morton, she could suspect anyone and perhaps everyone. The guest list might not prove as useful as Amelia first thought. Still, Amelia added Leo Morton's name to an invisible list of thieves. 'Did you notice anyone leave the party early? I was so occupied I can't recall.'

A sardonic smile crossed Tabitha's lips. 'Besides Mr Radcliffe?'

Of course – Mr Radcliffe. His departure had caused the perfect distraction for a thief. Perhaps the thief even precipitated it. It was possible that the two occurrences were connected, but would someone commit murder to obtain the jewel? The heirloom was priceless, and people had certainly killed for less. 'Benjamin Worth was anxious to get him out of the house, but they went out of the front door. I cannot see how their departure had anything to do with the theft.'

'Neither can I, but the fact remains that two crimes might have been committed last night, and that's two more than have ever occurred at Amesbury Manor.'

What Tabitha said was true. A man was dead, and the famed Amesbury jewel was missing. Although Amelia couldn't see the connection, it didn't mean there wasn't one. 'I plan to talk to Kitty. She had a watchful eye on the party. Perhaps she has information that will prove helpful.'

'Be careful, Amelia.' Tabitha's bright blue eyes darkened with concern. 'I cannot help but wonder if something dark lurks beneath the surface here.'

Jones interrupted to inform Amelia that Grady Armstrong was waiting for her in the drawing room. She patted Tabitha's hand, soft and wrinkled. 'Grady might also have information regarding crimes in the area. Keep hope, Aunt.' She stood. 'I'll let you know what I find out.'

TEN

Dear Lady Agony,

The children at the Ragged School at Petticoat Lane and Gouston Street require our assistance. They are in need of clothes, and this is the time of year when some are cleaning out their closets. The smallest gift can help. Would you please inform your readers?

Sincerely,

A Plea for Help

Dear A Plea for Help,

It is often said, 'What the eye does not see, the heart does not feel.' So is the case at the Ragged School. Dear Readers, please see what is needed there, and give with your whole heart. Your return will be twofold in spirit.

Yours in Secret,

Lady Agony

Grady Armstrong was a cool wind on a warm summer's day. Despite his ink-smudged fingertips and dishwater-blond hair, his accent sang of Somerset and his and Amelia's childhood days. Hearing his voice always put a smile on her face.

'You keep calling on me, Amelia, and people might start wondering about your motivations.' Winking, Grady waved his flat cap in front of his face, creating a small breeze over his flushed face. 'Your note seemed important.' He checked over her shoulder, lowering his voice. 'Is it about a letter?'

'Not this time.' She took the seat next to him.

He leaned back with a sigh, clapping his heart. 'Thank the epistolary gods.'

'We had an eventful evening – and morning – and I wonder if you might be able to help me with some information.'

'That's right,' he said. 'It was your sister's debut. That's one wildcat I wouldn't want to meet up with in the forest. Let me guess. She scratched someone's eyes out.'

She shook her head. 'Not exactly, although there was an argument, and a man ended up dead.'

'Blimey.' Grady's large Adam's apple bobbed in his throat.

'Madge had nothing to do with it, but it doesn't look good. The police were here this morning. And that's not my only problem.'

He covered his face with his cap. 'Do I dare ask?'

'Promise not to tell a soul?'

He dropped the cap, a wrinkle of annoyance on his brow. 'I never would.'

'It's the Amesbury diamond. It's gone missing.'

His brown eyes were wide and sympathetic. 'If I had to wager a guess, it's large and expensive.'

'Both. The brooch has a large diamond in the center and twelve smaller diamonds surrounding it. It's very old and very special to Aunt Tabitha. What's more, it's the third theft I've heard about in the area. A correspondent told me about two similar occurrences in Mayfair. I thought you might have more information on the crimes.'

'You think someone nabbed the diamond brooch during the party?' Like a good newspaper man, he always had more questions.

'Tabitha's dressing chair was propped up next to the window. We have no other explanation for it being there.'

'Are you sure it wasn't Madge trying to make a secret getaway?' The corner of his mouth kicked up in a smile.

Amelia swatted his knee. 'I'm certain. She's the one person I had eyes on all night.'

'I've heard about a recent uptick of fences at Petticoat Lane, or "the Lane" if you're averse to talking of undergarments. No matter what you call it, it's where they sell stolen jewelry. The police placed more bobbies in the area at night for that reason.' He shrugged, and she noted his oversized coat, too large for his sharp shoulders. 'Maybe that's where your jewel is.'

'It's an idea.' The street that had been renamed Middlesex decades ago but was still known as Petticoat Lane. Some said one could have her petticoat stolen at one end of the lane and sold back to her at the other end before knowing what had happened.

'I know what you're thinking.' He pointed a stubby finger at her. 'Petticoat Lane is not a place for ladies. All sorts of riffraff. Especially at night.'

She smiled. 'It's kind that you worry about me, Grady, but I've seen my share of malefactors, and so have you. We had all sorts pass through the Feathered Nest.'

'Not like this, you haven't. Trust me. Your father would have never let one of these men set foot inside his lodgings.' He knew as well as anyone what the Feathered Nest was: a reputable inn with keepers as particular as their patrons. As a young man, he'd worked in the stables, watering and feeding horses. But he and Amelia always found time to sneak in a horse race or fishing expedition as well as a quick detour for newly delivered news-papers. Some of her best memories came from the plans they shared while perusing the inn's dailies. If only they could get somewhere exciting – like London! – they would lead exciting lives. When it came to the future, they were of the same mind: they would leave Mells as soon as they were able. And that's exactly what they had done.

'All right.' Amelia held up her hands to stop his barrage of warnings. 'I understand. Petticoat Lane is a dangerous place. Now tell me what you know about Arthur Radcliffe.'

Grady rattled off a few particulars, most of which Amelia already knew. Arthur Radcliffe's father was a baron. Being the eldest son, Arthur would have inherited the title and estate. Arthur had a younger brother, trained at Oxford to be a physician, who would now inherit. It was a respectable occupation but not one in which he was particularly interested or well suited, and he might be relieved to know his profession would be short-lived. The family's title wasn't old or distinguished, but what the Radcliffes lacked in prestige, they made up for in wealth. According to Grady, Arthur Radcliffe was invited to all the popular parties.

Money was the first place Amelia's mind went. 'The baron is still alive, so his wealth—'

'—is of no consequence.' Grady buttoned his coat. 'At least, not yet. He's active and in good health. You'd better start some-place else.'

'But where?'

He stood, and she joined him. 'Let the police decide, Amelia. I mean it.'

'And leave Madge's fate up to them?' She shook her head. 'I cannot risk it. My parents entrusted her to me. I cannot let anything happen.'

Grady took her hands, silently pleading with her to reconsider.

His rough skin reminded her of their childhood days, when she had no worries about smooth skin, good posture or fashionable dresses. Her greatest concern back then was whether they would catch a fish and who would keep it – she or Grady.

'I'll be careful.' She gave his hands a squeeze before releasing them. 'I promise.'

'Make sure you are,' he said pointedly and was gone.

Before he was out of the door, she was devising a way to disguise herself. Goods were being fenced at Petticoat Lane after dark – maybe even the Amesbury diamond. Chances were that the thief would want to get rid of it as quickly as possible. Which meant Amelia needed to visit soon. Which required a disguise.

Amelia bit her lip. She'd gone plenty of places in search of an answer for Lady Agony. Dressmakers, dens, even the London docks. But Grady warned her of Petticoat Lane's dangers after dark. She needed to take someone with her.

Just then, Madge walked into the drawing room, took off her hat and flopped onto the chair. 'Winifred has the energy of ten boys. I love her.'

Amelia smiled. 'I love her, too.' But her love for Winifred was not the cause of the smile. She was smiling because she'd found the perfect person to accompany her to Petticoat Lane. Madge was used to donning disguises and acting out parts in the plays at the Feathered Nest. Furthermore, she was not above physical violence when the situation called for it, and a trip to Petticoat Lane after dark could be such a situation.

'What is it?' Margaret sat up a little straighter in the green chair. The color was beautiful against her red-brown hair. 'I haven't seen you make that face since you decided to race me to the pond. I won, if I recall . . .'

'You are aware Aunt Tabitha's brooch has gone missing.'

Margaret rolled her eyes. 'Who isn't? The entire house is in uproar.'

'As it should be,' said Amelia. 'It's a family heirloom and worth a lot of money.'

'What can I do about it?'

Amelia's smile grew. 'I'm so glad you asked. I want you to go with me to Petticoat Lane. By day, it's a market filled with anything one's heart desires. But by night, fences sell their stolen goods through any means possible. I need to see if Tabitha's brooch is there. If it is, I'll buy it back and return it to its rightful owner.'

'With what money?'

Amelia shook her head. 'Mine, silly.'

Margaret settled back in her chair. 'Oh, right. You're a countess now. But I don't think Lady Tabitha would want you down there if it's as bad as you say.'

'She won't know.' Amelia lowered her voice. 'We'll be in disguise.'

Now a smile reached across Margaret's face, too, and her hazel eyes flicked wide, the light allowing a yellow hue to creep in. '*In disguise*. I think we can manage that.'

Despite the seriousness of the situation, Amelia's heart lifted. No one knew her as her family did. As Madge did. No title. No corset. No conventions. Amelia felt as if she were a child again – a child with a very important mission, she reminded herself. 'I need to find us clothes.'

'What kind of clothes?' Margaret's voice ticked up in anticipation.

'That's a good question.' Silently, Amelia considered a few options and dismissed them. 'We'll need to buy the brooch. Our clothes must be credible. Women's clothes, but not mine. I cannot be seen with fences at Petticoat Lane. Still, we need to convey a certain amount of wealth to be taken seriously.'

'Money is always taken seriously,' Madge reasoned. 'As long as you have it, I don't think they'll care what you're wearing.'

'True.' Amelia admired her sister's sensibility and unique point of view. 'We won't want to draw unnecessary attention, though. We'll be plain. Practical. A little bit secretive.'

Madge slapped her hands on her knees. 'I know a person with just that fashion sense.'

'Who?'

Madge stood and grabbed her hand. 'Me.'

ELEVEN

Dear Lady Agony,

Do you work in disguise? One of my friends thought they saw you make a quick getaway at a milliner's on the corner of Haymarket and Pall Mall, wearing a flowered hat two sizes too large. According to her, it concealed your face but not your clandestine retreat out of the rear door. Was it you? I have to know.

Sincerely,

Too Hard to Tell

Dear Too Hard to Tell,

If I donned a disguise, surely I would avoid flowers as obvious as the ones your friend described. They alone would give me away. Regarding my penchant for costumes, however, I will leave that question up to you and your friend's fine imaginations.

Yours in Secret,

Lady Agony

A few hours and alterations later, Amelia and Margaret were stealing down the servants' staircase, holding their breath. Amelia was holding her breath at any rate; Margaret was stifling a giggle. Madge, who'd always claimed she'd grow taller than Amelia one day, was supremely happy to be proven right. Amelia had to pin her borrowed skirt several inches to avoid tripping over its length. Their father, it appeared, had given his height wholeheartedly to Margaret.

And his litheness, too. Amelia pulled at the snug skirt waist. Other than the small discomfort, the outfit worked supremely well for all purposes. It was plain, it was dark and it was respectable. With her hair pinned up under a black hat and veil, a garment she'd worn in her early widowhood, Amelia was confident no one would recognize her. Her sister's red hair, impossible to disguise, was transformed by a black wig from Amelia's old costume trunk, and she, too, was indistinguishable. They could go about the city undetected. At least, that was Amelia's fervent wish.

Amelia signaled for Bailey, who was waiting with the driver and carriage. She hated to involve her staff, but Bailey understood the importance of the errand. The Amesbury jewel was at stake, and Petticoat Lane was in the East End, across the city from Mayfair. Amelia would have him deposit them far enough away that their approach wouldn't be noticed, and if anything went wrong, he would be waiting to whisk them away.

'Or tumble with a fence,' he'd put in quietly when she told him of the plan. At over six feet tall with broad shoulders, a small waist and fists as large as a fighter's, Bailey was her most imposing footman and also the one her women friends swooned over. He would certainly give a fence a challenge. But with any luck, it wouldn't come to that.

As they made their way across the city, the fog moved over them in murky waves, the carriage rolling up and down streets like a small boat in a large sea. Nightfall was upon them, and out went the lamplighters, carrying ladders, wick trimmers and whale oil. One man whistled a happy tune that carried all the way to the carriage. With a cheerful face, he lit the dark street, making it friendly and more passable. The work, so important, had perhaps been passed down from his father and might again be passed on to his son. With the myriad changes taking place in London, it was hard to say what the future held, but Amelia knew humankind would always find new ways to chase out the dark.

As they crossed Bishopsgate, the coachman slowed to a stop, and a new buzz hovered over the carriage like a beehive. Around the corner, men's voices hummed in low tones, the air electric and dangerous. Amelia felt the singular pressure of being an older sister then. She must not only find information about the Amesbury jewel; she must also keep Margaret safe.

Bailey caught Amelia's eye as she descended the carriage steps with her parasol. 'We're only a stone's throw away if you need us. I can run as fast as any man here.'

'I know.' Amelia smiled briefly. 'If anything goes amiss, I'll call for you.'

'We'll be fine.' Madge gave him a cheeky grin. 'Don't worry about us. The Scott sisters can hold their own.'

Bailey ignored her. 'I'll listen for you, milady.'

Amelia turned the corner at Middlesex, better known as Petticoat Lane, and the noise that had been a buzz became a quiet roar. The smell of shoe leather and worn clothes accosted her, not to mention fried fish perhaps hours or days old. The mixture wasn't exactly unpleasant but became more arresting with each step. Margaret must have thought differently, for she scrunched up her nose, her chin tucking in as they passed a particularly strong odor wafting out of a pork sausage shop.

A man stepped in front of them with an offer of cigars. 'Direct from 'Avannah. Or if they don't interest you, a bit of silk for a dress might. I know the best qualities.'

'No.' Amelia shook her head briskly, intoning her voice with more courage than she felt. 'We're in the market for jewelry. Nice jewelry.'

The man closed one of his hooded eyes, the wrinkled lid craggy in the gaslight. 'Aye. I know where to find baubles for fine lasses like yourselves. Follow me.'

Amelia and Margaret exchanged glances before falling in step behind the old man, who was short and made shorter by the stoop of his shoulders. Although he was old, Amelia sensed he was streetwise by his steady gait. He knew the area well and steered them around obstacles like a shepherd herding sheep. Amelia was no lamb, however, and neither was her sister. They remained watchful for the danger that lurked around every corner.

Crossing Wentworth Street to Bell Lane, Amelia was surprised to see a jeweler appear before them with a decent window display, albeit unlit. She never imagined he'd take them to an actual shop instead of a vendor or street seller. The closer they came, the more Amelia understood about the business. Beyond the display, perhaps in a back room, a few customers crowded around a table to exchange bits of news and perhaps stolen goods. A single lamp illuminated four heads bent over in discussion. The shop might be a front for illicit activity.

The old man knocked on the back door. One tap, two taps, one tap.

A secret code maybe.

A man swung open the door. His forehead was high, and his nose was as sharp as a bird's beak. His small eyes were made larger by long, arching eyebrows, and his chin softer by a set of brown side whiskers. 'Mr Barnes. What have you brought me?'

'These two ladies is in the market for some fine jewelry.'

'Is that so?' The man studied Amelia first and then her sister. Amelia kept her shoulders straight, refusing to give in to her knees, which felt as if they would buckle. Margaret didn't budge either, although Amelia noted her nervous swallow.

Finished with his inspection, the man handed Mr Barnes a shilling.

'Thank you, Isaac, sir.' Mr Barnes stuck the coin in his pocket, turned and left.

The air grew heavier the moment he was gone, and for a moment, Amelia wished him back.

'Come in, ladies.' The man named Isaac flourished a hand. 'See if I have anything to your liking.'

Amelia took a step forward and regretted it when he shut the door behind her.

'Whatever brings you in on a foggy eve such as this? It must be important, perhaps a special gift you've been unable to locate.' Isaac's voice was cordial but restrained, leading the conversation in the direction he desired. 'Do you search for something particular?'

'Yes, we do.' Amelia kept her face away from the light. One lamp burned in the corner, and three men hovered over it. A woman, perhaps Isaacs's wife, was displaying an emerald bracelet that even in the dim light took Amelia's breath away. She'd never seen so many green gemstones in a row. 'Diamonds. One diamond, specifically. A brooch.'

'Ah, diamonds. The world's most beautiful jewel.' Isaac laced his fingers, and Amelia noted an enormous diamond ring on his pinkie finger. 'I don't know if you've come to the right place.'

In the corner, the woman paused for a moment, then kept talking. Amelia was certain it was some kind of signal, but for what she didn't know. Amelia swallowed. 'I believe we have. Mr Barnes said it was.'

Isaac nodded toward an isolated corner display, and they had no choice but to follow him. He went for his keys, as if to show them the merchandise, but then he grabbed Amelia's hand, studying her fine kid glove.

Amelia began to speak, cursing her blunder. The expensive material had given her away.

He held up a silencing finger, examining the clothing, front and back. 'What are you doing here, Lady?' he whispered. 'These hands have never seen a day's work in their life. You do not belong here.'

'Yes, I do.' Amelia stilled her hand from shaking as she drew it back.

'Yes, they have!' added Madge.

Amelia silenced her with a look, wondering how she could have ever thought bringing Margaret Scott was a good idea. Her temper was too hot, her inexperience a detriment to their efforts. She should have brought Kitty. She was a friend with a calm head in a tenuous situation. But it was too late now. She needed to work with what she had: a scapegrace sister, a dubious jewelry store and a suspicious owner. Only one thing could save her now.

Money.

'I assume this is an establishment that esteems money, and I have much to spend. For the right jewel. The right diamond.'

'Lady, you mistake me.' Isaac clicked his tongue in disapproval. 'I'm a craftsman, not a thief.'

Amelia needed to prove to him that she wasn't a lady and she wasn't jesting. To back down now would mean failure, and she hadn't come to Petticoat Lane to fail. 'Perhaps you're correct. Perhaps I'm in the wrong establishment. I'll check another.'

In a low voice, he said, 'Be careful, Lady.'

Amelia was confused by his comment but also committed to following through with her threat to leave. 'Thank you for your time.' Catching Margaret's eye, she nodded to the door, and they left.

When they were a few steps away, Margaret asked, 'Do you think he has it?'

'I don't know.' A breeze caught Amelia's veil, and she pulled it down. 'My status alarmed him.'

A steady click, click, click sounded behind her. *A man's boot*s. She checked over her shoulder. Isaac, if that was his real name, was fast on their heels, head down, the side feather on his low bowler hat dipping up and down despite the still night air. They couldn't outrun him. They couldn't outfight him. The best they could do was ditch him.

Amelia grabbed Madge's arm and took a sharp left, then a sharp right. An old woman with claw hands reached out, stopping her. Amelia squealed.

The woman, who had the face of a witch, with sunken eyes and a missing tooth, thrust a pair of old boots in her face. The curb was filled with Wellingtons and ankle-jacks. 'Tomorrow these will be gone, but tonight you're in luck.' She smiled an avaricious smile. 'Come, child. Take a pair.'

Amelia jerked her arm free. 'No, thank you.'

'How about these?' She shoved a pair of dingy wedding boots in her face. 'Try them on.'

'She said no.' Madge's voice was firm.

The old woman let out a cackle, and two men leaning against the building behind them looked up from their whittling. Amelia noted the size of their knives.

Isaac appeared from around the same building like smoke from a pipe.

The witch woman shrank from her own laughter, her eyes focused on the old shoes in front of her. Her lips still moved, but she muttered nothing aloud. Isaac owned this street, even its witches. Amelia knew it by the way people parted, silencing their conversations, paying him respect without words.

'There you are, Lady.' The whittlers turned from the building as Isaac approached. 'We have business to finish.'

'Do we?' Amelia squeaked. 'I'm not certain we do.'

His low hat disguised his sharp features. 'Follow me. There is no time to talk.'

'We're not going anywhere with you,' Madge stated flatly. 'If you try to take us, I'll scream.'

'Calm your fight dog, Lady. It is making much noise.'

Madge opened her mouth.

'No,' cautioned Amelia. 'Wait.'

'Those men in my store. They are following you. I promised my wife I would warn you.' Isaac's voice was insistent, the words rushing out without pause. Amelia detected real concern in them

and was surprised by it. 'You must hurry,' he added. 'They are
very bad men – cracksmen.'

Madge crossed her arms. 'And you're a saint?'

Isaac ignored her, talking to Amelia. 'Through that door. It's
the only way.' He pointed to the building behind them, whose
front door had opened as if by magic.

If it was a ruse, Amelia and her sister would be lost forever.
It was a three-story stone building but might as well be a cavern
or deep-dug well. No one, including Bailey, would hear their
screams from inside it. If it wasn't a ruse, the cracksmen from
his shop might slit their throats for their money and leave them
for dead. She'd been in bad situations, but none that involved
her sister. Her younger sister, at that. She cursed herself for
putting a family member in this situation.

'Lady?'

At least he was asking. The other men might not be so kind.

'Fine.' Amelia grasped Margaret's hand and pulled her along
the street, Madge hissing her disapproval with each step. Amelia
pushed the cracked door open and noted one of the whittlers
from earlier inside. He wasn't threatening, just dirty. His pants,
shirt and face were besmirched with dust and mud. His eyes,
however, were sky-blue and light enough to pierce the dark.

As soon as Isaac shut the door, his tone changed. 'You come
into my store looking for a diamond, talking of money? You
foolish woman. Have you not heard the Amesbury diamond has
been stolen? Everyone is looking for it.'

'Including me,' Amelia put in.

'Get in line, Lady.' Isaac lit a cigarette.

'You don't have it?' asked Amelia.

'No, I don't have it.' He waved his match, the flame disappearing in the dank air. 'And if I did, I wouldn't sell it to you.'

Incensed, Amelia felt her chin jut out automatically. 'Why
not?'

'She's got the money,' added Madge.

'Because I don't know where you come from. Wherever it is,
you need to return there.' Isaac nodded at the whittler. 'Archie
will take you out the back door.'

Archie shifted in the corner.

'Wait.' Amelia rubbed her forehead. She couldn't return to

Petticoat Lane. That much was certain. Now that she had gained the cracksmen's attention, it would be too dangerous. They would watch for her, wait for her. 'You do not understand. I need that diamond.'

Isaac threw his cigarette on the floor and snapped his fingers. Archie shrugged forward. 'So does every thief on this street.'

It was now or never.

Amelia took off her hat, straightened her shoulders and took a deep breath. 'I need the diamond because I'm Lady Amesbury. The jewel belongs to my family.'

TWELVE

Dear Lady Agony,

A falsehood is following me, and no matter which way I run, it is there, like a shadow, darkening my days. I cannot tell the truth, so please don't suggest it. What else might I do?

Sincerely,
Small White Lie

Dear Small White Lie,

You state it is a small white lie, yet it seems to cast a long shadow. Do not lie to yourself, Dear Reader. If it is darkening your days, it is not small, nor is it white. You know what you must do, but I will state it anyway. Tell the truth. It will set you – and the shadows – free.

Yours in Secret,
Lady Agony

Isaac quit stomping out his cigarette.

Archie cursed under his breath.

'I am willing to pay a reward to whomever returns the diamond to its rightful place,' continued Amelia. 'The Amesbury home.'

'How do I know you are who you say you are?' Isaac dipped his head, his nose pointy at the angle.

Amelia dug into the folds of her dress, rummaging in the pocket for the single card she'd placed there for an emergency such as this one. She gave it to him.

'The peelers will jail us for sure, Ike,' Archie muttered.

'No one need worry about my telling the police of this affair. I've come in disguise. I don't want my name mentioned any more than you do. On that you have my word.'

Margaret nibbled her lip, a habit from childhood that Amelia hadn't seen appear for years. It was rare that Madge was afraid or without words; Amelia must have frightened her more than she realized with the revelation. Amelia grasped her hand and squeezed it, pulling her closer. Madge had come to London for a reprieve from her problems and instead faced even more difficult obstacles. Clearing the path would be arduous, but Amelia was determined to bring her peace and happiness at last even if it took her all season.

'I admire your courage, Lady, and I will keep a look out for your diamond. But Archie is right. You must go. We cannot be seen with you. If something happens to you, God forbid, it will be us who swing for it.' Isaac attempted to hand back the card.

'Keep it,' said Amelia. 'If you have any information, you'll know where to find me. Your effort won't go unrecognized or unrewarded. I am in debt to you for saving our lives and wish to repay the favor.'

A smile twitched on Isaac's lips. 'You'd have a known fence darken a doorway in Mayfair?'

Amelia gave him an appraising look. Isaac was a good man to know, a link to London's East End, where she had few connections, especially criminal. Grady was her source of information, and an excellent source, too, but even he didn't know all the goings on in the vast city. With the spate of crimes in Mayfair, meeting Isaac Jakeman was fortuitous. 'Absolutely,' she answered. 'We've had recent thefts in the area, besides the Amesbury diamond. Jewelry is the thief's object of desire. Maybe you've heard?'

The smile fell from Isaac's face. 'Only in the papers. That thief plays a dangerous game.'

'Nobody wants nothing to do with Mayfair,' Archie put in.

'Where might the thief sell the goods?' she asked. 'Here?'

'You keep to your business. I'll keep to mine.' Isaac nodded at Archie. 'It's time for you to go, Lady.'

'But if you hear—'

'I will come.' He dipped his head. 'And claim my reward.'

'Of course,' Amelia answered, but Isaac had already turned to leave.

'This way,' said Archie, pointing in the opposite direction, a dark hallway presumably leading to an even darker alley. 'Do you have a driver?'

'Yes.' Amelia stuffed on her hat and motioned for Margaret to go first. 'On Bishopsgate.'

'And he let you go it alone?' grumbled Archie.

'I insisted.'

'You insisted,' Archie muttered, shaking his head. 'Thank the stars above Isaac Jakeman took pity on you.' He ducked around the corner while they waited. He returned, motioning them forward with the tips of his dirty fingers. 'Hurry now. Keep your heads down.'

Amelia didn't need to be told twice, and, for once, neither did her sister. They crossed Wentworth to Middlesex, keeping to one side of the lane. Moments later, three men came around the corner opposite them. Amelia recognized them from the jewelry store, and a breath caught in her throat. Noting her pause, Archie and Madge followed her gaze to the other side of the street, where the men peeked through windows and checked doors. One man grabbed a woman's shoulder, perhaps thinking it was Amelia or her sister. The woman took her shoulder back with force, her hat spilling to one side, revealing blonde hair. Then she went back to sorting her silks, neatly arranged by color.

'Shoes, miss.' The old woman from earlier was in her face with the same pair of dingy boots. Amelia had been too distracted to notice her approach. 'You forgot your shoes.'

Amelia shook her head, ignoring her.

The woman wouldn't be dissuaded and reached for her. 'Try them on.'

Amelia tore her elbow from the woman's grasp. 'No.'

'Yes.' The woman's voice was louder and insistent.

Archie paused. 'Take a rest, Yolanda. She's not buying nothing.'

The woman spat on the ground, and another vendor skirted around it. 'Disgusting old bird.'

The old woman howled at the insult, alerting the entire street – and the cracksmen. For a split second, Amelia locked eyes with one of the men. At that moment, it felt as if her soul was being sucked out of her body by the menacing blue eyes, and she slammed into Margaret, who was still in front of her.

Madge turned around. 'Ah . . . Archie?'

Archie took in the scene in seconds. 'Oh, Christ. Run!'

They did, swerving in and out of clumps of people. Heat surged through Amelia as she passed something hot. A street fire? A boiling pot? She couldn't look and perhaps imagined it anyway. Her chest was on fire. A noise was pounding in her head – she didn't know if it was her feet or her heartbeat.

Bailey was just around the corner. If they could make it to him, they would be safe. But between the people and the fog, she couldn't see a thing except her sister's dress flying in front of her. At least Madge was safe. Right now, that was all that mattered.

She heard a whistle. Then another whistle.

'You there. Stop!'

Margaret was not stopping, so neither did Amelia . . . until Margaret fell, and Amelia tripped over her, falling, too. She reached out for Archie, but he was gone. Like a ghost, he'd vanished into the fog, abandoning them to face the trouble alone.

'On your feet,' said a voice from above.

Amelia looked up to find Detective Collings staring down at her.

'What'd you take tonight, street urchin? Something that doesn't belong to you, no doubt.'

'Who are you calling street urchin?' Madge's wig was halfway off her head. Her hair was a tumble of red and black, like a ladybug's spotted shell. She sat up and pulled the wig off completely. 'I'm Margaret Scott, the countess's sister. I ask you to take that back, sir.'

At that moment, Amelia wished the ground would swallow her whole. She closed her eyes waiting for the street to crack, but nothing happened. Not a quake, not a quiver. When she opened them, Detective Collings was still there, squinting at her with his coal-colored eyes as if she were a monkey at the zoo.

Amelia stood and dusted off her dress. There were things one didn't want to do – like face Detective Collings – that one did anyway. It was best to do them without delay and with courage. Or at least in an upright position. 'Good evening, Detective. If you would kindly escort us to my carriage, I would be forever grateful.'

He blinked.

'I believe it is just around that corner,' added Amelia, indicating the direction.

Margaret stood also, shoving the wig under her arm.

'A moment, first.' The detective's voice was dark and gritty, like a cup of coffee that had sat too long, growing cold. 'I imagine you have a good reason for being on Petticoat Lane at this hour. In disguise.'

Amelia considered telling him the truth. The sooner they involved the police, the sooner the Amesbury jewel might be returned. But Amelia knew from her letters that both thefts in Mayfair had gone unresolved, despite the information being shared with Scotland Yard. She had just as good a chance of recovering the item as they did, and perhaps even better since she had the funds to buy it back – an exchange that would be considered illicit by the police. Telling him was out of the question.

'As you know, my sister is new to London. She wanted to see the market, but naturally, I did not want to be seen at this hour. So I indulged her, by going in disguise.' Amelia was proficient in concocting excuses on her missions as Lady Agony and was satisfied with how reasonable the lie sounded.

'And you were in the market for . . .?' pressed the detective.

Amelia tipped her head to the old witch behind her. 'Shoes.'

'Shoes,' the detective repeated.

'Shoes.' Amelia cleared her throat. 'Now, if you would be so kind as to escort us to our carriage. The area is much more hostile than I imagined.'

Detective Collings nodded in reluctant agreement.

'My feet are killing me,' whispered Madge. 'I should have bought those boots from that old lady.'

Heaven knows she offered enough.

Around the corner was the Amesbury carriage, and when Bailey spotted them, he jumped to attention. As they came closer, his eyes darted between Amelia and Margaret. 'My lady! Miss Scott! What happened to your—' He frowned at the detective. 'Hair.'

Margaret untucked the wig from her arm. It might have been a fishing net by its tangled appearance. 'It fell off.' She shook the wig. 'Little beasty.'

Bailey raised his eyebrows but said nothing as he opened the carriage door.

'Oh, and Miss Scott?' The detective's voice was light in a curious way.

Margaret paused at the carriage entrance.

'I met Mr Radcliffe's brother today.'

'You did,' said Amelia.

'I did.'

Amelia guessed his cordial expression had to do with information he was about to bestow. His mouth, although not smiling, was turned up at the corners, and his voice was overly eager.

'Jonathan Radcliffe is a trained physician. *Oxford* trained.' The detective emphasized the university. 'He attended his brother last night, and it's his expert opinion that his brother was murdered.'

Margaret sank farther into the seat.

The detective narrowed his dark gaze on her.

Amelia wouldn't allow Collings to intimidate her little sister, which was easily done on a remote street in a bad costume after a harrowing escape. It wasn't so easily done at Amesbury Manor, and Amelia tried to channel Aunt Tabitha in her response. 'I understand Jonathan Radcliffe tended to his brother many times – for gastric attacks. In fact, I heard he'd given him a new tonic. Perhaps it was his homemade brew that caused his brother's death.'

Detective Collings's eyes widened with something akin to surprise. Amelia guessed the thought had not occurred to him, but it had certainly occurred to her. Jonathan Radcliffe could be concerned about his own medical mistake and pointing the finger elsewhere.

The next moment, the surprised look fell from his face, however, and his eyes were hard as onyx. 'If that were the case, the doctor could have said his brother's death was natural. Expected, even.'

Margaret watched the volley of claims like a ball being hurled back and forth over a net, and her eyes returned to Amelia.

The detective was quick; Amelia would give him that. It hadn't taken him long to follow the thought to a conclusion that suited his purpose. 'Would he? The medical examiner will have something to say about the death, and the doctor might need an excuse.'

'The medical examiner.' Madge crossed her arms. 'Hadn't thought of that, had you?'

Detective Collings leaned closer to the carriage door, and Margaret sank into her carriage seat, looking fearful.

'I've thought of everything, Miss Scott, including reasons for your little escapade to Petticoat Lane. None of which include shoes.'

Amelia gave him a poke with her parasol. 'Excuse me, Detective. We really must be going.'

Detective Collings stepped out of her way, and with the impasse removed from the carriage entrance, Amelia climbed inside.

He grabbed the door. 'I will see you soon.'

'I look forward to it.' Amelia motioned to Bailey who immediately shut the door, leaving the detective to stare after them.

Madge released a breath. 'What an ordeal! I thought we were dead for sure. And where did Archie go? A fine guide indeed.'

'Not a guide, Madge, a Petticoat Lane fence who took pity on us. Thank heavens he got us as far as he did.' Amelia lifted her veil. 'One more minute and I would have hollered for Bailey.'

Margaret stared at the seat cushion in front of her, perhaps reliving the events in her head. Her shoulders shivered, and her eyes snapped back to Amelia's. 'What about the detective? Do you think what he said was true?'

'Every word,' Amelia muttered. 'The physician's opinion is expert, as the detective said. It would be given full weight at an inquest.'

'*Inquest!*' The freckles on Madge's face appeared darker. 'You don't think it will come to that, do you?'

Amelia gave her a brave smile. 'If it does, we'll be ready.'

THIRTEEN

Dear Lady Agony,

Yours must be in a taxing position. A lady in one life, a penny paper authoress in another. Where do you turn for comfort? I'd like to go there as well.

Sincerely,
Comfort & Joy

Dear Comfort & Joy,

When the world is topsy-turvy and my correspondents' problems turn into mine, I find great comfort in books. Nowhere else can I escape so fast to another time, another place, another me. My problems fade, and I am at once a lovelorn hero, a Turkish explorer or a Scottish maiden in plaid. Thank heaven for books. Without them, the world would be a less joyful place.

Yours in Secret,
Lady Agony

The next day felt almost normal. Yes, the entire house was upside down about the missing diamond, and her sister was dodging a murder accusation, but here in the two-story library, Amelia felt safe and secure. The cherry-wood bookshelves were filled with pages that assured her that life could and would go on. People greater than she had overcome insurmountable obstacles; a missing diamond and a dead party guest were hardly challenges in the shadows of wars and battles. Had not Oliver Hamsted just delivered a terrific tome on the Battle of Waterloo that still sat on her desk? The brown leather cover assured her he had.

Amelia packaged her responses in a parcel for Grady. All would be righted, including the lives she was assisting from afar. Bad hair, gowns and skin were no match for time – or Lady Agony. Life would move forward as it had since Adam and Eve.

Jones's shuffle sounded at the door, and Amelia looked up

from her parcel. 'Captain Fitz is in the drawing room, my lady. He is asking to see Miss Scott.'

'How nice . . .' Amelia had no idea why the visit pertained to her. It was earlier than usual for callers, yes, but she didn't mind the intrusion, and neither would Madge. In fact, Amelia sensed her sister enjoyed the captain's company a good deal and would welcome the call, no matter the hour.

Jones cleared his throat. 'None of the maids are available, and Lady Winifred's governess, Miss Walters, has taken her to the museum.'

Amelia blinked. 'All right.'

'Perhaps she shouldn't be alone with him?'

Amelia stood, knocking her knees on the desk. Margaret was beginning to be her Waterloo. 'Of course not, Jones. Thank you.'

And the old maid becomes a chaperone. Gracious, she grumbled to herself as she went up the stairs. *Next I'll be carrying a sewing basket*. 'Madge.' She knocked on her sister's door. 'You have a visitor.'

Madge flung open the door. Her skirt was a stunner, a lovely peach silk that made her hazel eyes appear browner, a perfect hazelnut color, and her coordinating collar accentuated her shading. 'What a relief. I thought I put on this dress for nothing.' She set her shoulders. 'Who is it? Lady Ann? The Farnsworth chit?'

'Captain Fitz.'

'Captain Fitz!' Madge stepped back into the room, checking the mirror. 'How does my hair look?'

'Beautiful,' answered Amelia. 'But when did you start caring about your hair?'

Madge swept a stray lock from her face. 'What do you think he wants?'

'To better make your acquaintance.' Amelia sighed. 'Let us not keep him waiting.'

Madge nodded, and Amelia led the way down the stairs to the drawing room, where Captain Fitz stood near the low table in the center of the room, looking very tall. His sandy blond hair was easy like his manners, and side whiskers outlined his handsome chin. When his blue eyes landed on Margaret, they flicked wide with excitement.

He bowed. 'Lady Amesbury. Miss Scott.'

The dimple appeared in Margaret's cheek, the one Amelia saw only on special occasions. 'Captain Fitz.'

'I'll ring for tea,' Amelia said to no one in particular. Neither of them was listening to her.

'Actually, I was hoping to take Miss Scott to Hyde Park. And you as well, of course,' he added hastily.

'Might we, Amelia?' Madge touched her arm.

Amelia smiled. 'It *is* a lovely day for it.'

Captain Fitz collected his hat and Amelia her parasol, and a moment later, they were in Captain Fitz's carriage. The park was so close that they could have walked, and Amelia always did every morning. But the intimate setting gave her a chance to inquire about Mr Radcliffe's gastric attacks and his brother's treatment. She hoped the captain, being an acquaintance of his, would know more about both.

'I'm glad to see you, Captain Fitz,' said Amelia. 'I understand it's a difficult time for you and your friends.'

Madge frowned, perhaps upset at Amelia for introducing the sad topic of conversation.

'It is.' Captain Fitz clapped his hands on his thighs. 'But we weren't close friends, only acquaintances. He was a peculiar man.'

'And an underhanded man, in my opinion,' Madge put in.

Captain Fitz laughed, unperturbed by the criticism. 'I understand you didn't get along with him. He must have been surprised at your disapproval. Most women adored him.'

'Not this woman.' Madge's lip kicked up on one side into a half-hearted smile.

As you've stated many times for all to hear. Thank you once again, sister. Amelia attempted to move from the topic of Madge not liking Mr Radcliffe. 'You said he suffered from gastric attacks, and his brother treated them. Is that correct?'

'Yes.' Captain Fitz was still smiling at Margaret. 'Jonathan Radcliffe is his brother.' He sat up straighter in his seat, pretending to preen a little. 'An Oxford scholar.' He dismissed the comment with a wave. 'He's smart – I'll give you that – but as exciting as January. He prefers dogs to people. Nothing like his brother.'

'Did the brothers get on?' Amelia asked.

Captain Fitz frowned as if he'd never considered the question. 'I suppose they did. Arthur thought a lot of him, or his education anyway. He thought Jonathan would find a cure for his stomach pains. Maybe in time, the new tonic would have helped him.'

'Or hurt him.' Amelia raised her eyebrows.

'What do you mean?'

'You said he took the new tonic the night of his death.' Amelia shrugged. 'Maybe it had something to do with his sudden passing.'

The captain was considering a response when the carriage wheel hit a rut in the road, causing Margaret to fall against the window and Amelia to follow suit.

'You bloody fool!' he called to the driver. Captain Fitz's voice was angry, and his blue eyes flashed storm-gray. 'Mind the road.'

The tone startled Amelia more than the dip in the road.

'Sorry, sir,' came a voice from up front. 'I didn't see it there on the turn.'

'In future, watch where you're going, Evans.' The captain shook his head in disgust. 'I apologize, ladies. My driver is more interested in talking than driving. He and the footman are like two old women.'

Amelia accepted his apology, and a moment later, they were in the park and out of the carriage, the blessed blue day upon them. As the sun seeped into her skin, she felt less troubled – or at least warmer. Her sister was enjoying Captain Fitz's company a good deal, and that made her happy. Margaret seemed more like herself in the park, comfortable amid the green grass and blue sky. Freer. The thought comforted Amelia, and she slowed her pace, allowing the gap between her and the couple to grow. Every woman should feel as unencumbered as Margaret did right now.

'Astonishing,' said a voice behind her. 'From London's most formidable penny paper authoress to her sister's keeper in less than two days. It must be a record.'

Amelia spun around to see Simon hurrying to catch up with her, holding his hat on to his head as he did. His smile spanned the distance, and she ignored the warmth she felt earlier as it spread all the way to her toes. He'd rebuffed her in the garden. She was angry with him. She was not going to smile back.

Yet she felt her treacherous lips lift upward. *Blazes!* Did he command the oceans and her face, too?

'Chaperones are supposed to follow closely, not dally,' he said.

'I'm new to the task.' She attempted a snarl. 'What can I say?'

He paused. 'Are you angry with me?'

'Hmm?'

'May I ask about what?'

She pulled her glance from the clouds. She couldn't possibly admit she was dismayed that he hadn't kissed her. Besides, it wasn't that, exactly. Was it? She shook off the question. 'Why would I be angry? Tell me about Captain Fitz. My sister appears smitten with him.'

Simon let the topic change and continued walking. 'Fitz is a good man. Your sister is in good hands.'

'Do you know him well?'

'No, not well, but enough.' He touched his hat as he passed an acquaintance. 'He fought valiantly in Crimea and earned a commendation for his efforts. He saved a troop of ten men with his quick thinking. One would think he would be able to save one Scott sister from further scandal.'

'If only that were true,' she muttered.

'I recognize that look.' He stopped walking. 'What has happened?'

'So many things.'

He gestured to Margaret, who had stopped to examine a particularly colorful lupin. 'We have time. Tell me.'

First hair and now flowers? Her interests are certainly diversifying.

Amelia leaned closer. 'The Amesbury diamond went missing the night of the ball.'

'*The* Amesbury diamond?' he whispered.

'Is there any other? I think someone absconded with it out of the window.'

His shapely black eyebrows lifted in question. 'It could be misplaced. Lady Tabitha is growing older.'

'It isn't misplaced. Tabitha's dressing stool was beneath the windowsill. It had no reason to be there.' He looked doubtful, so she continued. 'And Grady informed me that Petticoat Lane has seen an uptick in business.'

That got his attention. 'You think the jewel has been stolen by a Petticoat Lane fence?'

'I cannot say for certain.' She shrugged. 'Margaret and I went in disguise last night, but our inquiries didn't lead to the return of the diamond. A gentleman named Isaac Jakeman might prove to be valuable, however. He promised to keep his eyes open for the jewel.'

He reached for her arm. 'Isaac Jakeman is no gentleman, Amelia. He did time on the *Graystone* prison hulk. In fact, he should be on his way to Australia – God knows why he's back in the East End. More than likely his wife. They're devoted thieves and partners.'

That must have been the woman in the store. She and Isaac Jakeman had exchanged a look that didn't require words. In a moment, they had agreed what to do: get Amelia and her sister out of the store. He might have done time on a prison ship moored on the Thames, but he was also a decent human being, no matter what Simon claimed. If it weren't for Isaac's quick thinking, the night might have ended differently.

'Regardless, if he gains information about the jewel, he promised to let me know.'

'*Promised?*' Simon repeated. 'Did you not hear what I said? A man like Isaac Jakeman is out for one thing and one thing only: money. Promises mean nothing to him.'

'But a reward might.' She glanced down at her arm, letting him know to remove his hand. 'I offered him one for returning the item.'

Simon did and smacked his forehead. 'Of all the reckless propositions.' He pointed a finger at her. 'You made a deal with the devil.'

Margaret gave them a backward glance, perhaps overhearing the hostile male voice.

Amelia smiled brightly and waved. The second her sister turned around, she dropped her smile. 'If my propositions are wrong-headed, please share some of yours. Pray tell, what ideas do you have for retrieving the jewel? It's an heirloom and means a good deal to Tabitha, to our entire family.'

'I have a proposition,' he hissed. 'I propose I throw you over my shoulder and lock you in my room until I find the diamond myself.'

The idea isn't without appeal . . .

Simon closed his mouth, a rare pink hue traveling up his neck. 'My *house* is what I meant. Lock you in my house.'

He missed a step, knocking her parasol out of her hand and behind a bush. They both leaned down to fetch it, their heads nearly brushing. As he reached for it, she noted his eyes were as green as the thickest blades of grass, a dense expanse, verging on black. They flicked over her face, studying the curve of her forehead, the slant of her cheekbones, the dimple in her chin. They lifted to her lips, seeing the smile that his misstep had placed there.

He scowled. 'You will be my undoing.'

'I hope so,' she shot back.

He closed his eyes briefly. 'Do not go back to Petticoat Lane. Promise me.'

'Maybe.'

'Amelia . . .' His voice was no more than a whisper.

She cast a glance in her sister's direction. Margaret and Captain Fitz had met with Benjamin Worth and his betrothed, Theodora Castlewood, on the footpath. Amelia felt her chaperone – and investigative – duties call. 'I need to catch up with my sister.'

'Of course.'

She turned to leave.

'Lady Amesbury?'

She spun around.

He stuck out her umbrella. 'Don't forget your parasol.'

FOURTEEN

Dear Lady Agony,

Do you believe in love at first sight? All my friends do, but I have yet to see any evidence of the phenomenon. Perhaps you can convince me.

Sincerely,

Love at First Sight Skeptic

Dear Love at First Sight Skeptic,

Ah, the skeptic! There's one in every batch of letters. I do believe in love at first sight, but what might I say to convince you? I've seen it with my own eyes? I have. I've heard of it from correspondents? I have as well. Yet I have the distinct feeling no amount of evidence would be sufficient to convince you, so I will end with this: I hope, Dear Skeptic, cupid aims his arrow at you!

Yours in Secret,

Lady Agony

Amelia's parasol ticked along the ground as she hurried to catch up with her sister. Simon was so stubborn. He would never cross the imaginary line he had drawn in his head. In fact, he would stay several yards away from it, treating the boundary like a snake in the grass. What was it that kept him at a distance? His friendship with Edgar? His previous engagement to Felicity Farnsworth? His fear of Aunt Tabitha?

She is a trifle scary.

If Amelia weren't entangled in her sister's affairs right now, she would stomp right back and ask him. Put the question to him and force an answer. Isn't that what she would advise one of her correspondents? Indeed, she would.

But another problem had more of her attention: a big red-headed one in front of her. Even from afar, Amelia noted Margaret's arm linked with the captain's in too-casual closeness.

Did she want to invite more scandal this season? Amelia picked up the pace. She should know by now that Margaret was a full-time job, one that did not allow breaks. Her sister was new to London and did not realize that, even outdoors, her actions would be observed – and judged.

Amelia joined Margaret at her elbow. 'It appears you're having a fine time.'

Madge started. 'Goodness! You scared me.'

'It's Mr Worth and Miss Castlewood.' Captain Fitz let go of Margaret's arm, nodding at the approaching couple. 'Would you like to say good afternoon?'

'Very much,' replied Amelia.

'Not at all,' Madge muttered under her breath.

Benjamin Worth greeted his friend warmly, but when he spied Margaret and Amelia, his acknowledgment cooled. He was reminding himself to behave – or perhaps his betrothed had reminded him how to behave moments before. 'Lady Amesbury. Miss Scott,' he said in a clipped voice. 'Good afternoon.'

'Good afternoon,' Amelia said. Margaret bobbed her head. An awkward silence fell over the group, and Amelia rummaged for something to say besides the obvious.

'I haven't had the opportunity to congratulate you on your betrothal, Mr Worth,' she said. 'How are the wedding preparations coming?'

Miss Castlewood's glance alighted on Mr Worth, and when his eyes sparkled in kind, Amelia understood how much they meant to each other. The knowledge made Amelia dislike him a little less.

'Thank you, Lady Amesbury.' Mr Worth's voice was kinder, as if he couldn't keep the happiness out of it. He was definitely a man in love. 'They are progressing nicely.'

'My mother has been planning the wedding breakfast for a month. She won't know what to do with all her free time once we're married.' Miss Castlewood was cheerful, like a spring day, a weight removed since the day of the call upon Amelia and her sister. The change made her prettier and less plain, like a morning glory at daybreak.

'I, for one, could not be more pleased.' Captain Fitz beamed at Miss Castlewood. 'You deserve much happiness.' He nodded at Mr Worth. 'You both do.' His look was one of real friendship and even admiration. The men had survived Crimea together, and their experience might have made them value life more. They obviously wanted the best for each other and had the other's interest in mind, not just during the war, but now and forever. The bond couldn't be broken by space or time or hardship, and Amelia's respect for the soldiers grew twofold.

'And what of your efforts, Lady Amesbury?' Mr Worth attempted to include her and her sister in the conversation. Miss Castlewood looked on approvingly. 'Did your ball illuminate any new acquaintances for your sister?'

'One new acquaintance to be sure.' Captain Fitz turned to Margaret, his dashing side whiskers making a handsome profile.

Margaret's long eyelashes swept down, nearly grazing her high cheekbones. And was that color rising in them? *Gracious!* Amelia had only seen her sister blush . . . Actually, she never had. Margaret had met the captain only a few days ago, and somehow he had transformed her little sister. It was shocking and, if she was being honest, a bit frightening. 'Plenty of new acquaintances, Mr Worth. Thank you for asking.'

'I think it's delightful,' Miss Castlewood gushed. 'Visiting from a small town, discovering the city, having a ball thrown in your honor. It must be a bit overwhelming.'

'It is.' A flicker of exhaustion crossed Margaret's face like a cloud moving quickly over the sun. 'But in a good way.'

An older man hailed Captain Fitz from afar, and he turned to Amelia. 'Would you mind if I introduce Miss Scott? Cordell is one of my oldest and dearest friends. It will only take a moment.'

'Please do,' Amelia said. The pair headed off in the direction of a man who looked very much like the captain, except he had a beard instead of side whiskers and was perhaps twenty years his elder.

Amelia turned to Mr Worth. 'Is that a fellow soldier of the war?'

'Vice admiral. He served in Crimea also.'

'Such a hard-fought war.' Miss Castlewood's eyebrows furrowed, making her round face a little sharper. 'I'm only glad they returned safely.'

'Safe but not unchanged.' Mr Worth stared at the men or the

space; it was hard to tell which. Wherever his mind was, it wasn't here.

The glance was vaguely haunting, and Amelia understood that his time in the war, which ended four years ago, still affected him a good deal. 'What do you mean?'

The question took him out of his reverie. 'War changes a man, and not always in a good way. Some men come back with different lives, perhaps leaving loved ones behind in another country. Others suffer the effects of the damage they've witnessed, the damage they've inflicted. Outbursts. Nightmares. Tremors.'

'You mean Captain Fitz?' Now that he mentioned it, the captain had been easily agitated in the carriage ride. She assumed it was because the driver had made the mistake before, but perhaps his irritation was a result of the war. The idea made her question whether leaving the captain alone with her sister was a good idea.

'Who is to say?' Mr Worth shrugged off the direct question about his friend. 'I would have never imagined seeing him in Hyde Park with Miss Scott after what happened to Radcliffe, yet here we are, all of us, as if the misdeed hadn't happened.'

No one was nearby. Amelia could speak plainly and took the opportunity. 'I hope you're not still suggesting my sister had something to do with Mr Radcliffe's death.'

'Of course he's not,' Miss Castlewood was quick to put in. 'It has been a difficult few days, for Mr Worth particularly. But I, for one, am glad we're together at the park, able to enjoy some fresh air.' She touched his arm. 'And a good thing it is, too. It does no one any good to grieve alone.'

Amelia agreed with her, to an extent. It didn't do anyone any good to be alone for an extended period of time, especially in hardship. Friends could help one another deal with problems that seemed insurmountable when one was alone. Indeed, Amelia would have never been able to weather Edgar's passing without Kitty Hamsted. She'd been a friend when Amelia had needed one most. Miss Castlewood was that person for Mr Worth now.

Mr Worth must have agreed because his frown melted. The plum-colored skin beneath his eyes appeared less slack for a moment, and he released a breath that he might have been holding for days. The ordeal had taken its toll on Mr Worth. It was *still* taking its toll for that matter. Only Miss Castlewood's calm demeanor seemed to allay his angst.

'Has the family decided on a date for the funeral?' Amelia asked.

'No.' Mr Worth shook his head, and a brown coil of hair came loose from his hat. 'Doctor Radcliffe is still working with the surgeon to determine the cause of death.'

It made sense for Dr Radcliffe to oversee the procedures, but what if the overseer and the murderer were the same person? He could cover up his own wrongdoing and leave someone – like Amelia's sister – to assume the guilt. That would never do. Amelia needed to talk to the brother.

'The sooner the funeral takes place the better, in my opinion.' Miss Castlewood grasped Benjamin's hand. 'Then he will be at peace.'

'Peace.' Benjamin Worth squeezed her hand in return.

'The world certainly needs more of it,' Amelia agreed. But if her sister waving goodbye to the vice admiral and disappearing behind a chestnut tree was any indication, peace wouldn't be granted anytime soon. Amelia said her goodbyes and speedily caught up with the couple, informing them it was time to return home.

Madge pouted. 'We only just arrived.'

'It might seem so, but it's quite late, and I promised Winifred I'd listen to her latest piece of music. She's been working on the interlude a fortnight and is finally ready to play it for me.' Rain, wind or infatuated sisters, Amelia did not miss Winifred's piano performances. Her daughter's music was very important to her, and thus it was important to Amelia. Like books, Winifred's music had the ability to transport Amelia to a different place, one without murder investigations looming. It was the one time in the afternoon that belonged to the two of them absolutely, and Amelia would no more miss it than miss a formal occasion.

'Of course, Lady Amesbury.' Captain Fitz led the way to the waiting carriage.

Once inside, Amelia took the opportunity to ask about Jonathan Radcliffe, Arthur's brother. 'Have you ever met the man?'

'Yes, a few times. He lives on Harley Street and has a small

surgery where he takes patients. His brother was a great admirer, and we stopped once or twice.'

'What was your impression of him?' Amelia asked, feeling as if she already knew the answer.

'He was smart, as I said . . . quiet.' Captain Fitz seemed to be fumbling for the right words to describe him. 'Honestly, he didn't talk much about medicine. He talked about their estate back home in Staffordshire. Seemed quite enamored with it.' He lifted his eyebrows, which matched the sandy color of his whiskers. 'Though he did offer me some up-and-coming liver pills, now that I think about it. I didn't take them, of course. Why would I? I'm right as rain.'

'Anyone can see that.' Madge fluttered her eyelashes.

Amelia thought her behavior was positively bizarre. *One moment a girl is in the barn taking apart a spinning mule and the next she's in a black four-wheeler hitched to a pair of bays batting her eyelashes.* Jonathan Radcliffe and his medicine be damned. Young love was the most powerful tonic of all.

When they arrived home, Amelia quickly took her leave, giving Margaret and Captain Fitz a few precious moments alone. She wanted to send Kitty a note post-haste. Amelia thought they might be able to see Jonathan Radcliffe today. Kitty still had that bad ankle that acted up once in a while, and if the doctor had to treat her, it would leave Amelia free to search for information about his brother's death. Certainly, most upper-class families such as hers and Kitty's would have their family physician pay a house call. But if the ankle flared while they were out shopping? A sneaky smile crept upon her in anticipation. They'd have no choice but to stop.

Amelia was listening to Winifred play Beethoven's 'Sonata No. 5' when Kitty's return note arrived. Kitty was definitely in the mood for shopping. The better question was when *wasn't* she in the mood for shopping? Amelia couldn't ask for a better friend or more compulsive shopper. A plan made, Amelia relaxed, watching Winifred's small hands seemingly fly over the keys of the pianoforte. Even from afar, Amelia noted the razor-sharp focus in her eyes, the irises the color of blue topaz. Admiration swelled in her chest. To be so talented and determined at her young age was a rarity. Amelia felt lucky to be a witness to her journey.

Winifred played the last note, and Amelia stood and went to the piano. 'You are a beautiful musician, Winifred. Your music takes my breath away.'

'You always say that.' Winifred hugged Amelia's waist.

'Because it's always true.' Amelia inhaled the scent of strawberries that followed Winifred wherever she went. 'Next time you play, ask Margaret to accompany you.' She leaned closer to her ear. 'You would never guess it, but she has a lovely voice. She's just shy when it comes to performing.'

Winifred's crystal-blue eyes grew wider. 'I know how to help with that.'

Amelia gave her shoulders a squeeze. 'I know you do.' Winifred herself had fought off a case of stage fright before her first recital, but they had weathered the trouble together. With time and practice, she had performed to a packed house of admirers, all of whom were eager to hear her play again. When the time came, Winifred would be more than ready.

Amelia gave her a peck on the cheek. 'I'll see you later.'

The keys were tinkling before Amelia was out of the room. As she fetched her parasol, she heard Margaret's tentative voice join a familiar refrain of a popular song. She stopped and listened to her sister's voice, which she hadn't heard for more than two years. With each note, it grew stronger, more assured. Winifred's volume grew also, and by the time Amelia reached for the door, the two musicians matched each other in sound and soul. To hear them together was indescribable, two pieces of Amelia's heart coming together in a joyous melody.

Simply lovely.

This season had its problems, but it also had its rewards.

Margaret coming to London was one of them. Amelia refused to allow Arthur Radcliffe's murder to make it feel otherwise.

FIFTEEN

Dear Lady Agony,

Do you know the remedy for wrinkles? I've heard onion juice is good for them but am hesitant to try the suggestion without instruction. I hope you may provide it.

Sincerely,
Wrinkles Away

Dear Wrinkles Away,

I have also heard onion juice might provide assistance for saggy situations. Before I provide instruction on the vegetable, however, let us address the issue: wrinkles. Many consider them a problem, but I do not. In my opinion, they are signs of experience. I would no more erase them than erase the laughter that created them. If you are still inclined to try, though, follow these steps: Mix the juice of two onions with white lily, white wax and Narbonne honey, all of the same amount. Melt in a pipkin, and mix well until cool. Apply at night, and do not remove until the morning. Let me know if it provides progress – or problems. I'm sure readers would like to know if the tear-inducing remedy is worth the effort.

Yours in Secret,
Lady Agony

Moments later, Kitty was in the carriage, and Amelia had the sinking feeling that she actually thought they would be shopping for the remainder of the afternoon. Kitty wore a velvet bonnet and a pink lace mantle that made her heart-shaped face look as pretty as a porcelain doll's. But this doll grew peevish when she learned they were going to call upon the good physician, Jonathan Radcliffe.

'You mean, I won't be able to stop at Lock and Co. Hatters or Storr and Mortimer?'

'Perhaps that draper you like, but only because it's close to Doctor Radcliffe's practice on Harley Street. It presents the opportunity for an authentic accident. We want it to appear as if you've reinjured your ankle.' Amelia tapped her chin. 'You might even scuff your boot a little to provide evidence of the accident.'

'Scuff my boot!' Kitty drew back as if bitten by a serpent. 'These are my new burgundy Balmorals. They are the most comfortable boots I own at the moment. I would no more scuff them than gouge my eyes out.'

Hardly a fair comparison. 'Forget about the boots. We'll stop at the draper, you'll twist your ankle on the way out, and we'll go straight to Harley Street, where the doctor will examine your limb. While he's performing his duties, I will look for clues to his brother's death.'

Kitty sniffed. 'Not exactly an ideal day.'

Amelia frowned. 'It's perfectly ideal. You want to shop; I want to know what happened to Mr Radcliffe. Everyone wins.'

Kitty clasped her hands, which were covered in a lovely pair of pink kid gloves with mauve rosettes. 'I also want to know what happened to Mr Radcliffe – and free your sister from suspicion. Be assured I will get as much intelligence as possible out of him while you are ransacking his house.'

Amelia smiled. If the past was any indication, Kitty would find out as much information as Amelia. She had a beautiful and trusting face. Once, she was able to out a dressmaker who was making her seamstresses work eighteen-hour days. All Kitty had to do was hold up a blue fabric, don a dreamy look while fluttering impossibly curly eyelashes and beg for a new creation. The dressmaker promised her then and there to have a dress sewn in less than forty-eight hours. This confirmed the rumors were correct, and Amelia warned her readers of the dressmaker's practices the very next week. It was one of the highlights of their year.

'The viscountess thinks her nephew is quite smitten with Margaret by the way,' said Kitty, looking out of the window for the draper. 'She is not pleased by it.'

'I got that impression also.'

Kitty tossed a look in her direction. 'Lady Hamsted indicated he is not as well-off as one might imagine. She said her brother has been careless with the family's wealth, and money is of the utmost importance. I do not know if it is true, however, or if she wants to avoid a connection with your sister.'

'Probably the latter,' Amelia muttered. 'Madge did her reputation no favors with her rebuke of Mr Radcliffe on the dance floor. Yet Tabitha did mention a similar scenario. He could be as reduced as Lady Hamsted suggests.'

The carriage stopped at the draper that had recently advertised imported brocade satin and embroidered shawls in *The Times*. Kitty dropped the conversation, hardly waiting for the stairs to be set down before taking off at a quick walk.

If she continues at this pace, she truly will sprain her ankle.

Thirty minutes later, Kitty was satisfied with the fabric she'd chosen for her mother-in-law's yearly country house grouse-hunting party in August. It was a pretty emerald-green brocade satin with flowers of coral, pink, and gold. Amelia didn't have the confidence to wear such a dress but knew it would look lovely on Kitty. She had the uncanny ability to suit every occasion, making each creation feel as if it was just what the hostess would have wished for if she'd had all the fabrics in the world to choose from.

'And, you'll be happy to know,' Kitty said as the footman shut the carriage door, 'my skirt was accidentally soiled.' Kitty lifted the hem of her dress. 'See? I took a step backwards and brushed along a neglected cupboard. Jonathan Radcliffe has to take my word about the reinjury.'

'It does look convincing.' Amelia gave her what she hoped was a grateful smile. 'Thank you, Kitty.'

Dr Radcliffe saw patients in his home office, as did most newly graduated physicians. In time, he might pay house calls on people in the upper echelons, such as Amelia and Kitty, but for now, he operated his practice out of his house like many other physicians on Harley Street.

As they approached his residence, Amelia reminded herself it was Dr Radcliffe's concerns that had summoned Detective Collings in the first place. The Metropolitan Police would have never become involved – let alone call on an aristocratic family unannounced – had the doctor not proclaimed his brother's death was suspicious. And because of his accusations, Margaret was suspect number one.

It was rather convenient for Jonathan Radcliffe, in Amelia's opinion, whose tonic could have gone terribly wrong. He was new to the occupation, after all. How much did he really know about gastritis, or any other ailment for that matter? Amelia supposed she was about to find out.

She held Kitty's arm, as if for support, as they approached his home office. They were greeted by a woman whose smile was too large for her face, hospitable and kind. Lines creased the sides of her mouth as if she'd welcomed hundreds of patients in the same manner, but Amelia understood it was more likely her good-natured attitude than a demand of the doctor.

'We have a bit of an emergency, I'm afraid,' Amelia explained. 'Mrs Hamsted and I were shopping when she reinjured her ankle, which only healed weeks ago. I expect it needs wrapping for our return trip home.'

With a sympathetic look, the woman ushered them into the front parlor. The room was prettily papered in a rich brown color with elaborate fans of gold. The desk chair was also cushioned in brown with a red brocade, and a cabinet with bright green drawers was new and untarnished. The shade of the oil lamp was also green and sat atop a curved side table. Amelia and Kitty each took a chair on either side of it.

'Please wait here.' The woman flashed her infectious smile again. 'The doctor will be in to see you momentarily.'

Jonathan Radcliffe entered moments later, and he was not entirely what Amelia was expecting. Whereas Arthur Radcliffe was fashionable, small-statured and crafty, Jonathan was broad-shouldered with a head of dense blond hair and eyes the color of Cretan waters. The epitome of health and wellbeing, he was a man who probably enjoyed hunting, fishing and other outdoor pursuits. His coat was comfortable, and although it was nice-looking, it was several years old. His shoes, too, were scuffed, and no amount of polish could disguise their wear. Amelia imagined he walked every day in them, long distances and in every kind of weather. He was the type of person, like herself, not to be deterred by a little rain.

He took *The Times* off his chair and placed it on his desk, dusting off the seat of the chair before sitting. 'Miss Deveraux mentioned an ankle sprain?' Dr Radcliffe looked between the two women.

'I have a sprain – or I *had* a sprain.' Kitty smiled, the apples of her cheeks flushed from shopping. The color agreed with her dress. 'It was fine until I had a spill at the draper a few moments ago. I thought it best to have it looked at right away, and Lady Amesbury had heard good things about you from your brother.' She paused respectfully. 'My condolences on his passing.'

Dr Radcliffe's eyebrows, which were as light as his hair, lifted slightly. 'Lady Amesbury, the host of the ball Arthur attended the night of his death?'

Amelia nodded. 'I'd only met him that evening, but I'd like to express my sincere condolences as well.' Amelia braced herself for accusations or at least guarded looks, but they didn't come. He was milder-mannered than his brother and didn't seem to enjoy attention as much as his brother did. He was a second son, after all, and probably wasn't used to it.

'Thank you.' He clasped his large hands on his lap. 'I'm only in the office because I've been assisting the medical examiner. Not that I have many patients, mind you. Most days are quiet whether the door is open or not.' He tapped his fingertips together. 'You talked to my brother that evening?'

'Yes, he knew of the incident with Charlie Atkinson – or you did, rather. My sister is Margaret Scott, and we spoke of the encounter.' Amelia treaded cautiously with her next words. 'I was chagrined to learn the injury was much talked about.'

A smile flickered across his broad face. 'I wouldn't say it was much talked about – except by my brother, perhaps. He was a bit of a gossip-monger that way. I did hear of it, though.' He leaned in slightly. 'It isn't every day a *woman* breaks a *man's* arm.'

Despite its truth, Amelia felt her pulse jump in her throat. She didn't like hearing her sister talked about in a way that made her sound like a perpetrator. In fact, Margaret had been a victim of unwanted affection. If she'd acted violently, she'd had every reason to. She'd had no idea if or where the advancement would end. 'And it isn't every day that a gentleman kisses a woman who isn't willing. Oh, wait. Yes, it is.'

'Indeed, we need more Margaret Scotts in the world,' Kitty added enthusiastically.

That might be taking it a bit far. 'Or at least more appreciation for women who are willing to fight back.'

Jonathan Radcliffe surprised her by saying, 'I agree. You would not believe the hardship I've seen women suffer at the hands of men. I say fight back with all your might.'

Amelia's estimation of him immediately went up. 'It must be a very trying time for your family.'

'It is, and I'm afraid it will only become more trying when the autopsy is finished.'

'You believe something happened to your brother that night?' asked Kitty.

'Something *did* happen to him. He was ill.' He didn't say anything for a moment, his brow creasing with confusion. 'So very ill.'

'He fainted in my supper room.' Amelia wasn't certain he had all the facts and decided it was better if she told him than have him rely on Benjamin Worth's account. 'At the time, I thought he was overly warm or drank too much champagne.'

'Whatever happened took a dreadfully wrong turn.'

'I was told he had gastritis,' Kitty put in. 'I know a few people who suffer with the condition.'

'He did,' Dr Radcliffe exhaled a loud breath, the memory seeming to pass. 'Or at least he thought he did. He never had the constitution I had. He'd been ill since childhood. Some stomach upset or another always plaguing him. A very weak person, health-wise. He wished for my endurance. Perhaps with enough time and tonics, I would have convinced him he was cured. But that night was different.' He shook his head. 'Whatever struck him was real.'

'Do you have any idea what it was?' asked Amelia.

Dr Radcliffe's eyes flicked to the window. 'I did work at the Brompton Hospital but never witnessed a death like his.' His eyes returned to hers. 'By the sight and smell of the contents of his stomach, I would wager he was poisoned. Furthermore, poison would account for his thirst. He wasn't a heavy drinker by nature.'

Poisoned. Hearing the doctor utter the word aloud brought on a new wave of panic. 'He mentioned a new tonic to one of his friends.' Amelia phrased the next words carefully. 'Perhaps it had adverse side effects?'

'Side effects?' Dr Radcliffe let out a laugh and stood up. He walked to a small shelf of bottles that shook as he approached and selected a dark blue one. 'The tonic is no more than ginger and aloe.' He took a large glug of it and set it down. 'My brother loved trying new concoctions. He wanted perfect health. A perfect life. I gave him everything from Beechams Pills to this. It didn't make any difference, I'm afraid. Even if it did, it wouldn't have satisfied him. Only divinity would have been enough.'

They lapsed into silence, and Amelia considered the doctor's words. Arthur Radcliffe had been obsessed with his health. As a soon-to-be baron, he might have wanted to build himself up as much as possible. He would surely never be as strong as his brother. That was as clear as the doctor's steady hand.

Jonathan Radcliffe walked over to Kitty, gesturing to her foot. 'You didn't come here to listen to me discuss my brother's problems, however. You have your own.' He touched a padded bench. 'Take a seat here, and I'll look at that ankle.'

Kitty moved to the elevated position, and Amelia knew they would be occupied for several minutes. 'I'll step out.'

Amelia meandered into the adjoining room, where Miss Deveraux was situated behind a desk, which was larger than Dr Radcliffe's, with a fine leather ledger and appointment book. Amelia asked how long she'd been working for the doctor.

'Since he began his practice,' said Miss Deveraux. 'He likes someone to greet his patients and manage his appointments. I imagine he'll be in high demand one day.' Her chin lifted earnestly, and all joviality disappeared from her face. Her position was one she took very seriously. Amelia understood why the doctor employed her. If she had any say in the matter, the practice would grow as popular as she predicted.

'Indeed, he will.' Amelia's eyes flitted across the desk. 'I must say, those are very fine ledgers. I wouldn't mind having one of those in my morning room.'

Miss Deveraux smoothed them protectively. 'Dr Radcliffe sees very important persons in his day-to-day affairs. His father is a baron, you understand.' Her larger-than-life smile flitted across her face, so pleased she was to relay the information.

'Yes, I do.' Amelia cleared her throat a few times. 'I apologize, Miss Deveraux, but I seem to have swallowed wrong.' She coughed a few times, hoping the woman would understand her need for refreshment.

'Goodness!' Miss Deveraux stood, the lines around her mouth pressed into a concerned frown. 'May I get you something to drink?'

Amelia swallowed hard, tapping her throat. 'A cup of tea would be wonderful.'

'Of course.' If she was surprised by the request, she didn't mention it. She was just as accommodating as her employer. 'It will just be a few minutes.'

Amelia hated making herself a pest, but she needed Miss Deveraux out of the room for as long as possible so that she could peek at the appointment book. How many times a week had Arthur Radcliffe paid a call on his brother? That was the question on her mind, among others.

The second Miss Deveraux was gone, Amelia reached for the ledger. Miss Deveraux had very neat handwriting, and it was easy to scan the dates and names. Amelia flipped the gilded pages, thoroughly impressed with the quality of the paper. She admired fine stationery as some ladies admired fine hats. A designer quill or rich-colored ink could make her heart flip-flop.

Perusing the pages, she discovered Arthur Radcliffe had been here three times last week. And the week before that. He was as bothered by his stomach as Dr Radcliffe said he was. Other than his brother, Dr Radcliffe had a lot of time on his hands as far as she could see. Hours at a time were unmarked by appointments. He was a young physician with not many patients and perhaps not many prospects. If his clientele didn't pick up, he might have to change his lifestyle – or at least his expensive tastes in stationery. Inheriting the baronetcy, however, would fix the problem – if not immediately, then in the distant future. Elder relatives had certainly been encouraged to their final resting place for less.

She glanced up, checking the door, and then returned to the pages. She thumbed through a few more weeks. It was a month to the date when she spotted a familiar name on the schedule: Ann Harding. Lady Ann from the party. Amelia frowned. What was her reason for an appointment with Dr Radcliffe? Surely, she had a family doctor who came to her home. All the upper classes did. It didn't make sense that she would find a different doctor. What purpose would she have?

Kitty let out a nervous laugh from the other room, giddy and not quite herself. 'I was worried for no reason, it seems. What a relief.'

That was Amelia's cue. She glanced at the appointment book one last time. Arthur Radcliffe had an appointment immediately before Lady Ann's, suggesting that their paths had crossed before the night of the ball. She had to wonder if there was more to their history than Lady Ann had revealed.

Without time for further consideration, Amelia rejoined Kitty and Dr Radcliffe.

'Not *no* reason,' Dr Radcliffe was saying. 'The ankle is obviously weak and will continue to cause you problems until it's fully healed. The more you can rest, the better chance you have of not reinjuring it later. Ankles are finicky to say the very least.'

Kitty tilted her head. This was her prettiest look, the one that had the power to ensnare a man a mile away. 'And I assume I can return if it doesn't progress?'

What a friend! She was planning for a return trip, but that trip took a detour with the doctor's next words, leaving both listeners stunned.

'I'm afraid I'll be shutting down my practice soon. As the baron's only remaining son, I won't be needing it any longer.'

SIXTEEN

Dear Lady Agony,

I've been invited to sing at a concert, as have two of my acquaintances. I do not have a bad voice, but they have been practicing together every day. When I asked if I might join them, they said we did not possess the same vocal ability. I feel slighted, and the slight has led to nervousness. What might help?

Sincerely,

A Slighted Soprano

Dear A Slighted Soprano,

An insufferable situation! I'm glad you count them as acquaintances and not friends because their behavior is exclusive and rude. Who crowned them queens of the concert? One thing will help, however, and that is to forget they exist. Sing your heart out, brave bird! Leave the crows to caw between themselves.

Yours in Secret,

Lady Agony

T he next day, Amelia was still thinking about Dr Radcliffe – which was to say, the would-be baron. She considered whether he could have killed his brother for the title. He had no passion for his practice. That much had been obvious by the turn of conversation over her well-made cup of tea. What he enjoyed was rowing for Oxford. He'd been quite an athlete, from his accounts, and was still in very good shape, if appearances were to be trusted. Dosing his brother would have been easy. Jonathan Radcliffe saw him three times a week. It could have been a slow, gradual poisoning with the final dose oversetting him the night of the ball.

And yet . . .

Amelia put down her quill.

If Dr Radcliffe had been poisoning him, he'd have no reason to tell the Metropolitan Police his suspicions about the death. He could have blamed the death on his brother's ongoing problems with gastritis – unless, as she told Detective Collings earlier, he knew the medical examiner would rule it a homicide and he would need a theory. The doctor had mentioned the word *poison* in their conversation. His opinion meant more than most. His father was a baron. The police might get away with harassing Margaret Scott of Somerset, certainly, but not a member of the peerage.

As if the thought summoned her sister, Margaret burst through the door without so much as a single knock.

'I look like a bloody canary in this contraption!' Madge's face was flushed, only a shade lighter than her hair. 'A big fat canary.' She held up her skirt, revealing stiff ivory petticoats. 'Have you ever seen so much material? My arse looks as big as a—'

'Madge!' Amelia hissed. 'Close the door.'

'I'm not going to the concert in this.'

'Yes, you are.' Amelia said each word with great deliberation. 'The viscountess was kind to invite you. Kitty insisted on the invitation.'

Madge fisted her hands at her waist. 'What will the captain say if he sees me in this?'

'He'll say you're very beautiful if he knows what's good for him,' grumbled Amelia. 'I paid a good deal of money for a rush on that frock. It's a personal recommendation from Kitty's modiste. Kitty assured me it's the height of fashion.'

'I don't care how much it cost. It's dreadful.'

Amelia stood from her desk. 'Not another word unless it's *thank you, dear sister.*'

Madge dropped her hands from her waist and rushed over to the desk. 'I'm sorry, Amelia. I'm very grateful for your generosity, of course. It's just that I'm not used to such . . . *finery*.' Her hazel eyes nearly matched the quill on Amelia's desk. 'I've always been plain, you understand. You hold your own under scrutiny, but I don't like being the center of attention. And I feel like this dress puts me square in the middle.'

Amelia came around to the other side and gave Madge a hug. 'You are not plain. You are exquisite, and this dress just happens to show it. Trust me when I say you will not be the center of attention. Lady Hamsted is known for her extravagant tastes. All the ladies in attendance will be dressed in their finest.'

'Ladies,' Madge repeated into her shoulder. 'Not little sisters playing dress-up in their big sister's wardrobe.'

Amelia pulled back, searching Margaret's eyes. 'That is not what you're doing. These clothes are your clothes. This is your season. And to be honest, it's been quite eventful already.' When Madge still looked doubtful, Amelia ticked off the highlights on her fingers. 'An argument in the ballroom, a visit from a detective, a discovery on Petticoat Lane . . .'

'Don't forget Captain Fitz.' Madge's lips curved into a smile, making her chin appear less square. 'He's been the best part so far.'

'You like him?'

'I do.' The smile on Madge's face reached her eyes. 'He doesn't put on airs. He seems honest, kind. Forthcoming. I like that in a person.'

Amelia saw those same qualities in Margaret herself. She looped her arm through her sister's. 'Come along. I'm certain Lady Tabitha is waiting for us, and you don't want to see what happens when she feels put off.'

Madge leaned in. 'Does she beat you with the walking stick?'

'Very nearly.'

Aunt Tabitha was impressed with Margaret's gown, and in the carriage ride to the viscountess's, she went as far as to ask why Amelia didn't wear something similar. It had taken all Amelia's fortitude not to answer, 'I was forced to wear mourning for two years by an elderly relative. I'm hardly accustomed to pale blue.' But the truth was Amelia probably wouldn't have worn it anyway. It seemed too youthful for her. It was the kind of dress worn by young maidens with lots of dreams and little experience. She had been that woman when she first came to London, but she was a different person now. She enjoyed her daughter, her work, her freedom.

And yes, Simon Bainbridge.

But he'd made his lack of romantic interest perfectly clear. He enjoyed their informal investigations. They gave him something to do. If she could help him with a problem, or vice versa, life was easier. He was satisfied.

the facts. The chemistry she'd felt was
...sy. She had little to no experience with
...Edgar, and she'd been his nurse and
...dn't mean she *couldn't* take a lover.
...rake the Rake only a few nights ago?
...ngaging, comical – dashing even.
...t Simon Bainbridge.

Simon Bainbridge had a piece of her heart, and she was afraid she might never get it back.

The carriage stopped, and Amelia put away her concerns and focused on her sister. It was her season, and it *would* be successful if Amelia had any say in it.

Lady Hamsted lived in a fine house in Grosvenor Square. It was a Georgian home, one she'd renovated with impressive results. The house had more land than many of the others surrounding the green square, which made it even more valuable. Space was not easy to obtain in London, even in the finest neighborhoods. Only families with houses that had been passed down carefully, from one male peerage to the next, counted themselves so lucky.

Although Amelia had been in the house before, she hardly recognized the drawing room for all the changes that had been made. It held a new pianoforte with an ornate bench seat and a golden harpsichord that took over one entire corner of the room. The maroon-and-gold-striped wallpaper remained the same, as did the dark paisley couch. But other furniture, such as tables and padded leather chairs, had been brought in to create seating areas where guests could comfortably enjoy the music.

Amelia, Margaret and Tabitha situated themselves near the window, an arched beauty adorned with rich gold brocade.

'Is that Miss Berg?' Amelia whispered to Tabitha while nodding toward a woman barely as tall as the music stand that she stood by. She was well known for her small stature and large musical skill.

Tabitha nodded. 'I heard she performed in *Orpheus in the Underworld* in Paris and brought patrons to tears. I had no idea she'd be in attendance.'

'Nor did I.' Kitty was at her elbow and wore a blue gown with a simple headdress of light-blue chenille, a dark blue bow and

ribbons at the ear. 'My mother-in-law kept her attenda[n]
even from me.' She turned to Margaret. 'What a visio[n]
in yellow. I'm completely jealous!' She pouted, and a
dimple appeared high on her cheek.

It was just what Margaret needed to hear. Amelia saw h[er]
exhale a visible sigh of relief, and she silently thanked her friend.

'You could not have chosen a better color for your hair, face
or figure.' Kitty leaned in. 'I knew you were beautiful, Miss
Scott, but next time, you must give the other young ladies a
chance.'

'Oh, go on!' Madge waved away the compliment. 'Everyone
can see you're the prettiest in the room.'

'I almost forgot.' Kitty passed them each a piece of fine linen
paper. 'I'm supposed to be handing these out. A program for the
afternoon's events.'

'Impressive,' Tabitha murmured, and she was rarely impressed.

They were to hear Beethoven, Weber, and Clementi, followed
by guest poetry readings and performances. *It should be a fine
afternoon*, Amelia thought.

Until Simon Bainbridge strode over as if he owned the entire
room and possibly the house, too. His white cravat was blown
open, showing what Amelia considered an indecent amount of
tan throat. He always appeared as if he'd just stepped off a ship,
the wind having had its way with him. A trill of appreciation
from the ladies followed in his wake, and Amelia forced herself
to study a minuscule piece of lint on her skirt as he approached.
It would do no good for him to see her observing him. He already
knew she was interested, and she already knew he was not.

'Mrs Hamsted.' Simon dipped his head, and even from her
preoccupied position, Amelia could see several strands of black
hair fall forward. It was shameful how nice the man's hair was.
Meanwhile, hers frizzed at even the suggestion of rain.

'Lord Bainbridge, my mother-in-law will be so pleased you
were able to attend.' Kitty curtsied enthusiastically. 'The more
future dukes, the better.' She lifted her eyebrows in the direction
of Lord Drake, who'd entered late, in his customary way. Amelia
might have said he did so to draw more attention to himself, but
after meeting him, she hardly thought it was the case. His tardi-
ness might be more blamed on lack of interest than conceit.

Tabitha offered her hand, and he took it. 'Always a delight to see you, my lord.'

Amelia glanced up vaguely.

He kissed it tenderly. 'And you, my lady. May I have the pleasure of sitting by you?'

Tabitha lifted her chin. 'I insist.'

Amelia just succeeded in not rolling her eyes.

Miss Berg was a master at the pianoforte, and Amelia wished Winifred had been present to hear her performance of Beethoven. When Miss Berg continued with a sonata from Clementi, Amelia was moved to tears. Had not all of popular society been in attendance, she would have let them fall, so full was her heart with emotion. As it was, she dabbed at them discreetly with the corner of her hankie. It was always this way with her and music. It would always remind her of *home*.

The Scott family didn't possess material wealth, but what they lacked, they made up for with music. Despite her father's long days, he never missed an opportunity to play his violin for road-weary travelers by the fireside in the evenings. It refreshed the family as much as the travelers, and when she considered it, all her family members were much the same way. Her mother always indulged them with dessert, no matter how hectic the day, and her sisters never refused to sing or play at the request of a lodger. How lucky she was to have grown up surrounded by good music, food and family.

She reached over and grasped Margaret's hand, and Madge smiled a sweet smile. Amelia knew she, too, was thinking of home. It was evident by the high color in her cheeks. Amelia only had to close her eyes and she would be back in the green hills of Somerset, the air mingled with the soulful strains of the violin and woodsmoke from the chimney.

Miss Berg finished, and Amelia was relieved for the interlude. She needed a reprieve after the momentous sonata, usually reserved for formal concerts and dark auditoriums, where audience members could listen without being observed. Several attendees must have felt the same, for they were taking the opportunity to mingle with others, including Lord Morton, whose approach she noticed not by movement but by his intense gray eyes, aimed at her sister.

Leo Morton's hair was perfectly parted on the side, smooth with pomade, and his side whiskers were equally sleek and cut just past the ears. His cravat was gray, like his eyes, and his look was one of confidence and sophistication. It should surprise no one that he was Lady Hamsted's nephew, and it certainly didn't Amelia, although his pleasing personality was a nice difference. Amelia wondered if he was bereft of funds (he certainly didn't appear such), or if Lady Hamsted had fabricated the lie to keep Madge at a distance. If so, the viscountess need not go to the trouble. As far as Amelia could ascertain, Margaret had no interest in Lord Morton beyond friendship.

'I'd planned on a few debutantes singing at the pianoforte. Perhaps a badly written piece of poetry or a sonnet.' Lord Morton gestured to the golden harp. 'I never imagined this. I do not get to London often enough, obviously.'

'Many times, drawing room concerts are exactly that,' said Amelia. 'For better or worse,' she added with a chuckle.

'I suppose that means I will not have the pleasure of hearing you sing, Miss Scott?'

'Me?' Margaret asked. 'No.'

'It *would* be a pleasure, my lord.' At first, Amelia only meant to distinguish Madge from the many bad singers she'd heard over the years, but then her voice took on that prideful and distinctive tone it often did when she was discussing a family member, the one she had little control over. 'She is the best vocalist in all of Mells, and most likely London, also. To hear her sing – simply, it is heaven on earth.'

Lord Morton's dark eyelashes lowered in Margaret's direction. 'I do not doubt that in the least, Lady Amesbury.'

Margaret's cheeks flushed.

'I was surprised not to see a singer listed.' Tabitha flipped her program over to make certain. 'Maybe it was left off the program by accident.'

'What surprised you, Lady Tabitha?' Lady Hamsted was at her elbow, waiting to hear what wonderful aspect of the performance astonished her.

Tabitha looked up from the program. 'The singer. I'm assuming you have one who will amaze us with a perfect falsetto or impeccable Italian.' She tapped her cane. 'Or is it French? They've certainly been popular this season.'

'I'd only planned instrumentals.' Lady Hamsted swallowed, her thin neck strained by the action. 'We might have one of the young ladies sing, of course.' She scanned the room, her gray eyes lighter than her nephew's and vaguely haunting. 'Miss Farnsworth is accomplished and so very beautiful. Do you not agree?'

'Lady Amesbury was just now telling me what a lovely voice Miss Scott has.' Lord Morton's eyes wandered over Madge's face. 'Perhaps she will treat us to a song.'

The action did not go unnoticed by Lady Hamsted, whose eyes snapped to her nephew's. 'It would be unfair to ask Miss Scott to perform after the music we've enjoyed.' Lady Hamsted studied Margaret as if she were a curious bird or insect. 'Have you ever performed in front of people, Miss Scott, or just at the festival in the town square?' She turned to her nephew. 'They always have one of those in small villages.'

'Oh, yes, my lady,' Margaret nodded. 'Often.'

Madge didn't recognize the condescension in Lady Hamsted's voice, but Amelia did, and she attempted a deep breath. Instead, she sounded like a badly used train engine. She, too, had suffered insinuations the first two years she was in London, but people disguised them more cleverly because of her wealth and – to be honest – Aunt Tabitha. Insulting Lady Tabitha was akin to social ruin. However, the insult to her sister stung twice as badly.

'I have heard Miss Farnsworth sing, and you're quite right,' Simon put in. 'She does very well at it.'

Of all the wrong things to say, this was the most wrong. Instead of defending her sister's talents, Simon had come out with a compliment for the fabulous Felicity Farnsworth. Amelia's response was immediate. 'I'm afraid, my lord, she could not compare to my sister.' Amelia tipped her chin in challenge. 'No one could.'

'I say she sings.' Lord Morton lifted a single dark eyebrow, giving him a debonair look. 'I, for one, would love to hear her.'

'My sister is being . . . overly kind.' Madge slid Amelia a look that said she knew exactly what was happening. Amelia's competitive nature had surfaced at exactly the wrong time and was drawing unwanted attention. 'I don't know how to play an instrument as fine as that one.' She nodded to the pianoforte. 'I'd ruin it.'

'Miss Berg is still here . . .' Lord Morton cast a quick glance around. 'She might do you the honor.'

'I'll play,' Amelia said, a little louder than she intended. 'A song you know. We both do.'

'"Sweet Nightingale"?' asked Margaret.

Amelia nodded. 'Yes.'

Lady Hamsted introduced them, and as she did, Tabitha pulled on Amelia's sleeve. 'I haven't heard you play the pianoforte in all the time you've been in London. Are you certain you know what you're doing?'

Amelia was certain, and as she took Margaret's hand and led her to the instrument, she'd never been more certain of anything in her entire life. Her nature had gotten her into this, yes, but instinct took over. She placed her fingers on the keys, willing them to remember the notes, and as the words floated from Madge's mouth and into the room, she forgot about everything else, including all the people staring at her.

She was back at the Feathered Nest, dishes clinking somewhere in the next room, a man's hearty laugh interrupting, perhaps, with a joke, and suddenly the voice, as sweet as the angel Gabriel's, falling over the room and stopping conversations.

Amelia felt it happening here, too. To herself. To others. The powerful silence and Madge's voice. They were all that existed in the world. Or at least all that mattered.

When Amelia stood from the bench and looked at the attendees, she saw it was true for them, too. She hugged her sister tightly, and Madge muttered into her shoulder, 'Don't you ever do that to me again.' And Amelia laughed through her tears, silently thanking her mother for bringing Margaret here.

SEVENTEEN

Dear Lady Agony,
    Do you know the identity of the thief? We are all waiting
for an answer.
    Sincerely,
    A Curious Reader

Dear A Curious Reader,
    I do not. Rest assured you will be the first to know when
I catch the Mayfair Marauder. (Does the name suit, Dearest
Readers? I do so enjoy alliteration.)
    Yours in Secret,
    Lady Agony

I f Margaret had admirers before the performance, she had twice as many afterwards, and a small flock of them encircled her as she moved away from the pianoforte. Lord Morton, for one, was smitten with her performance. Kitty was delighted. And Aunt Tabitha could only be described as flummoxed. She went so far as to say Margaret was the best vocalist she'd heard since Jenny Lind and that Amelia wasn't half as bad as she thought she'd be at the keys. Truth be told, if it had been any other song, Amelia would've struggled, but she couldn't have forgotten the family favorite in a hundred years.

Lady Hamsted briefly congratulated Margaret, but the peevish look on her face told a different story – one that didn't want Margaret Scott as the heroine. She quickly turned away, so quickly she bumped into a maid with a tray of tea things, dirtying the sleeve of her dress. She excused herself with all politeness, but as she glanced over her shoulder, Amelia noted her jaw clenched in jealousy. The viscountess was known for two parties during the season: her croquet tournament and her concert. Now the latter was seen as a success – for little-known Margaret Scott. And her dear nephew, Leo Morton, had all but forgotten about Felicity Farnsworth.

What a shame, thought Amelia, glancing at the viscountess's bevy of friends, who tipped their chins a little higher as she passed by. *They* were the people to know; Margaret Scott was not. Amelia didn't have to hear their conversation to know what they were saying. She'd been around people like them before. They would no more take in an unknown than a rabid mutt. What they didn't realize about Madge was that she didn't care in the least. She didn't need to be admired to feel worthy.

'You never fail to surprise me, Amelia.' Simon's voice was so low that it made Amelia notice the dwindling raindrops falling on the windowpane. The afternoon shower had stopped, and all that was left was a smattering of speckles.

'That's interesting because I find you rather predictable,' she said. 'I assumed you would come to Felicity Farnsworth's defense, and you did.'

'I came to *your* defense, you numbskull. How would I know your sister could sing like an angel? The viscountess put her on the spot, and I thought to give her an exit.'

Amelia had the good grace to blush. Of course he wouldn't have known. The entire room had been stunned. But like so many instances, when it came to Simon, she'd said the first thing that popped into her mind. 'Yes, well. I had it handled.'

'I see that now. I should know better than to underestimate you. It's a lesson I must keep learning, I'm afraid.'

She hazarded a glance at him, and his green eyes stared back at her with appreciation. Steeling herself against his charms, she kept her expression neutral, but on the inside, her heart did that thing it did when they were close. She took a breath, realizing how shaky it was as she released it. She dared not speak a word, and Lady Hamsted excused her from doing so by re-entering the room with an exclamation.

Lady Hamsted grasped at the viscount, who was in arm's reach of Amelia and Simon. 'Henry, a word, please.'

Lord Hamsted sensed her concern. 'What's wrong, dear?'

'My ruby necklace,' Lady Hamsted whispered. 'It's *gone*.'

'I'm sure it is only misplaced.' Lord Hamsted frowned, the puzzled appearance resembling his son's. 'Then again, you never misplace anything.' He quickly scanned the room. 'Oliver, Kitty.' He gestured to the nearby couple, and they came immediately.

'Would you help your mother find her ruby necklace? I gave it to her our first Christmas, and it is very special to her.'

'When did you notice it missing?' asked Oliver.

'When I went upstairs to tidy my sleeve.' Lady Hamsted sniffed. 'My jewelry box was open, and the piece was gone!'

'Just like Aunt Tabitha's diamond brooch,' Amelia whispered to Simon. 'If I had to wager a guess, it isn't lost. It's *stolen*, and the sooner we investigate, the more likely we are to find the culprit.'

Simon took half a second to agree. He touched her elbow. 'Let's go while everyone is preoccupied with Margaret, including your aunt.'

They ducked out of the room, turning right at the grand staircase.

The butler stopped them. 'Your carriage, my lord?'

'No, thank you. Lady Amesbury needs a breath of fresh air after her performance.' Simon lowered his voice as they walked by him. 'Playing always ignites her nerves.'

The butler, an old man with a barrel-shaped belly, frowned. 'But the rain, my lord?'

'Has stopped.' Simon flourished a hand toward the window.

'And I have my parasol if it starts again,' Amelia added.

'May I suggest the garden terrace?' asked the butler.

'An excellent suggestion.' Simon smiled. 'Lead the way, good man.'

The butler left them on the terrace, which had an overhang that would have protected them from the strongest storm. It extended the length of the patio and gave way to the enormous lawn where Lady Hamsted held her annual croquet tournament. Since all the guests were in the drawing room, the terrace was empty, and the privacy gave Amelia and Simon the opportunity to examine the layout of the house.

The private rooms were located in the south wing, so they started their efforts there, thinking the thief gained entrance from the outside. Amelia stuck to the grassy areas; the rain had made everything damp and messy. While Simon was able to go beyond the lawns, only worrying about his shoes, which could be easily cleaned, she had to hold up her skirt and petticoat to ensure no one would be able to detect a damp hemline.

If it did by chance get wet, she'd be able to give the same reason Simon had to the butler: she'd gone outside to calm her nerves.

Women and their nerves. Amelia sighed. At least the rote excuse came in handy when one needed it.

She scoured the lawn, looking for anything the thief might have left behind in a hurry. A button, a buckle, a torn piece of fabric.

'Amelia!' called Simon from around the corner of the house. 'I found something.'

She rushed to join him near a thicket of ornamental grasses, probably imported from the Far East if Amelia knew the viscountess's penchant for original design and topiary. 'What is it?'

Simon was hovering over a spot of patchy grass. He stood and moved to the side. 'A footprint.'

Amelia bent down to observe it more closely. It was recently made: a man's shoe.

'It's rather large. Though not as large as mine.' He extended his shoe for a comparison.

Something gave her pause, but she couldn't say what. Not the size, exactly, but something near it. 'Do you suppose the thief absconded out of the window?'

'Nothing so dramatic.' Simon pointed to the nearby balconet and steps. 'He probably walked away without notice.'

Amelia glanced at the house; it was the epitome of wealth, care and safety. It should have been the last place in London a thief had access to, yet he did.

It came to her then. The person wasn't an outsider; he'd been invited to every place he'd ransacked. The shoe print was evidence of it. 'Simon, this shoe.' Amelia motioned for him to take a second look. 'The sole is shallow – a gentleman's shoe. The sole of a lesser shoe would be deeper and more porous.'

Simon glanced from the shoe print to her. 'How the devil did you know that?'

'It was one of the first things I noticed when I moved to Mayfair: how none of the men's shoes were made for work, only leisure. Women's, too.' She shrugged. 'It surprised me.'

Their heads were nearly touching, bent over the muddy spot in silence. Simon studied her face as she studied the footprint, attempting to commit the lines to memory. 'As you continue to surprise me.'

'Amelia!' Kitty's voice called from the terrace. 'Is that you?'

'Kitty, come quick.' Amelia waved her over. 'I want you to look at something.' She turned back to Simon with an explanation. 'If anyone knows shoes, it's Kitty. For all we know, she can identify the brand and cobbler.'

Kitty had a pensive look on her face as her feet left the safety of the terrace. 'This had better be good,' she grumbled. 'If I mark my boots, you *will* find a way to clean them.'

Simon quickly went and lent her his arm, and together they traversed the lawn carefully.

'Kitty, take a look at this shoe print. I say it comes from the shoe of a gentleman. What do you say?'

Kitty squinted at the mark in the mud. 'I say it comes from the shoe of a *very fine* gentleman. Look at the narrow shape of the toe. It's the height of fashion.'

'How smart you are!' Amelia heard the trill of excitement in her own voice. 'We believe this is the print of the thief who fled with the viscountess's necklace.'

Her eyes widened. 'Truly?'

'It's been raining all afternoon.' Amelia gestured to the sky as if it could explain the theory. 'The only respite has been the past hour. It has to belong to a person who left recently.'

'Do you know who that might be?' asked Simon.

'It's been an eventful afternoon and is growing more eventful still.' Kitty grimaced.

Uh-oh. Kitty never grimaces.

'Which means . . .' Amelia prompted.

She released a breath. 'Which means that Detective Collings is here – the same awful man you told me about. The viscount sent a note to the Metropolitan Police, and he arrived moments ago.'

Amelia clapped her hands together. 'That's wonderful, Kitty. Bring him around immediately.'

Kitty's blonde eyebrows peaked in surprise.

'Don't you see?' Amelia continued. 'He might be able to do something with the shoe print. Scotland Yard has all sorts of new methods. He might be able to trace it, for instance, or even create a mold.'

'A possibility, if we hurry.' Simon turned toward the terrace.

'I hope he can do *something*.' Kitty looped her arm through Amelia's. 'Lady Hamsted has come unhinged. I know she has dozens of baubles, but this one really is special. Oliver says his mother has worn it every Christmas since he can remember. I would hate to have a family heirloom lost to bandits.'

'He's not a bandit, Kitty.' Amelia sidestepped a mud slick. 'The shoe tells us he's a gentleman, and a fashionable one at that. My guess is he has been invited into the houses he's stolen from.'

'But that doesn't make sense. If he's a gentleman, why steal at all?'

They reached the terrace, and Amelia released her arm. 'Perhaps for the thrill of it. For the excitement.'

Kitty pursed her lips. 'I, for one, will be checking every single shoe when I get inside. I can tell a shoemaker and size from halfway across a ballroom. You know it's true. If I find the culprit, I will confront him.'

'With me,' Amelia added. 'You'll confront him with me.' A large raindrop hit her forehead.

Then a second and third.

'Amelia, your parasol,' said Kitty, shielding her face with her hand.

She opened it, and they rushed to the terrace door, where Simon held it ajar.

They had just stepped through it when the rain started in earnest. Together, they looked out at the lawn in stunned silence, one thought and one thought only on their minds: the footprint. All thoughts of identification were washed away with the cloudburst.

Amelia closed her eyes briefly in frustration. It would be fine. They knew what the shoe looked like even if Scotland Yard didn't. They could describe it to the detective, tell him their suppositions. He couldn't possibly fault her or her sister with two other witnesses present.

Could he?

She found out the answer to that question a few moments later in the viscount's study, where Detective Collings stood as smugly as a stuffed guest at teatime. His coal-colored eyes were focused on her entrance alone, no one else's. His dislike was not for the crime but for her. Why? What had she done to offend the detective?

'In my line of work, we talk about common denominators, and I wonder if one might be found here.' The detective's eyes didn't leave her face. They were pebble-small and as cold as steel. 'Trouble seems to follow wherever you go, Lady Amesbury. First your ballroom, now here?'

'I am going to be frank with you, Detective. I have no need of the ruby.' Amelia made a half-circle gesture to the others in the room. 'None of us do. So I'd have you stop pointing fingers in here and start looking for suspects out there.' She signaled the window. 'Simon, Kitty, and I saw the footprint, and it was made by a man.'

'A *gentleman* with a taste for finery,' put in Kitty.

Simon lifted a finger. 'Or an ordinary man trying to appear as such.'

'A solid point,' Amelia conceded. 'But shoes would be a difficult item to steal. One has to consider the size and shape, not to mention the fit. A hard proposition to say the very least.'

Simon and Kitty shared a noise of agreement.

Lord Hamsted turned to the detective. 'Collings, we're wasting precious time. If they saw a footprint, *someone* left by the terrace, and I cannot imagine any of the guests choosing to exit that way. I'll talk to my butler Friese, but in the meantime, I'd appreciate your having a look around. If nothing else, it will settle my wife's nerves.'

Kitty snapped to attention. 'Where is Lady Hamsted?'

'In the drawing room.' Lord Hamsted answered in a gentler voice. 'She had to rejoin her guests, who are thankfully unaware of the situation.'

'I should go,' said Kitty.

'I'll come, too.' Amelia stood from the green leather chair. 'Unless you need anything else, Detective?'

Detective Collings stared at her for an unnecessary amount of time before answering the viscount's request. 'If you could have your butler bring my hat, I'll ask him a few questions on my way out. I'll survey the area, but with weather like this, I can be sure of a negative outcome.'

'I would not be so certain,' said Simon. 'Much might be learned by walking the perimeter.'

Amelia had heard his voice this dark one other time, and that was when a known crook had threatened his sister's reputation. Had he perceived a threat in the detective's look? Was it possible he cared for her in some way he could not show?

'The rain has been on and off all day.' Simon continued more lightly. 'You might be surprised what you find. I'd be happy to help.'

'A fine idea,' said Lord Hamsted. 'Lord Bainbridge was a captain in the Royal Navy and has overseen his fair share of problematic situations.'

The detective murmured in agreement, and Amelia mouthed the words *thank you* over her shoulder. Simon smiled briefly in acknowledgment.

'Do you know a smile from Simon puts a bounce in your step?' Kitty whispered as they made their way toward the stairs. 'He doesn't need to say a word. Not an iota. And suddenly your face lights up like St Paul's Cathedral.'

'Thank you, Kitty,' grumbled Amelia. 'I'll make certain to tame my enthusiasm when he's around.'

Kitty reached for her elbow, twisting to face her. 'When are you two going to face the fact that you're in love?'

Amelia shook off her arm, but the instant heat in her face told her she hadn't ducked an answer. Gracious! In love. She'd never been *in love* before. Just considering the idea would have made Simon, a jilted bachelor, run the other way.

'Ha!' Kitty continued walking. 'I knew it. Your face is never red, and it's as red as a pepper. Deny it all you'd like, but I know. You're falling in love with him.'

Amelia faced her at the top of the stairs. 'Even if I was, which I'm not, it wouldn't matter. Simon is not interested in me.'

Kitty swatted away the idea like a bothersome gnat. 'Of course he is. He just won't admit it – yet.'

'And when might he?' Amelia raised an eyebrow in question.

Kitty scrunched up her nose. 'When you stop getting involved with murders.'

EIGHTEEN

Dear Lady Agony,

You would have readers believe a Lady, a member of the peerage, could find out the identity of a thief and burglar terrorizing the city. It is highly irregular behavior, and I, for one, will not tolerate it. We know you are bound by the same rules we all are. Please stick to the facts. Your fiction has no place in the paper.

Sincerely,
Out of Bounds

Dear Out of Bounds,

What would I do without your not-so-gentle reminders about my audacious behavior? Thankfully, I know the answer to that question. I would go on writing my words and answering my letters. If it makes you more comfortable, cling to your tiresome rules. I will continue to circumvent them every chance I can.

Yours in Secret,
Lady Agony

Later that evening, Amelia had finished with dinner and was in the library, enjoying a glass of brandy as she perused the day's batch of letters to Lady Agony. With the musical event, she hadn't been able to get to them any earlier and considered it a nice way to end the day. She loved hearing from correspondents – most of them. She squinted at a familiar signature even though she very well knew to whom it belonged. Out of Bounds. Out of Bounds once again was writing to tell her she was pushing the boundaries of acceptable behavior. Had anybody ever told her? *Just you, three times.* Her readers were familiar with boundaries; they came up against them every day. What they wanted from her was a way to circumvent them. If they wanted boundaries, they would find them with Mrs Beeton or any of the other etiquette experts. Lady Agony would never be them. She would always be herself, for good, for bad – or for boundless.

Amelia had just tucked away the response when she heard a rap at her window. Her first thought was not of Winifred but of Margaret. It would be just like her to be out after dark with no good way to re-enter without notice. Winifred, ten years her junior, was more responsible than to be out after dark without a reason. But Madge acted first and thought later.

Amelia took a bracing sip of brandy and stood from her desk. *The library windows are certainly large enough to pass through*, she thought as she crossed the room. The windows and the books were two reasons she loved the room more than any other. And the fireplace. And the soft chairs placed in front of it. Obviously, she loved everything about the room. Even the emerald-green velvet curtains.

She pulled one back and screamed.

But only for a half-second. She knew who it was in an instant. A face like Isaac Jakeman's could not be mistaken: small eyes, hooked nose and face-softening side whiskers.

She unlocked and opened the window. 'Please accept my apologies. My guests do not usually enter through the window.'

Isaac stepped through and took off his hat. His graying hair fell over his forehead. 'I am not a guest, Lady. I am here to collect on a favor.'

The words should have disturbed her, but they didn't. His broad smile made him appear amenable. Which, in and of itself, was dangerous.

'Everything all right in there?' Margaret hollered from the dining room or maybe down the stairs, in the kitchen. She enjoyed late-night snacks, and Cook enjoyed her love of food. So did Tabitha. If she had to guess, they were concocting something special right now.

Isaac dipped back into the green velvet curtain, and Amelia gained a new appreciation for its thickness.

'Fine, Madge,' Amelia called back. 'I dropped a paperweight on my toe.'

'Ha!' Margaret laughed. 'Ninny.'

Amelia scowled at the door as she locked it. 'Take a seat, Mr

Jakeman.' She sat across from him in the paisley chair. 'What can I help you with?'

'You are so polite.' Isaac smoothed the green leather couch. 'Your furniture is so nice.'

'Thank you. I appreciate that.'

He leaned back. 'I think I could get used to Mayfair.'

'I certainly have.'

His brow furrowed, giving his nose even more the appearance of a hawk. 'You haven't always lived here?'

'You are surely jesting.' She laughed. 'I'm from Somerset.'

Isaac smiled. 'I hear it just there, in your voice.' He rubbed his hands together. 'Now then, I need you to do me that favor you mentioned.'

Amelia waited to hear what he could possibly want from her, besides money.

'My wife – you met her at the store.' He hesitated, moving his hat from one hand to the other. 'She'd like a new dress. We're attending a party for a gentleman who owns a textile mill, and she'd like to pay a visit to a modiste. A fine one. I thought . . . you might . . . which is to say, you must have one.'

Amelia stood and went to her desk. 'The best in the city. Let me write you a note of introduction.' Her modiste was creative, quick and forward-thinking. She wouldn't want her creations worn by just anyone, but she also would not dismiss an introduction from Amelia. They were as close as a dressmaker and her client could be. She knew all Amelia's unfashionable peccadillos – like pockets – and she never withheld them. In turn, Amelia never demanded more than her modiste could give her, nor did she ask for work to be done under unreasonable deadlines.

She handed him the note.

'Thank you.' He stared at it, and when he looked up, his smile was a little lopsided. It made him look younger, if not boyish. 'I was not sure how such things were done. In my business, it does not matter so much what the clothes look like. But my wife?' He shrugged. 'She likes the pretty things.'

'All women do. And you're welcome.'

He stood and put on his hat.

'Mr Jakeman, there was another theft today,' she said. 'This one in Grosvenor Square. A ruby belonging to Lady Hamsted.'

'I heard the news.' He pulled on the brim of his bowler hat.

'I found a footprint, and if I didn't know better, I'd say it was made by someone at the party. A gentleman.'

'You play with fire, Lady.' His eyes, twinkling like topaz, belied the warning. 'But you may be right.'

She leaned closer. 'You believe so?'

He buttoned his coat. 'The Amesbury diamond. The Hamsted ruby.' He pulled a cigar out of his pocket and put it between his teeth. 'This thief knows his wares. None in the East End know the details of such things.' He crossed the room.

'You're right.' His confirmation of her theory was exactly what she needed to hear. Only an insider would know where to look and – more importantly – when. 'The culprit knows exactly the right time to strike.'

Isaac surprised her by turning around and patting her on the shoulder. 'I like you, Lady.'

Amelia was certain the pleasure showed on her face. A smile crept up her cheeks and into her eyes.

A loud knock interrupted the farewell, and Isaac Jakeman slipped through the window without so much as a wave. She closed the window and stared at his shape until it disappeared into the inky darkness.

Another knock, this one louder.

'I'm coming, Madge.' Amelia stomped to the door. 'Really! Have you not heard that patience is a virtue?' She pulled it open.

A frowning Simon Bainbridge met her at the door. 'Why is this locked? It is never locked.'

She sighed. 'Good evening to you, too.'

Simon breezed past her, surveying the room. He squinted at the window. 'Was someone in here with you?' He sniffed. 'I smell cigar.'

Mercy, Jakeman hadn't even lit it.

'Keep your voice down.' Amelia looked around the corner, into the hallway. 'Where is Jones, anyway?'

Simon lowered his eyelids, his thick dark eyebrows giving him a daring look. 'Your sister has convinced everyone to make popcorn in the wire box. Even Jones couldn't resist the fun. He said I knew my way to the library and left me standing in the entry.'

She shut the door and plopped into the nearest chair. 'It does not surprise me. In fact, I wouldn't be surprised if she's had the entire household converted to her way of thinking by the time she leaves.' She smoothed her dress, a lovely navy silk she had donned for dinner. 'Do you know I overheard her and Aunt Tabitha discussing a new recipe? A lobster bisque, I believe it was.'

He took the chair across from her, his eyes still focused on her face. He steepled his hands, leaning over his knees, and she caught herself leaning back. 'Lobster bisque. Quite.' He tapped his fingertips. 'I don't give a damn about lobster bisque, Amelia. What I want to know is who was in here with you. I know it was a man.'

She arched an eyebrow. 'If it was, would you be jealous?'

'Excuse me?' The words came out as a hiss. 'Jealous?'

She didn't answer. He'd heard the question.

He raked a hand through his hair twice, and it dipped low over his brow in a black, messy wave. 'Dash it all! We are investigating a murder and a theft, and you're inquiring about my *feelings*?'

'That's correct.' Amelia enjoyed seeing the imperturbable Simon Bainbridge perturbed.

He stood up unexpectedly and stalked to the window. 'No. I am not jealous. I don't care a fig who was in here.' He peered past the curtain, then let it drop. 'Was it that Grady Armstrong? I have seen the way he looks at you, you know. Friend. My foot! He's always finding a reason to stop by.'

'Grady?' A puff of laughter escaped her lips. 'He doesn't need a reason. He's my editor and a very dear *friend* who, by the way, enters and exits out of the front door.' She paused, considering whether to tell him. His imagination was running amuck, and if she didn't, he might run through several unsavory scenarios. 'If you must know, it was Isaac Jakeman.'

Simon resumed his seat in the chair so slowly that one might have thought the chair was delicate, despite being a sturdy oak piece that would be in the family for another hundred years. 'Please tell me you haven't been conversing with the East End's most notorious fence in your Mayfair library.'

'That's exactly what I've been doing. I know he's a thief,

Simon, but he is also a decent human being. In fact, he wanted a dress for his wife.' She smiled, remembering the look on Isaac's face, half puzzled, half pleading. 'I gave him an introduction to my modiste, but not to worry. Her sensibilities are quite modern.' She raised a finger. 'He made a solid point regarding the thefts.'

'Which is?' Simon uttered through a clenched jaw.

'The Mayfair Marauder knows his victims. He goes for their most expensive jewels. He recognizes their value and location.'

Simon shook his head. 'The Mayfair Marauder?'

'That's what I'm calling him now in my letters,' she explained.

'He is a real criminal. *Jakeman* is a real criminal. They are not sport for your agony column.'

Her throat went dry. 'I never said they were. My readers have *real* problems, which I help them solve. Have solved, including two murders, one of which involved a suitor of your sister's.' She stood and reached for the glass of brandy on her desk. 'So please don't pretend that I don't know what I'm doing or act as if I'm playing at dress-up or jewelry. I know exactly what I'm doing.' She took a hefty swallow.

His footsteps were so quiet that she didn't realize he was behind her until he whispered the words, 'I know how important your work is and how good you are at it.'

His breath was as gentle as a flutter of a morning lark's wing, and the warmth of his body radiated behind her. It was impossible to ignore, but she tried to, taking another sip of brandy.

'You were right.' A hitch in his breath caught her attention. 'I was jealous. I care about you, Amelia, and the thought of another person – another man – in here made me unreasonable. Unthinking.'

She turned around.

'I am sorry.' He touched her cheek.

She closed her eyes, letting the touch wash over her. He cared for her. She hadn't been going mad. He felt something for her. But would he act on it, or would his pigheaded pride get in the way?

She found out a moment later when his lips brushed hers. Her eyes opened in surprise, but only for a second, until she felt him smile, and they closed again, not needing to see what her heart could feel. It was a side of him that she hadn't known, until now.

Not only vulnerable, but needful. He'd been denying himself for a while; the kiss – long, lingering, lustful – was proof of that. His strong hand stole around her waist, and she had to remind herself she was holding a glass of brandy. The kiss deepened, and then she had to remind herself she was standing.

The power was like no other. The power of him. The power of them. He was her equal in every way. To have this also was unimaginable. Her sigh echoed in her chest or in his – she really couldn't tell which – and he held her closer so that she wouldn't fall backwards or he forward. They stood that way, entangled with each other, exploring the untapped passion that flowed out of them and between them. His hand slid lower on her back, and she longed for them to be even closer, though she didn't see how that was possible. Her back arched, and he groaned, murmuring her name in her mouth.

She came undone, forgetting where they were, or who they were, or why they had to stay apart. Had someone said so, or had she imagined it just as she had imagined this moment a hundred times before? Whatever the reason, she didn't know and didn't care. What mattered was their affection for one another, and she wouldn't allow queen or countryman to tell her otherwise.

'What in God's name is happening in here?'

Tabitha Amesbury, however, was another matter altogether.

NINETEEN

Dear Lady Agony,

    What should one do when caught in a precarious situation? Face what's coming or run fast?

    Sincerely,

    Fight or Flight

Dear Fight or Flight,

    Every situation is different, and some situations are more precarious than others, but I am of the opinion that a problem should be faced directly whenever possible. Most likely, it will surface again if not dealt with, and confronting it once is so much better than twice.

    Yours in Secret,

    Lady Agony

Simon and Amelia tore apart from one another, a slosh of brandy emptying on the floor.

Tabitha slammed the door and locked it. 'Your sister could have walked in. A maid.' She half covered a gasp. 'Winifred!'

Or you. Who, in Amelia's opinion, was the worst option of all.

Simon took another step away from Amelia as if she were a wildfire or molten lava. She wished she were. At least then she'd have a chance of slipping out of the room. She'd rather face the devil himself than Tabitha Amesbury. By the look on her face, the two could have been related.

'Lady Tabitha.' Simon cleared his throat. 'I . . . apologize.'

Her wrinkled eyelids narrowed. 'Apologize? Is that what happens when two people are caught together in a compromising situation? An apology?'

Amelia glanced down at her personage. She was completely intact. It was only her brandy that had taken a minor spill. She set it down on her desk. 'Aunt, don't be unreasonable. Simon and I have been working together quite closely, regarding the thefts, and these things can happen.'

'These things *happen*?' Tabitha repeated incredulously. 'Have they happened before?'

'No.' Amelia had stolen a kiss in a carriage, but this was not that. This was something else entirely.

Tabitha released a breath. 'Thank heavens. If you'd compromised her, Simon Bainbridge, I would have you married within the week.'

Simon's face flushed a plum color, a cross between pink and purple.

Tabitha dismissed his embarrassment as casually as an errant servant. 'I am Edgar's aunt.' She punctuated the syllables with her cane. 'I won't hear of this! And in his very home!'

Simon looked abashed. Guilty, even. Amelia shared the sentiment. Having Tabitha witness the passionate moment was beyond the pale. But Edgar had cared for her. He wouldn't want her to be alone for the rest of her life. She knew it in her heart.

'Again, I apologize.' He glanced at Amelia. 'To both of you.'

'Please do not apologize,' Amelia said to him. 'We didn't do anything wrong.' She turned to Aunt Tabitha. 'I know Edgar was your nephew, and you loved him. So did I. But that does not mean we will never love again.'

'*Love?*' repeated Tabitha.

Amelia hadn't meant to say the word. She wished she could strike it from the air, but it seemed to reverberate off the walls, lingering for the entire world to see. Tabitha's mouth hung open, her jaw slack and unbelieving. Simon flinched, as if the idea physically hurt him. You'd think she said the word *Fire!* from the way they responded. Was it that unbelievable? 'What I meant to suggest is that one can enjoy someone's affection without it taking away from the memory of a person.'

Tabitha's mouth snapped shut. She poked her cane, a beauty with a shapely swallowtail handle. 'An unmarried woman cannot enjoy anyone's affection outside the bonds of marriage, Amelia.' She took a deep breath. 'I will hear no more on this subject. Simon, I'll bid you good evening.'

Simon replaced his hat on his head. 'Good evening.'

'Wait! What?' Amelia felt as if she were an audience member, watching a play pass before her eyes, not a participant at all. He walked by her without so much as a backward glance.

'Amelia, Winifred is waiting for you with a bowl of popcorn in her room. I told her not to take it upstairs, but she wanted to share it with you.'

With that, Tabitha turned and followed Simon out of the library, leaving Amelia to wonder what had just happened. The best and worst moments of her life had transpired within the span of fifteen minutes. Simon admitted he cared for her. And she'd felt his care in his kiss. So why had he left her without so much as a sympathetic word? Aunt Tabitha was hostile, naturally, but even Amelia had kept a modicum of courage in the unexpected circumstances.

Margaret peeked in the open door. 'Did I just see what I think I saw?'

'What do you think you saw?' asked Amelia.

Margaret stepped inside with an oversized dish of popcorn. 'Lady Tabitha showing the marquis the way to the door.'

'That's fairly accurate.'

'Here.' Madge held out the dish. 'You need this more than I do.'

Amelia took a handful, popping a buttery bite into her mouth. 'This is good.'

Madge glanced at the hall. 'Did she kick him out for good?'

Amelia laughed despite her bad mood. 'No, she did not kick him out. She was upset because – you see, she has expectations regarding the Amesbury family, and when those expectations aren't met, she can be incorrigible.'

Madge squinted at Amelia, a red twist of hair on top of her head falling forward. 'She caught you at something, didn't she?'

Amelia felt a wave of heat hit her face. 'Of course not.'

Madge tilted her head.

'Fine, she did.' It felt good to have a sister to talk to, even a younger sister. Certainly, Amelia was supposed to be the older, wiser woman, and heaven knows she'd been trying to be. But in truth, she wasn't always wise. Like Margaret, she was still sometimes puzzled to find herself in a world where rules mattered more than feelings.

'A kiss?' Madge's eyes sparkled like a blue ribbon on a package.

Amelia nodded.

'Was it satisfactory?'

Amelia sighed. 'Very much.'

'Good.' Madge popped a piece of popcorn into her mouth. 'It was worth getting caught, then.'

Amelia smiled. 'I suppose it was. But Simon acted so strangely afterwards.'

'I'd act strangely, too, if I were him.' She took another piece. 'Having Lady Tabitha walk in unannounced must've been his worst nightmare come true.'

'Still, he could have said *something* before he left.'

Madge shrugged. 'Sometimes silence is the best response.'

'This coming from a woman who has not remained silent a single moment in her entire life?' Amelia threw a piece of popcorn at her. 'Please.'

Madge laughed. 'You'd better pick that up. Lady Tabitha did not want the food leaving the kitchen.'

'I'm going upstairs to see Winifred.' Amelia dusted off her hands.

Madge glanced over Amelia's shoulder at the door with a look of horror. 'Here she comes!'

Amelia snatched up the thrown kernel.

Madge snorted a laugh. 'Got you!'

Amelia chuckled about the joke all the way up the stairs. It really was good to have family in the house. They never let one take oneself too seriously – Madge especially. The sisters had faced scarier people than Tabitha Amesbury. *Perhaps not scarier, but angrier.* Amelia remembered the time she and Madge had mixed up a man's and woman's valises. He opened the luggage to find women's underthings instead of paperwork. He was irate, but their father explained the man had been traveling and was unreasonable. Staying away from home too long did that to a person in his opinion.

Amelia knocked on Winifred's door as she opened it a crack. 'May I come in?'

'I've been waiting for you!' Winifred flopped on her bed cross-legged, and a few of the popcorn kernels fell on her coverlet. 'Come here.'

Amelia joined her on the bed, smiling at the vision her daughter was becoming. Her pretty blonde hair curled about the shoulders of her white nightdress, a white hair tie discarded beside her, and her button nose was scrunched up the way it did when she was perplexed or interested or amused. She was ten, soon to be eleven, and moments such as these seemed to grow further and further apart. Amelia savored every look and every second.

'This is not just popcorn.' Winifred lowered her voice. 'It's what Madge – may I call Miss Scott Madge?'

'Of course.'

'It's what Madge calls sweet corn. It has butter, salt and *sugar* on it! You must taste it.'

Her sister had made it for her many times, and Winifred was right: it was the perfect combination of sweet and salty. But she didn't say so to Winifred. She was much too excited, and Amelia didn't want to disappoint her. She popped a piece in her mouth. 'Mmm.'

'It is delicious.' Winifred took a piece and chewed as if to verify her statement. 'Madge is a most interesting person, isn't she?'

'She is.'

'I love having her here.' Winifred ate another piece. 'I don't care if she did poison a man in the ballroom.'

Amelia briefly closed her eyes. 'She did not poison a man in the ballroom. I promise.'

'Right.' Winifred tipped her head thoughtfully. 'But if she did, she would have a good reason.'

'And pray tell, what would be a good reason for poisoning someone?'

Winifred put the bowl on the bed, sitting up a little straighter. Her tiny brow furrowed in serious reflection. 'If the person hurt someone she cared about. Or if the person was about to hurt someone she cared about. She'd have to stop him, or worse, wouldn't she?'

'I suppose she would,' Amelia answered, but she wasn't thinking about Madge. She was thinking about Lady Ann and her argument with the man on the terrace. She'd said if he came any closer, she'd scream – or worse. Was it possible that Mr Radcliffe had been the man with her that evening? Her name was in his brother's appointment book, after all, and she'd been seated next to him in the supper room.

The longer Amelia thought about it, the more she thought it was entirely possible that Lady Ann's threat had come to fruition.

TWENTY

Dear Lady Agony,
   Do you think revenge is best served hot or cold?
Sincerely,
Hot or Cold

Dear Hot or Cold,
   I think it is best not served at all, for what purpose can it hold? It will not repair the initial damage. Trust me when I say any satisfaction will be fleeting. Then the anger will return, perhaps with sadness, leaving the exactor lower than before. Do not do it.
   Yours in Secret,
   Lady Agony

The next day, the rain had been forgotten, and the sun spotted the bright blue sky in spectacular fashion – a showy orb that illuminated every neighborhood in London, from Mayfair to Whitechapel. Amelia's day had started with a head-clearing walk in Hyde Park. The kiss was foremost on her mind. It gave her shivers to recall it, as did the aftermath of Aunt Tabitha finding her and Simon in each other's arms, albeit for completely different reasons. Amelia came to the optimistic conclusion that the awkward situation of last evening would be forgotten today. How could it not on such a morning? She took one last look at the pulse-pounding city, the beat in the street already hammering a busy tune, then turned the knob of her front door.

   The breakfast room smelled of meat, eggs, fresh pastries and fruit, and Amelia went to the sideboard immediately to fill her plate with all of them. It was a benefit of being an early riser: the best offerings of the morning for her picking. She selected two eggs, ham, sausage, kippers, and a large croissant, slathering it with butter and jam. Glancing woefully at the blueberry muffin, bursting with fresh fruit, she realized she had no more room on her plate and turned to the table.

And almost fell over.

Tabitha was seated with her traditional tea and toast and an unhappy look on her face. It appeared to be a cross between indigestion and irritation.

'Aunt.' Amelia selected a chair two away from hers. No reason to be too close to her in case the food began to fly. 'You're up early this morning.'

'I could not sleep.' Tabitha glared at her from over the rim of her teacup.

Definitely irritation.

'I'm sorry.' Amelia unfolded her napkin. 'I've suffered from that affliction enough to understand how debilitating it can leave one the next day.' She smiled and cut a piece of sausage. 'Try a little brandy this evening. It always helps me.'

'Nothing could have elevated my woes last night.' Tabitha set her teacup down, rattling the saucer. 'I was stunned into a stupor at finding you and Simon Bainbridge entangled in the library. I could not unsee the scenario no matter how tightly I closed my eyes.'

Amelia glanced at the window, a sliver of bright sun sneaking through the heavy drapery. Despite the beautiful weather, it seemed all would not be forgotten today. She put down her knife. 'It was only a kiss, Aunt. You must have sneaked a few when you were young.'

'I most certainly did not.' Tabitha put her palms on the table, and the teacup quaked in response. 'I knew my place, and I kept it. I wouldn't have indulged in untoward behavior for all the joys in Christendom.'

Jones saved her from defending herself with his timely entrance. 'Excuse me. Detective Collings is here. He is asking for Lady Amesbury.' He glanced at Amelia, then Tabitha. 'Shall I tell him she is not home?'

A twitch started in Tabitha's right eye, and Amelia wished she could warn the detective today was not the day to test her aunt. Tabitha had banished him from the house once already; she would never allow him to interview Amelia alone again.

'No.' Tabitha stood abruptly. 'Put him in the drawing room,

and don't bother lighting the fire. I'm not going to bend this house to his will.' She motioned to Amelia with a single finger. 'You come, too.'

Amelia glanced longingly at her plate. 'What of my breakfast?'

Tabitha's pursed lips indicated breakfast would be late if not skipped altogether.

A few minutes later, they met Detective Collings in the cold upstairs drawing room. The chill air might have been an intimidation tactic, but Amelia doubted it. Tabitha's tall frame, clothed in head-to-toe black, was intimidation enough. Even in her plain blue walking dress, Amelia felt overdressed.

'Detective.' Aunt Tabitha stumped to a chair, emphasizing her shiny black cane. Indeed, it had encyclopedic sound qualities, revealing all her moods: happy, content, peevish, angry and – today – fuming.

Detective Collings stood from his chair.

Tabitha selected the red damask chair across from him, and he returned to his seat. Amelia perched on the edge of the settee. 'Imagine my surprise at having breakfast interrupted,' Tabitha continued. 'I suppose you believe old ladies need not eat at all or would be better off dead.'

Detective Collings's lip curled in a half snarl. 'I believe nothing of the sort. I asked to speak to Lady Amesbury. I did not want to disturb your morning.'

'Well, you have,' declared Tabitha. 'So what is it we can help you with?'

Detective Collings fumbled a paper out of his coat pocket, and the sheet fell to the floor. Retrieving it, he flicked it with satisfied smugness. 'I have here an initial report from the medical examiner. He's a friend of Doctor Radcliffe's and was keen to complete the examination quickly and thoroughly. I've just come from his surgery, where he has informed me that Mr Radcliffe died of arsenic poisoning.'

'*Arsenic*,' Amelia repeated. The poison was easily attainable at any chemist's shop. All one had to do was sign his or her name in a book stating its reason for use, usually rats. London was overrun by them. During her investigations, Amelia learned the poison was also used in cosmetics and green color dye. Once, a woman had written to Lady Agony about witnessing a fellow seamstress fainting after working on a pair of green drapes for ten hours. The hours were long, certainly, but they'd worked longer before. Upon investigation, Amelia discovered the material was latent with arsenic, which wasn't lethal but could make one ill all the same.

'The death is officially a murder, and I will be investigating it as such.'

Amelia felt a trickle of sweat start at her brow.

From her vague countenance, Aunt Tabitha had no such physical problem. 'That does not explain why you are here.'

'Let me be plain, Lady Tabitha.' Detective Collings leaned in, perhaps to alarm her. 'Mr Radcliffe was murdered the night of your ball, perhaps at the gathering itself. That means I will be investigating your home, your family members and your friends for clues to what transpired that evening.'

Amelia willed the sweat bead to stay on her forehead and not drip onto her dress.

'I will talk to the Yard about this,' Tabitha declared.

'Talk to whomever you'd like.' Detective Collings had the face of a cat that'd just swallowed a mouse. 'I have authority from the Chief Officer to investigate.' He stood. 'Now, if I may have a look around? I'd like to interview the staff who were present at the dance and dinner. Precious time has been lost already.'

'I really think it unnecessary, Detective.' Amelia stood also. 'What can anyone tell you that my sister and I have not shared in your previous visit?'

'That's to be determined.'

'Here is what I have determined,' said Tabitha in a startling low voice. 'You have dug your heels into this case for one reason and one reason only.'

Detective Collings inched back.

'Did you think I would not find out that you were in the Royal Navy with our beloved Edgar? That you loathed him for gaining the rank of Lieutenant Commander when you could not?'

'A position reserved for aristocrats,' he said in a low growl of his own. It was evident to Amelia that Tabitha had hit a nerve, and his reaction was that of a lone dog, angry and fearful.

'Lies!' Tabitha shot back.

Amelia watched the volley in stunned silence.

'Even in death, you cannot admit his merit,' continued Tabitha. 'He was a younger son. He earned the position through toil and perseverance, two characteristics that evade you still today.'

The detective struggled to find the words. His eyes bulged a little, protruding from their sockets, and his weak chin jutted out in defiance. 'I deserved that commendation.'

He didn't. Amelia knew he would never obtain the rank of inspector either.

'Enough.' Tabitha silenced him with a word. 'I will allow you to talk to our staff, but let this be known.' She stood, and Amelia and Collings did as well. 'I will not have you smear the Amesbury name out of spite. If you do, I will speak with the Chief Officer myself. What I say about you will not be kind.' She cleared her throat. 'Mr Jones will assist you with the interviews.'

The butler must have had incredible hearing, for he appeared seconds later at the door.

'The detective would like to speak to some of the staff, Mr Jones.' Tabitha dipped her chin. 'If you could direct him accordingly.'

'Of course, my lady.'

Amelia blinked at the pair as they walked out. She turned to Tabitha. 'I knew his dislike was out of bounds. Why didn't you tell me earlier?'

'I only learned it recently, when I paid a second call on Lady Sutherland. She found out the story from her man at the Yard.' Tabitha closed the door halfway before telling her the rest of the account.

Edgar, as a second son, had not expected to inherit the title of earl. It was only when his father and brother perished in the same accident that he became the Amesbury patriarch. He and his Aunt Tabitha, along with his now-orphaned niece Winifred, were the remaining family members in a long and stately history. Edgar had not been handed a senior rank as some first sons had. He'd earned it, as Tabitha had said, with hard work and perseverance. But Collings, who'd served at the same time, thought the office had been handed to Edgar because of his newly bestowed title. He himself had applied for the position and been denied. It was easy for Amelia to understand why the Royal Navy came to the decision. Collings was resentful, not one to be put in a position of authority. Yet here he was, leading what would most likely prove to be the most important case of his life – and certainly hers. If only the Yard could see what the Navy had years ago.

Yet it might not have mattered. With London's increasing crime, officers were needed more than ever before.

Just not this officer.

'So you see,' Tabitha finished, 'his petulance is to be expected. Unwarranted and offensive, but expected. He is looking for a reason to implicate us in this crime, and I am worried he will find it.' Tabitha put up a hand before Amelia could respond. 'Which is not to imply your sister committed the deed. As I said, the art of subtlety is beyond her reach. But it hardly matters when one is as steadfast as he is in a particular outcome.'

Amelia wouldn't put it past him to manufacture evidence against them. 'Does Jones know of your suppositions?'

'I informed him this morning while you were circling Hyde Park.' Tabitha tsked. 'Jones will be vigilant against all attacks.'

The reminder of Aunt Tabitha's disfavor fell like a raindrop after many wet days. Amelia hated being at odds with Tabitha, but what could she do? She refused to swear off Simon for good, and that's exactly what Tabitha wanted. Amelia knew it was the one way to quit the subject altogether and go back to being friends – or, if not friends, relatives.

Amelia ignored the barb, focusing on the case itself. 'Thank goodness Mr Jones is aware of the situation. As you say, he won't allow the detective to manufacture evidence against us.'

At that moment, the out-of-breath butler appeared, his comb-over hairstyle definitely not combed over. The wispy brown flap of hair fell over his forehead, and his eyes, small but not uncaring, implored them for help.

'What is it, Jones?' asked Tabitha. 'Has something happened?'

He nodded aggressively, calming his breath.

'Take your time,' Amelia said. 'Whatever's happened, we will take care of it.'

He shook his head just as aggressively. 'It's Detective Collings.' He swallowed hard, trying to regain his composure. 'He's found something in the ballroom and is admitting it for evidence. A little container of white powder—'

He no more had the words out of his mouth than Amelia hitched up her skirts and raced down the hall and into the ballroom, where the detective stood near a potted fern. When he heard her enter, he held up a bag. 'I'm afraid I have bad news. I found this hidden in your plant, and although I cannot be entirely certain, I'm fairly sure it is the arsenic that killed Mr Radcliffe.'

'That cannot be.' Amelia felt a little like Jones, shocked and out of breath, as she crossed the room.

'Oh, but it is. I decided to take a cursory tour of the room before interviewing staff, and, lo, I find the method of murder discarded under some leaves.'

'There must be an explanation.' Amelia had the idea that he placed it there himself, yet Jones had been with him the entire time. He would have noticed. Still, she would put nothing past the duplicitous detective.

'There is not,' Detective Collings said with finality. 'Mr Jones witnessed the discovery, and although he believes rat poison might be kept in the household for pest control, he's never seen it contained in a little glass vial.'

Amelia squinted at the bag but only for a moment before he snatched it out of her view and put it into his pocket. Someone had put the poison into an ornamental glass bottle. But who and why? 'It doesn't belong to us. It might be in our house, but that does not mean it is ours.'

'Another coincidence, Lady Amesbury?' He buttoned his coat. 'I've had enough of them from you to last a lifetime.'

'What of the staff?' Amelia followed him to the door. 'I thought you were going to speak to them. They'll tell you we had nothing to do with this. One of them may have seen something that will tell you who did.'

Collings patted his pocket. 'I will process this first. When I know it is arsenic, be certain I will return.'

The smug smile appeared again, the one that told Amelia she was under his thumb, and he would not be allowing her up anytime soon. She was a victim of his envy for her departed husband and she refused to allow him to exact revenge on her two families. Whatever it took to clear the Amesbury and Scott names was her objective, and she would not stop until it was accomplished.

TWENTY-ONE

Dear Lady Agony,
Recently, I caught my friend in an untruth. I did not
confront her with it at the time. I thought she would tell me
eventually, but she has not. It bothers me. Should it?
Sincerely,
Wounded Wilhelmina

Dear Wounded Wilhelmina,
It does not matter if it should or not. It does. Therefore,
you must talk to your friend. I suspect the real hurt comes
from your friend's lack of trust. Assure her you are trust-
worthy, and see what becomes of it. If she refuses to talk,
you might consider if you wish to remain friends. Lies
between friends are ill-sewn seeds.
Yours in Secret,
Lady Agony

That afternoon, Amelia was in her carriage with Kitty, relaying her harrowing morning on their way to pay Lady Ann a call. Amelia rarely made calls, so having Kitty along was welcome, not to mention advantageous. Kitty was well-liked by popular society. Everyone enjoyed seeing her calling card on the salver. Today she was wearing blue Byzantine, a detail that didn't escape Amelia's notice even with a new piece of evidence collected against her sister. And not just any evidence: most likely the method of murder. That, in and of itself, spoke to her friend's captivating fashion choices. Kitty, however, was not distracted from her task. She seemed more determined than ever to discover the reason behind Lady Ann's appointment with Dr Radcliffe since learning of the arsenic; she'd promised to do whatever it took to uncover the connection between the two people.

'If I need to describe the intricate weave of my Byzantine blouse while you pilfer a nearby room, simply tap your chin, and I will receive the signal.' Kitty adjusted the black velvet hat with blue feathers that dipped low on her brow. 'I will not have our dear Margaret arrested for a crime she did not commit.'

'Nor will I,' Amelia replied. In spite of Madge's take-it-or-leave-it attitude, she had won everyone's good favor, including Kitty's. It warmed Amelia's heart to know people saw in her sister the same qualities she had forever known. Amelia had always respected her younger sister's unwavering independence, but here in London it had become an obstacle, something Amelia had to overcome or explain. She felt it had more to do with London than her sister.

'How the devil did the poison get there in the first place? Arsenic is not something one leaves lying around.'

'Unless you are the murderer,' Amelia thought out loud. 'And it could have been. Arsenic is not prepared in glass vessels. The perpetrator could have planted it there – no pun intended – after poisoning Arthur Radcliffe. The detective, also, might have hidden it in an attempt to frame the Amesburys. Yet you would think Mr Jones would have noticed.'

'True enough.' Kitty tipped her head to one side. 'But if it was the murderer, why choose the night of your ball to kill Mr Radcliffe?'

'Perhaps the number of people, and therefore suspects, appealed to him. He could mask his identity by being one in a sea of many. I daresay it worked.'

Kitty set her chin. 'Not if I have any choice in the matter.'

The carriage stopped, and the footman collected the steps.

Amelia reached over and touched her hand. 'Thank you, Kitty.'

Kitty smiled. 'What are friends for? I rely on you for every-thing, and you must do the same.'

'I am glad to hear you say that because I need help with a problem of similar magnitude when we are finished here.'

Kitty arched an eyebrow. 'A problem on a par with arsenic poisoning?'

'In my heart, yes, but not actually.'

Kitty squeezed her hand. 'Lord Bainbridge?'

Amelia nodded, and the footman opened the door, leaving the question to linger in the carriage as they collected themselves for the call.

Lady Ann lived in an old home on Bedford Street, a sprawling square building that must have taken a good deal of money to heat in the winter months. The drawing room was a beautiful sage-green with ornate gold arches that matched the frames of the paintings on the walls, which included a particularly stunning vase of roses. The bow window was enhanced by a brocade salmon-colored curtain as well as a crystal chandelier, which hung high on the ornate off-white ceiling. Lady Ann was seated in the alcove with another caller when they arrived and greeted them graciously as they entered.

'Lady Amesbury, Mrs Hamsted.' Her voice was warm and tinged with real enthusiasm. 'How good of you to call. This is Miss Murphy. She is new to London.'

They exchanged greetings and selected a settee near the women. Miss Murphy had a square face, fair and clear, and wide eyes the same color as her cornflower-blue dress. Her gown was plain, without ruffles or frills, and suited her disposition, which was open and forthright. Amelia immediately liked her.

'On a day such as this, I must be close to a window, if not outdoors altogether.' Lady Ann smiled, and her blue-gray eyes appeared lavender in proximity to her headdress, a light purple chenille with a ruche of darker ribbon. 'I cannot imagine better weather.'

Amelia nodded. 'I feel the same. I took a long walk in Hyde Park this morning, and it was glorious.'

'You describe all your walks in the same manner,' jested Kitty. 'No matter the weather.'

'Very true,' Amelia agreed. 'I enjoy the exercise, I suppose. Do you enjoy time outside, Miss Murphy?'

'I enjoy nothing less.' Miss Murphy's robust bosom shook with laughter. It was the kind of warm laughter that made other people smile if not join in. 'Give me a good book or game of cards, and I'll stay indoors forever. I suppose I shouldn't admit it, but it's true. My health is not amenable to the outdoors.'

Amelia gave her a sympathetic look. 'Sneezing, coughing, watery eyes? I have a sister who suffers from the affliction. A terrible condition, but it got her out of a good many chores in our childhood.'

'I suffer from the very same, but I'm sorry it never relieved me of any tasks as a child.' Miss Murphy laughed her easy laugh again. 'Summer can be torture at times, and the city has been hard to handle.'

'Our local physician prescribed my sister a tonic that helped, but I imagine you have a family physician who has tended to the condition. I am happy to recommend mine.' Amelia gestured to Lady Ann, hoping she might mention Dr Radcliffe. 'And I'm certain Lady Ann would do the same.'

'Oh, yes,' said Lady Ann. 'I'd be glad to recommend Doctor Devin. His card is an excellent one to have on hand when illness strikes. One doesn't want to be without assistance in this city.'

'Did you ever meet Doctor Radcliffe, Arthur Radcliffe's brother?' inquired Amelia. 'I've heard his name mentioned once or twice recently. He is new to the practice and probably easy to reach for an appointment.'

The slightest pause was noted before Lady Ann answered. 'I don't believe I knew he had a brother who was a physician.' She stood. 'If you'll excuse me, I'll fetch Doctor Devin's card for you before I forget.'

'I'd appreciate it.' Miss Murphy glanced at Kitty, her bright, square face open and direct. 'It can be difficult to make contacts when one doesn't know a soul in town. Lady Ann has been incredibly kind to me.'

'She's a thoughtful person,' added Kitty.

'But I believe she's mistaken about Doctor Radcliffe.' Miss Murphy's brow furrowed. 'I could have sworn I spotted her talking to him at the chemist's shop on Hampstead Road. Everyone knows that man – or his brother, at least – even I.' She shrugged. 'I could be mistaken.' Her lips lifted into a smile. 'I cannot find my way from Piccadilly to Regent Street.' Another laugh bubbled out of her. 'I don't know how you Londoners stay sane.'

'Wine. Lots of wine.' Kitty chuckled, but the knowing look she slid Amelia did not escape her notice. Lady Ann was hiding her acquaintance with Dr Radcliffe, but why? Amelia needed to know, and she needed to know now. Time was running out for Margaret. If Detective Collings determined the powder was indeed arsenic, which he could do with the Marsh test, his next step would be to accuse her sister. His history with Edgar only assured her of the notion. But how to go about asking Lady Ann? Talking about one's ailments was not done in polite society.

Lady Ann re-entered with the card, and Miss Murphy stood to take her leave. 'Thank you, and for tea also. Lady Amesbury, Mrs Hamsted.' She bobbed her head in their direction. 'It was good to meet you.'

'You as well,' said Amelia.

'I hope we meet again soon,' Kitty added.

After Miss Murphy left, Lady Ann returned to her chair near the windows. She reminded Amelia of a wren, petite and pretty with a voice that could be just as sharp as it was beautiful. The night of the ball, she'd proven just how severe it could be.

'Miss Murphy seems like a very nice person,' said Amelia. 'Is she here for the season with her parents?'

'With her cousin,' corrected Lady Ann. 'Lady Adamson? She wed the earl last year and was reported to have brought a dowry to the marriage of ten thousand pounds.' She raised her eyebrows as she took a delicate sip of her tea. 'Miss Murphy is reported to have the same amount.'

'Goodness,' Kitty exclaimed. 'They are lucky women.'

'Lucky indeed,' murmured Lady Ann. 'And now so too is the earl. His estate in Northumberland has fallen into disrepair, as have so many of the old houses, and someone must pay for them.' Amelia noted her jaw tightening. 'Usually young women on the marriage mart.'

Kitty frowned. 'I count myself fortunate to have made a love match in this town.'

Lady Ann sighed. 'It is rare. London is not known for them. If it's not money that's wanted, it's something else, and a woman rarely knows what until it's too late.'

Amelia leaned in. 'It sounds as if you speak from experience.'

'Of course not. It is only my second season, and—' Lady Ann stopped abruptly. A brief smile passed her lips, then faded. 'I don't see why I should dissemble. You are kind, and you are women of experience – one married and one widowed.' She took a breath before continuing. 'I once thought I'd made a love match and doomed courtships were a thing of the past, but I was wrong. Men can be very deceitful when it serves their needs.'

Kitty's blue eyes were sympathetic. 'An unfortunate truth.'

Lady Ann lowered her shoulders. 'Rest assured I will not be caught off guard again.'

Amelia didn't believe she would. In fact, whoever she confronted on the terrace the night of the ball was evidence of the fact. Was it Mr Radcliffe or Mr Briggs? She'd spoken to both men at the ball. If only Amelia could ask. But even if she could, she couldn't do so without revealing that she was eavesdropping – not intentionally, but eavesdropping all the same. And there would go Lady Ann's good opinion of her. Amelia wanted to remain in Lady Ann's good graces, so she would have to go about finding the information another way.

The Royal Botanic Society was holding a horticultural exposition tomorrow, and she and Margaret were attending, along with half the people who attended the ball, including Mr Briggs. The events were wildly popular, especially among the aristocracy. Madge insisted on going with Captain Fitz, so Amelia would be performing her duties as chaperone. If Kitty accompanied her, Amelia could ask a few questions in her spare time.

Amelia told Kitty the idea the moment they left Lady Ann's.

Kitty's nose scrunched up as if she smelled something foul. 'Me a *chaperone*?' She moaned. 'I'm too young to be a chaperone.'

'No, you're not.' Amelia tsked. 'You are married. That's as close to an old maid as one gets.' The idea wasn't without merit, in Amelia's opinion. Old maids didn't have to adhere to the senseless rules young women did. When she was old, she would go anywhere she liked and say whatever she pleased. That is, if Tabitha wasn't still alive, which she probably would be. Amelia could see her living to be one hundred and ten.

Kitty lowered perfectly curled lashes. 'Speaking of old maids, you were about to tell me of a recent relationship problem . . . something akin to poisoning?'

As Amelia relayed the story of her passionate kiss with Simon, Tabitha's unexpected arrival and the lingering consequences, Kitty's expression changed to one of empathy. Two lines appeared between her perfect blonde eyebrows. 'I am sorry, Amelia. I didn't mean to be snide. How awful!'

'I forgive you.' Amelia tried a smile and failed. 'Truly, it was awful. Not the kiss, mind you, but Simon's reaction. Just as I believed he'd crossed a bridge, he retreated in full force. Do you think he will ever come around?'

'I wish I could say,' Kitty said pensively. 'I'm afraid his loyalty to Edgar will prove to be an obstacle. Never mind what Edgar would have wanted for you – and his niece for that matter. Men can be obtuse when it comes to emotions.'

'This man in particular.'

'You need to talk to him. Tell him how you feel. I know you care deeply for him.' Kitty held up a hand. 'Don't try to deny it.'

Amelia released a breath. 'I do care for him, but I care for my freedom, too. This is the first summer I've fully enjoyed in two years.'

'Because of him.'

'Or the murders,' Amelia jested. But in her heart, she knew Kitty was right. Clothes, callers, invitations – yes, they had changed this year. But they didn't matter. What were her feelings for Simon? With each passing predicament, they'd become more than partners. They'd become friends. And something else.

Whether or not Simon felt the same way, however, was soon to be seen.

TWENTY-TWO

Dear Lady Agony,

My grandfather passed away, and I feel dreadful. I truly do. However, my grandmother has removed all the looking glasses from the house, and I dare not leave the house without a glance in the mirror. My mother states I'm being selfish. Am I?

Sincerely,

No More Mirrors

Dear No More Mirrors,

My sincerest condolences on your grandfather's passing. It must be harder still with your grandparents being close, living in your household. However, I do not think it's selfish for a young girl to desire a looking glass. You want to look your best, and a mirror would assure you. Do you have a friend who might loan you one? If so, tuck it in your drawer and use it when you must. I hardly think it will bother anyone, especially your grandfather's spirit, which has most assuredly left for its heavenly home.

Yours in Secret,

Lady Agony

Amelia had just settled in with a stack of letters when Jones informed her that she had a caller waiting in the drawing room. She gave the letters a look that said, *Excuse me; I'll be back.* That's how she thought of her correspondents – as friends, and now they were friends who were left waiting for a response. She would tuck the letters away for safe keeping once Jones left the room and return to them later that afternoon.

Amelia was not used to being called upon so frequently, and her sister's presence was to blame. Madge had been busy from sun up to sun down. She and Amelia's maid, Lettie, had to have been to most of the houses in Mayfair returning calls. Then there was shopping, which Madge had taken to surprisingly well. All went as smoothly as silk – of which they bought much.

Jones added, 'It's Lord Drake, my lady.'

She paused. 'Here?'

'Quite so.'

This was a surprise. Was it possible Margaret had snagged the attention of London's most eligible bachelor this season? If she had, she wouldn't have it for long. Lord Drake was notorious for his short-term relationships and inability to be captured by money-hungry mamas. Which made him more desirable. Which made him more aloof. Which reset the cycle to occur each year.

When Amelia entered the drawing room ten minutes later, she could understand why. Lord Drake was handsome with a style that outperformed any man's. His dark coat was well fitted, despite some men's preference for looser articles, and he wore a double-breasted waistcoat of two colors, one which matched his powder-blue cravat perfectly. He was kind and easy to talk to and surprisingly unpretentious. Apparently, being infamous hadn't gone to his head.

After exchanging warm greetings, Amelia gestured to a chair across from hers. 'I'm afraid you've missed my sister, my lord. She's left for St James's Park.' She frowned. 'Something about an origami demonstration.' When she said it out loud, she realized how unbelievable it seemed. Madge would rather hammer a nail than fold a piece of paper. Amelia really needed to be more mindful of her sister's comings and goings.

'I'm here to see you.' He smiled, showing off a dimple in his left cheek.

'Oh.' The thought was so incredible that Amelia might have blushed. 'How nice.'

'Today is the first opportunity I've had to thank you for the dance and the conversation the other evening.' Lord Drake steepled his hands together. 'I rarely discuss my father's condition with anyone, yet I felt comfortable doing so with you.'

Amelia was immediately put at ease by his words and manner. 'I am happy to talk whenever you'd like. It is difficult nursing a loved one. I had Edgar's aunt and Winifred for support, but I understand you have no brothers or sisters.'

He nodded. 'And my mother, God rest her soul, passed away five years ago.'

'I am sorry.'

'Thank you, although I'm grateful she hasn't had to witness my father's deterioration.' He swallowed. 'It has been difficult.' He tossed his head a little, perhaps shaking off a recent memory. 'The estate is a great comfort to him, to both of us.'

Amelia smiled. 'It's good of you to offer your assistance. Everything is easier to handle, I find, when I am at home, surrounded by the things I love. Is Cornwall as beautiful as they say it is?'

His brown eyes took on the color of the rocks on the Cornwall coastline, and his sadness seemed a distant memory. 'Even more so. When the tide comes in, you've never heard such a sound as the water crashing on to the rocks.' His eyes flicked to the window. 'When I was a child, the sound used to lull me to sleep.' He came back to her face. 'Even today, it calms me. It reminds me that everything is transient – even suffering.'

Amelia understood how much his father's illness had affected him then. If it had been up to him, he'd probably be in Cornwall right now. But his ducal duties and the season called, and he was here now, paying all the calls and attending all the parties. He had to plan for the future, and he was the future duke. He must marry and have children, a son to whom to pass down the dukedom. 'It sounds beautiful. I imagine you wish you were there right now.'

He smiled. 'I didn't mean to insinuate that I did not want to be here. The parties and soirees have had their rewards this season, such as Lady Applegate's lawn ornaments, which were more garish this year than last.' Lady Applegate was known for decorating her house to the extreme, and Amelia smiled at the joke. 'And our conversations,' he added seriously.

'Then we must talk again soon,' suggested Amelia.

'Indeed,' Lord Drake agreed. 'You are a good listener. Has anyone ever told you that?'

'Not in so many words, but thank you.' She was thinking of her letters now, never far from her mind, and how many problems she listened to, via letter, from her correspondents.

He stood, and she did as well. 'You are, and that is a rare thing in London.'

She smiled at the compliment.

'Most residents love the sound of their voices too much to stop talking.'

'Luckily, I do not suffer from that problem,' Amelia said, laughing.

The smile didn't leave his face as he dipped his chin. 'Good day, Lady Amesbury.'

Amelia bid him goodbye, and her mind immediately returned to her letter from No More Mirrors. When people passed on, mirrors were often covered with black cloth so the spirit wouldn't become confused and would move on to the next life without difficulty. *If only I could solve my difficulties by brandishing a cloth.* At any rate, she hoped her answer was satisfactory.

Amelia stepped into the hallway and paused. Lettie, her lady's maid, was talking with her mother, Patty Addington, on the landing of the stairs. That was interesting. She was supposed to be with Margaret at the paper-folding event. Perhaps Madge had realized crafts were not her forte, and they had left early.

Noticing her stare, Lettie made her way down the stairs. 'Do you need something, my lady?'

'No, thank you, Lettie. I assume origami was not the pleasurable activity Margaret thought it would be?'

'Miss Scott does origami?' Lettie mused. 'I never would have imagined.'

Amelia put her hand on Lettie's arm, drawing her into an alcove. 'You were not with my sister this afternoon?' she whispered.

Lettie had large, almond-shaped eyes like her mother, and they blinked back at her now. 'I have not seen her since breakfast. Three eggs and a side of meat that would have fed a grown man. I've never seen women who eat such hearty breakfasts as the likes of you two.'

Amelia groaned internally. The letters to Lady Agony would have to wait. 'Margaret must have a good reason for disappearing by herself, and I imagine it has something to do with Captain Fitz.'

'Lady Tabitha won't like that at all.'

'No, she won't, which is why I must find Margaret.' Amelia took a step toward the umbrella stand in the entry to fetch her parasol.

'I'll come with you.' Lettie began to untie her apron. 'Two sets of eyes are always better than one.'

Amelia held out a hand. 'I'll be all right. I need you to make excuses if anyone asks for our whereabouts.'

'*Lie?*' Lettie's voice was tinged with panic.

'Not lie,' assured Amelia. 'Obfuscate.' She winked. 'With any luck, I'll be back before anyone notices.'

A few moments later, with the help of her very discreet footman, Bailey, Amelia was on her way to St James's Park in her carriage, where Margaret had suggested the origami event was taking place. While Amelia realized her sister was capable of lying to her about her activities, Amelia did not think she was proficient enough to hide her whereabouts altogether. Where else would a pair of lovers wanting a spot of privacy go besides a park? St James's was the first place to check, because, one, Madge mentioned it, and two, it was the nearest, besides Hyde Park and Green Park. If her sister was anything, it was rash, and Amelia found rash people did not always think past the first step of action. She knew the fact too well because she was one of those people herself.

Despite all that had happened, the day was still beautiful, warm without the slightest dampness in the air. The kind of day that happened once in a summer in London. The fog had lifted, like a curtain at daybreak, and wouldn't come down again until evening. As Bailey placed the steps, Amelia took in a steadying breath.

Inside, she was fuming.

A vial of arsenic had been found only this morning in a fern in her ballroom, and Madge, never one to be deterred from anything, especially trouble, had fled from the house alone to cause more of said trouble. It was maddening. She should be helping her case, not harming it.

Amelia forced herself not to stomp as she made her way along the path, crossing a footbridge near Duck Island. It would do no good to upset the birds on such a lovely day as this. She would find her sister. It was just after four o'clock. How much damage could Madge have done to her reputation in a few hours?

Plenty, answered the voice in her head, but still she kept walking, searching for the couple.

Instead, she found Felicity Farnsworth, who was behind a particularly large fig tree. Her head was down, but Amelia would recognize that raven-colored hair anywhere, even beneath her empress hat, which had a flat crown and upturned brim that was tilted at a jaunty angle to show off the lines of her face.

'It is settled, then,' said Miss Farnsworth. 'My father has promised you my dowry.'

'Quite so.' A man's voice was clipped. 'In exchange, you'll receive my decades-old title.'

'You make it sound as if it is a business transaction.'

The man cleared his throat. 'I suppose it is one of sorts.'

A sharp intake of air, then, 'You will obtain the special license?'

'Immediately.'

'I will prepare,' Miss Farnsworth replied. 'Good day, my lord.'

Felicity Farnsworth turned without another word, and Amelia had to step to the side to avoid contact. She desperately wanted to see with whom Miss Farnsworth was speaking but had to act quickly to avoid a collision. 'Excuse me.'

'Oh!' Felicity jerked her head up, and Amelia noted her eyes glistened with tears. Why was she upset? This is what she wanted, wasn't it? A title? Perhaps it didn't belong to the man she desired, or maybe the man wasn't as attentive as she hoped. The conversation had sounded brisk, but then again, Amelia found most of her own conversations with Miss Farnsworth were.

'Lady Amesbury, I didn't see you.' Miss Farnsworth discreetly brushed at her eyes.

Amelia found herself in the peculiar position of feeling sorry for her and made an excuse. 'I was watching the ducks, I'm afraid, instead of watching where I was going.'

Glancing at the lake, Miss Farnsworth seemed relieved to have something else to look at other than Amelia. 'They are quite peaceful.'

'Indeed.' Amelia searched for something else to say, but she and Felicity Farnsworth had nothing in common, and any time Amelia had tried to engage her, it had ended badly.

'I . . . Uh.' Miss Farnsworth started and stopped. 'I suppose you are here with your sister?' Her voice was hopeful, almost pleading.

'Yes, I am.' *At least, she'd better be here.*

'I saw her just there, past the mulberries.'

'Thank you.' Amelia couldn't keep the relief out of her voice entirely. 'I had better return to my chaperone duties.'

'Of course.' Miss Farnsworth nodded eagerly. 'Good afternoon.' Then she was off, walking quickly across the footbridge with her chin tipped and the encounter seemingly forgotten.

Amelia didn't forget quite as quickly. She veered in the direction of the fig tree, but whoever Felicity Farnsworth had been talking to was gone. A man. *A man with a title*, Amelia corrected. Not surprisingly, Miss Farnsworth would get what she wanted all along.

Amelia did not have time to ponder the situation and didn't care to anyway. She had a sister to find and scold. She was certain Miss Farnsworth could handle whatever life threw her when it came to men and relationships. She'd certainly handled Simon artfully, and he was a difficult man to master.

Amelia found Madge and Captain Fitz near the mulberries, as Miss Farnsworth had said, Margaret with her head thrown back in raucous laughter. It was almost impossible to be angry at her with such a smile on her face and her auburn hair falling out of its pins around her shoulders. *Almost.* The expression reminded Amelia of when they were children and how easily she could make her laugh – really laugh as she was now. All it took was a stumble on a step or a drink coming out of the nose to make her giggles begin.

From what Amelia could surmise, Captain Fitz had dropped his hat, and one of St James's Park's famous pelicans was pecking at it. The captain was shooing the bird away in a desperate attempt to retrieve the article. Amelia smiled. It *was* kind of funny. The big bird scooped up the hat and sailed away, and her smile turned to laughter.

Margaret and Captain Fitz turned at the sound.

'Amelia!' Madge called happily. 'What are you doing here?'

Amelia joined the couple, her step a little lighter. 'Chasing after my charge, who is becoming more and more difficult to keep track of.'

Madge stared at her toes.

'I apologize, Lady Amesbury.' Captain Fitz swiped at his hat-dented hair. 'It is my fault. I should have told you about our meeting this afternoon.'

Madge touched his elbow reflexively. 'No, it's my doing,

Amelia. We only wanted an afternoon to ourselves without everyone watching us.' Her blue eyes looked almost hazel in the reflection of the trees. 'I don't know how you Londoners do it. Never a moment's peace to oneself.'

Ironically, it's what had attracted Amelia to the city. She'd had enough of peace and tranquility in Mells to last a lifetime. The same people, the same dirt roads. She'd longed to leave, to explore the rest of the world, and although she hadn't had the opportunity to travel yet, she'd enjoyed every second in London. From coster-mongers to high society, she loved the multitudes of different people who inhabited the city.

Amelia exhaled, some of the ire leaving her body. 'I under-stand, Margaret, but after the problem this morning, you cannot invite more controversy. As much as I detest the rules myself, you must follow them or be subject to more talk.'

Captain Fitz tilted his head, and a filtered beam of sunlight bespeckled his sandy brown whiskers. His eyes flew to Amelia. 'What happened this morning?'

Amelia frowned at Madge. It wasn't like her to conceal anything, at least not real problems. 'You have not told him?'

'No, Amelia, I have not.' Madge's face turned as red as her hair. 'Excuse me if I didn't want the captain running in the opposite direction.'

'Is this about Mr Radcliffe?' asked Captain Fitz.

Madge flung a hand in Amelia's direction as if to say *finish what you started.*

'Yes, it is.' Amelia hesitated. 'A suspicious powder was found in our ballroom this morning. Detective Collings is testing it as we speak. Margaret is his number-one suspect.'

Captain Fitz surprised them both by laughing. 'The detective must be a dimwit. As if Miss Scott would implicate herself so easily. She could have hidden it in a dozen different places – her bedroom, for instance.'

'That's what I said,' Madge agreed.

Captain Fitz stooped, trimming his height to meet Madge's eyes. 'Please don't concern yourself with his suppositions – or the idea of me running in the opposite direction. I've fought in a war, Miss Scott. It'd take more than an errant detective to send me scurrying.'

Madge's long eyelashes fluttered with happiness. The captain was right. Had Margaret decided to poison Radcliffe, she could have hidden the poison anywhere, such as in their personal living quarters, which wouldn't have been so easily found by a member of the Metropolitan Police. That fact alone told her that the person who did the deed probably didn't have access to that part of the house.

Furthermore, Amelia believed the poisoner placed the poison in the potted plant on purpose. The murderer wanted Madge to be accused of the murder to take the suspicion off himself or herself. It was the only explanation that made sense, and the first thought she had was of telling Simon. Then she remembered the awkward moment when he left last night, and she decided to return home.

'We really must be going.' Amelia nodded in the direction of the carriage. 'Bailey is waiting.'

The drive home was blissfully quiet, which should have given Amelia more time to think about the murder. Instead, she found herself studying her sister, who seemed as ebullient as a bride on her wedding day. She practically radiated happiness out of the carriage windows, her hair a bright coppery red and her cheek color high. If Amelia didn't know her sister better, she'd say that Margaret had fallen in love with Captain Fitz. But Madge had never even had a serious suitor. Yet the idea was as clear as the bright summer day. Murder – and love – were both in season.

TWENTY-THREE

Dear Lady Agony,
    Have you caught the Mayfair Marauder? Many doubt your progress, but I do not. If anyone has a chance of catching a thief in the night, it is a woman. First, we are historically bad sleepers, and second, no one pays any mind to our activities. My bet is on you.
    Sincerely,
    A Rooting Reader

Dear A Rooting Reader,
    Thank you for your kind words. They give me encouragement, and even a giver of advice needs reassurance once in a while. I am so very close to capturing the culprit. Continue to watch this space, Dear Reader. All will be revealed soon.
    Yours in Secret,
    Lady Agony

The next morning broke with a howl of surprise. Amelia, an early riser, was taking her meal in the breakfast room when the sound twisted through the room like an errant wind. Although she was reluctant to leave her breakfast, yesterday's all but ruined by Detective Collings, she stood and went to the door to see where the sound came from. She didn't have to wait long before Tabitha stumped down the stairs with something shiny in her hand.

Amelia squinted. She'd never seen Aunt Tabitha in her dressing gown or – *her hair in papers*? Who was it that told her women did not come down to the breakfast room with their hair undone? Oh, that's right. *Tabitha.*

'Amelia! Look. Look what I found.' Smiling from ear to ear, Tabitha held up a jewel in her hand.

Not just any jewel: the Amesbury diamond.

'I awoke this morning, and it was in my jewelry box, as if it'd never been gone.' Tabitha, half done up for the day, wore one ear bauble. 'Did you have something to do with its return?' She beamed at Amelia as if she already knew the answer.

'I wish I could say I did, but no.' Seeing the joy on Tabitha's face, Amelia couldn't contain her own. 'That's wonderful, Aunt.'

'Maybe one of the servants misplaced it.' Tabitha lowered her voice. 'They could have told me. I'm not without compassion, you know.'

Amelia decided silence was the best response to that statement.

Tabitha sighed at the jewel. 'It is beautiful, isn't it?'

'Quite.'

'From now on, I'll have eyes on it every day.' Tabitha glanced at her own gown, seeming to remember that she was only half dressed. 'Enjoy your breakfast, dear.' She turned on her heel, her eyes never leaving the jewel.

After a moment, Amelia remembered to close her mouth. She didn't know if Tabitha would ever forgive her and Simon's indiscretion, and here she'd called her *dear*. She supposed the retrieval of a timeless heirloom had that effect on people.

Amelia returned to her plate in the breakfast room, wondering how the jewel came to be back in its proper place. It was hard to believe, as Tabitha did, that the staff had misplaced it. Surely one of them would have come forward when they found it. Was it possible that Tabitha had misplaced it herself? It seemed unlikely, but Amelia couldn't dismiss the idea altogether. Tabitha was growing older, and all women, young and old, misplaced a piece of jewelry now and then. But the *Amesbury diamond*? Amelia finished her last bite of sausage, deciding that it was a bit of overdue luck. Fortune had smiled on their family, and Amelia was smiling back.

After breakfast, Amelia responded to letters from her correspondents until Kitty arrived to take her, Margaret, Winifred and Miss Walters to the exhibition by the Royal Botanic Society at the Regent's Park. The Society managed about eighteen acres, and their exhibitions were always popular with the *ton*. Amelia imagined today would be no different. While the sky was overcast, the day was mild, a light wind chasing away the dampness of the morning rain.

She heard Madge's footsteps – heavy, hurried and loud – on the stairs and pushed away from her desk. Work of a different nature called. Margaret wore a pink chiffon dress with ivory lace gloves, and Amelia had to check twice to see if it was her sister under the straw shepherdess hat with flowing pink ribbons tied under her chin. Indeed, it was Margaret, wearing a smile angels would envy. No one would guess she'd been accused of hiding a bottle of arsenic in a potted fern only yesterday.

Madge talked of nothing but Captain Fitz on the way to the Regent's Park, and by the time the carriage stopped near the entrance on Chester Road at two o'clock, Kitty gave Amelia a sly look and whispered, 'Cupid has been busy this month.'

Cupid is busy every month during the London season, Amelia thought as she descended the carriage steps. Hungry mamas made sure of it. The Inner Circle of the park was likewise busy, debutantes with chaperones in tow filling the lawns where large marquees held flowers and fruits from the best and most illustrious gardens in England. Prizes would be awarded to praiseworthy fruits, including pineapples, melons, grapes, nectarines, peaches and others. The gardener of the Duke of Norfolk would surely be on the list if a particularly large strawberry was any indication. If Amelia remembered correctly, he'd won a gold medal last year for an interesting group of pineapples.

Amelia was more interested in the bands from the First and Second Life Guards and their merrymaking music than fruits or flowers. She tapped her toe to the beat of a familiar tune while watching Winifred and Miss Walters disappear down a hill to a small lake. Winifred had a new toy boat she wanted to sail, and Miss Walters was to help her until Amelia could join later.

Right now, her investigation called, and she surveyed the crowd for any of the people in attendance the night of the ball. She spotted Mr Briggs talking to the Duke of Newcastle near a particularly showy bowl of grapes. Grady had told her that Mr Briggs was entering his prized white Frontignac grapes, which he'd brought all the way from the West Coast of North America. She decided fruit would be the way to the newcomer's heart.

Madge was already mooning after Captain Fitz, her face staring

up at his in a way that spelled trouble. Kitty, watching the couple
with an adoring smile, didn't seem to comprehend the issue, but
Amelia did. She knew if the couple was left alone, they would
find a copse of trees or an oversized rhododendron bush to disappear into. That couldn't happen, but neither could the escape of
Mr Briggs.

Amelia took Kitty's arm. 'Mr Briggs is just there, with his
grapes, and I must talk to him. Watch over my sister. She isn't
to be trusted for a single second alone with Captain Fitz.'

Kitty's smile turned sour. 'When did you become a stickler
for rules?'

'When my sister was accused of murder.'

'I understand, but truly, Amelia, you're being too severe with
her.' Kitty tsked. 'She's unfamiliar with society, but so were you
a few years ago. Remember how it felt when Lady Tabitha forced
instructions en masse upon you? Not very nice.'

Was Kitty seriously comparing her to Aunt Tabitha? *Blazes*.
The older woman was rubbing off on her more than she would've
liked to admit. Mentally, Amelia ticked off excuses and then just
as quickly dismissed them. Kitty was right. She was being too
harsh. 'Fine. Let them have fun – but not too much fun. Keep a
respectable distance at all times.'

'I will.' Kitty shooed her in the direction of the American.
'Now go.'

Amelia considered an approach as she took her first step toward
Mr Briggs. She liked grapes. She drank wine. She could easily
ask about his newly acquired country estate in Kent. Goodness
knows he had enjoyed talking about it enough in the supper
room. According to his account, the estate had been home to a
Franciscan monk four hundred years ago. Mr Briggs was determined to bring the holy act of winemaking to the estate, and
from the appearance of his grapes, he was well on his way.

He stood with his feet shoulder-width apart, more suited to a
boxing match than a garden exhibition, nodding at a compliment
from Lord Drake, whom Amelia was pleased to see at the exhibition. Mr Briggs's torso swelled with pride at some praise, and
Amelia had to remind herself he was a dilettante, not a prize fighter.
When Lord Drake moved on to the Duke of Norfolk, Amelia
approached him, commenting on his handsome bowl of fruit.

'Thank you, Lady Amesbury.' Mr Briggs preened. 'These are the finest grapes in all of England, or my name isn't Thomas Briggs.'

The man didn't have a modicum of humility, and Amelia could see why some people were drawn to his larger-than-life personality. Being with him was like watching a play or reading an entertaining book. One was always waiting to see what he would say next.

'I'm not sure if you recall, but my estate was once owned by a Franciscan monk who devoted his entire life to prayer. He left the monastery in 1701 and lived until the ripe age of ninety-seven years.'

'Fascinating,' Amelia replied. 'The estate must be a beautiful respite from town life.'

Mr Briggs nodded, and Amelia realized his face was an open book, something she could peer into without him realizing it. So many Londoners veiled their emotions, but here was a man who did not bother to hide his feelings – or conceit. Amelia found it refreshingly honest.

'It is.' He took a jaunty step forward. 'In fact, I'm having a house party in August. I've heard grouse is in season, and I'm a great shot. Can kill anything within a hundred yards. I'll send you an invitation.'

'Thank you, Mr Briggs.' Amelia couldn't help but smile at his braggadocio. 'I suppose you'll be inviting debutantes, like Lady Ann?' She nodded at Ann, who happened to be at the next table examining a vase of roses. 'I believe you met her at my party.'

'Lady Ann?' asked Mr Briggs. 'Oh, I invited her, but I don't think she cares for me. I think she's taken with that Radcliffe fellow. I saw them go out on the balcony for a bit of *fresh air*.' He winked a big blue eye. 'We all know what that means.'

'Mr Radcliffe?' Amelia was stunned to have the fact confirmed.

He shrugged. 'She's a lady. He's a lord. Or he will be someday. They're made for each other.'

Amelia wasn't surprised he was not aware Mr Radcliffe was dead. Mr Briggs was an outsider and not privy to any information of real consequence. 'I regret to inform you that Mr Radcliffe is dead. He passed away the night of the party.'

'What a shame.' Mr Briggs frowned. 'I suppose the title will pass on to the next man and the next and the next until the end of time.'

'Something like that,' Amelia murmured.

'At any rate, you'll be getting an invitation.' He glanced over her shoulder, and she realized a gardener was waiting to discuss grapes with him. 'Look for it in the post.'

She murmured her appreciation and scooted along, pretending to study a particularly large pineapple. What she was really doing was considering her conversation with Mr Briggs. Lady Ann had the means and now the motive to kill Mr Radcliffe. He was the one on the balcony with her; they'd fought. A few hours later, he was dead. It made sense.

Except . . .

Lady Ann was intelligent, too intelligent to leave behind a bottle of poison.

Unless she meant to implicate Margaret, and in that case, she was very stupid, for Amelia would not rest until her baby sister and her family's name were cleared. She had only one way to find out: confront Lady Ann.

Amelia quickly glanced over her shoulder. She was pleased to find Margaret listening to the band with the captain, Kitty and Oliver. With all well on that front, she turned her attention to Lady Ann, who was almost as pretty as the roses she admired. Her hair was as light as the yellow flower and twisted into a golden plait at the back of her head. Amelia took a step closer.

'My goodness!' Lady Ann touched her chest. 'You startled me.'

Amelia apologized. 'You seemed so intent that I did not want to interrupt you.'

'I love flowers.' Lady Ann touched a velvety petal. 'They are my weakness.'

Suddenly, Lady Ann's desire to leave the city made sense. She'd been ill-used this season, perhaps by Arthur Radcliffe. Whatever had happened, it hurt her enough to threaten him. The encounter might have soured her of London altogether. 'Lady Ann, would you mind if we spoke in private?'

A furrow puckered her brow. 'I hope nothing is wrong.'

'Not at all.' Amelia motioned toward the lake, where an empty bench was available. 'I'd like to ask you something, but even the flowers have ears.'

Lady Ann chuckled with understanding, and they remained silent until they were alone on the bench. The only sounds were that of a pelican's wings as it landed on a rock near the shore, the soft roar of collective voices from the marquees and the band fading behind them.

'You have something you wish to ask me?' Lady Ann's eyes were as wide and blue as the lake. 'I must admit I *am* curious.'

'It's about the night of Margaret's ball.'

'Yes?' Lady Ann folded her hands on her skirt.

'Let me be frank.' Amelia studied her carefully. 'I know you argued with Mr Radcliffe on the terrace. I'd like to know why.'

'I'm not sure what you mean.'

'I saw you.'

'Oh.' Lady Ann's curious look changed to one of agony, and the pain in her face seemed almost physical. Whatever had happened between her and Mr Radcliffe brought on a visceral reaction, a memory that hurt her whole body.

'I know it's dreadful, and I would not ask, except my sister is in danger,' Amelia pleaded. She hated prying into Lady Ann's problems, but it had to be done. 'A detective at the Metropolitan Police believes she killed Mr Radcliffe. He found evidence to support his theory just yesterday morning.'

'No!' Lady Ann covered her mouth with a gloved hand.

'Yes,' replied Amelia. 'I need to know what happened that night – and why.'

'I cannot tell you.'

Amelia grasped her hand. 'I told you my sister is being investigated for murder. Surely you can trust me with your secret.'

Lady Ann closed her blue-gray eyes, perhaps deciding whether or not she could trust her. When she opened them, Amelia knew she'd decided she could. 'You're correct. I did fight with Mr Radcliffe on the balcony. He and I used to see one another, and I thought he was fond of me.' She smiled weakly, but no happiness was on her face. 'His parents were friends with mine, and we had many opportunities to spend time alone together.' She paused to see if Amelia understood her meaning. She did. 'I assumed he would ask for my hand. I gave him certain . . . allowances I shouldn't have. When consequences ensued, I went to his brother for help. He knew of herbs to help me with my dilemma.' She cleared her throat. 'When Arthur approached me on the balcony, I was mortified. I told him never to come near me again. Do you know what his response was?'

Amelia shook her head.

'He said, "Or what?"' Lady Ann blinked as if she still didn't quite comprehend the words. 'He knew my secret. If he had lived, he would have used it.'

Amelia heard the sharp intake of her own breath. Arthur Radcliffe was an even worse human being than she believed, a scoundrel who used information and people to get what he wanted. Not only had he used Lady Ann, but he would have done it again and held her hostage with blackmail. She'd had every right to kill him . . . but did she?

Lady Ann seemed to comprehend the unasked question. 'I did not kill him. On that you have my word.' She tipped her chin ever so slightly, and with the reflection of the lake, her eyes looked a little icier. 'But I am thankful to whoever did.'

TWENTY-FOUR

Dear Lady Agony,
My daughter is prone to excitability. Any time we play a sport, she becomes insufferable. Her exclamations are boastful, unladylike, and very near hysterical. I've heard carraway seeds prevent hysterics. Do you recommend them for this trouble?
Sincerely,
Worried Mother

Dear Worried Mother,
Given on a daily basis, carraway seeds and ginger, spread on bread with butter, are said to prevent hysterics. However, I do not believe your daughter suffers from that condition. Her exclamations are completely warranted and even healthy. There is nothing wrong with becoming excited by competition. My advice is to let her play.
Yours in Secret,
Lady Agony

Amelia walked away from the bench with a new understanding of Arthur Radcliffe, a realization that should have come much sooner than it did. All along, Margaret had predicted he'd wield his information against her like a loaded gun. And with enough time, Amelia believed he would've used the knowledge of the incident with Charlie Atkinson to his advantage. As Amelia surveyed the beau monde at the exhibit, she wondered how many other people he blackmailed and for what reason. They, too, had to be relieved by his death.

Her eyes landed on a particular person in the crowd: Jonathan Radcliffe, who even from a distance looked out of place. Then again, perhaps he was in the perfect place. Now that he would inherit the title of baron, he needed to be acquainted with the

right people. He was speaking with Lord Morton, who was such
a person.

'Lady Amesbury.' Lord Morton greeted her affably. 'How good
to see you again. I've thought about nothing but you and your
sister since her stunning performance at Lady Hamsted's.' He
turned to Dr Radcliffe. 'I imagine you attended the concert.'

'I did not have the opportunity, I'm afraid.' Dr Radcliffe pulled
at his cravat. 'Next time.'

'Unfortunately, you'll have to wait an entire year,' said Amelia.
'Lady Hamsted blesses us with the concert only once a season.'

Lord Morton bent slightly at the waist, his hat creating a
shadow on her dress. 'By that time, Miss Scott will be married
with her singing days behind her. I cannot imagine her lasting
another season.' He dashed a look in Margaret's direction. 'A
stunning . . . voice.'

Jonathan Radcliffe followed his gaze. 'It sounds as if her talent
caught your fancy.'

'I imagine she's fancied by half the men in London.' Lord
Morton's eyes reluctantly returned to the doctor's, which had
flicked to Felicity Farnsworth. He gazed at her as a child gazes
upon a sweet in a bakery.

'As is Felicity Farnsworth,' added Amelia. 'She's very popular
this season.'

'Yes.' Lord Morton paused. 'For different reasons.'

'Such as the Farnsworth equestrian estate?' Jonathan Radcliffe
jested, but when Lord Morton cut him a look, he stopped his
laughter short. He still had much to learn about the rules of
decorum. The joke might be made between the two men in a
club, but never in front of a lady. He slipped his hands in his
pockets, visibly uncomfortable.

'She is there, near the topiary, and I must talk to her before I
go.' Lord Morton touched the rim of his hat. 'If you'll excuse me.'

Amelia was left with the doctor, who seemed a different person
than he had been at his office. There, he was sure of himself.
Relaxed, if not content. Here, he was nervous, pulling at his
neckwear and adjusting his shoulders as if his coat didn't fit quite
right. It was new, and perhaps he wasn't as used to fashionable
dress as his brother had been. 'Are you enjoying your afternoon?'
Amelia asked.

'Mostly,' he replied. 'Everyone knew my brother, which is a blessing and a curse. I've been welcomed with varying degrees of enthusiasm.'

She paused, considering the statement. 'Your grief would have excused your absence.'

'My father needed me here. He fancies a new gardener for the estate, and the Duke of Norfolk promised a recommendation. The position must be secured before the end of the summer.' Dr Radcliffe removed his hands from his pockets. 'Arthur was adept at negotiation.' He adjusted his shirt cuffs. 'I must figure out a way to be so as well.'

Adept at blackmail, you mean. 'I've heard his negotiations were often one-sided.'

He gave the material a final yank and straightened his shoulders. 'I suppose that idea comes from your sister. Word is, she argued with my brother the night of her debut.'

Amelia focused on his eyes. 'It does. He blackmailed her with her past – a past which he knew of because of you.'

'He was a knowledgeable man, Lady Amesbury. He acquired information from all sorts of places.'

'It is what he did with the information that bothers me, Doctor Radcliffe.' Amelia dug the tip of her parasol into the ground to root her anger. 'He used it for his own benefit.'

'Who in this town wouldn't do the same?' he defended.

'Is that what you plan to do?' she shot back. 'Use your knowledge for power?'

'No.' Dr Radcliffe's answer was immediate. 'I . . . I never wanted power, only peace. Power is a dangerous desire, a lesson my brother learned too well.'

Jonathan Radcliffe knew. He knew what his brother was, even if he didn't say so outright. Of course he did. He'd helped Lady Ann and perhaps others his brother had burdened. 'Do you believe he was murdered because of it?' Amelia asked.

He clasped his hands in front of him. 'Arthur was drunk on power. It changed him. He used to be a good man. Then he became influential. He liked that better.'

'Do you know who might have killed him?'

'I do not.' He shook his head quietly. 'He'd be disappointed in me, you understand. He would want me to seek retribution. I

only want to seek refuge in our country house with our dogs.'
He glanced past the park. 'It's all I've ever wanted.' His sad eyes
landed back on hers. 'I suppose you think I am slothful.'

'I do not think that,' she assured him. 'I'm *glad* you're different
from your brother.'

The sentiment appeared to make a difference, for the corners
of his small mouth turned up briefly, and he released a breath
he'd probably been holding since he arrived at the park. He
dipped his chin in thanks, and Amelia turned toward the water,
where she spotted Winifred talking to a boy several years younger
than herself. Winifred was ten years of age, nearing eleven more
quickly than Amelia would like, but still enjoyed playing when
the opportunity arose. It was nice that she had another child to
talk to at the park. Miss Walters's companionship must get tiresome, and Amelia had been busier with suspects than she'd
intended.

The boy was shorter, although height certainly wasn't an indi-
cator at this age. She'd seen Winifred tower over boys a year
older than her. They would find their height later in their teens.
Winifred was a little too close to the water for Amelia's taste,
perhaps showing off, and when she skipped a rock, it set her
momentarily off balance.

'Careful!' Amelia called out automatically, and Miss Walters,
on a nearby bench, looked up from her book. Winifred turned
around.

Was that an eye roll? Amelia was certain it was as she came
closer. Winifred wouldn't appreciate the warning, especially in
front of a boy, but Miss Walters was distracted by her novel and
not watching closely enough.

'Careful not to dirty the hem of your dress.' Amelia attempted
a casual tone. The truth was, when it came to Winifred, she had
little control over her emotions. She cared for the girl so dearly
that her feelings were sometimes nonsensical and overreactive.
Her reactions were on a par with those of a bare-knuckled boxer,
and although she reminded herself to count to ten in these
instances, she often reached only five before acting.

'I won't,' Winifred replied. 'This is B.J. He brought a boat as
well.'

'How do you do, B.J.?' asked Amelia. Although he was about

six or seven years of age, his crystal eyes held a look of experience that belied his age. He had curly brown hair under his cap
and a dimple in his chin that was a tell of his youth.

'I am well. Thank you, ma'am.' He had an accent she couldn't
place.

'Who are your parents?' Amelia asked.

'I'm here with Mr Worth.'

She nodded. She remembered Miss Castlewood mentioning a
nephew during her call.

'B.J. is showing me how to skip stones,' explained Winifred.
'Have you ever done it?'

'Of course I've skipped stones.' Amelia picked up a nice flat
rock next to her shoe. 'Grady and I were the best stone skippers
in all of Mells.'

B.J. frowned. 'Where is that?'

'Don't ask,' whispered Winifred.

'Somerset.' Amelia rubbed the stone, checking for suitability.
'Watch and learn, children.' She gave the stone a toss, and it hit
the water – and sank.

Winifred and B.J. shared a laugh. It was a happy sound, and
despite Amelia's blunder, she enjoyed the lightness of the activity.
Children had a way of taking one's mind off everything, including
murder.

'I am out of practice. That's all.' Amelia picked up a smaller
stone. 'Let me try again.'

'Give me that, city girl.' Margaret appeared at her elbow and
snatched the rock from her hand. Captain Fitz looked on, amused.
Madge threw the rock, and it skipped across the water with five
bounces. Placing her fists on her waist, Madge sported a devilish
grin. 'Ha!'

'I said I needed practice.' Amelia picked up a rock and pitched
it across the water. It bounced twice.

Now not only were Winifred and B.J. laughing, but Margaret
and Captain Fitz were, too.

More determined than ever, Amelia picked up another stone.
Margaret followed suit.

'It's all in the wrist.' Madge grabbed her wrist with her free
hand and waggled it. 'Loosen up.'

'I *am* loose,' Amelia stated tightly.

This brought more giggles from Winifred and B.J.

Amelia flicked the stone across the water, and it skipped five times. 'See there!'

'Wait.' Captain Fitz interjected before Madge could throw her rock. 'I have an idea. Children, fetch a stone. The best you can find. Ladies, do the same. We will have a contest right here. The person with the most skips wins . . .' He looked around. He walked over to a bush and plucked a small yellow flower from it. 'This.'

Winifred and B.J. searched for stones. Amelia did the same. When they were ready, they lined up near the water. To Amelia's chagrin, a small crowd formed to watch the fun. Lady Hamsted was looking on with a frown of distaste, but her husband seemed excited to see who would win.

Despite the Scott sisters' best efforts, it was B.J. who won the contest with seven skips. His action garnered applause from the small group of onlookers, and he acknowledged the win with a wave of his cap. Captain Fitz placed the flower in the buttonhole of his small jacket, and B.J. preened a little.

Benjamin Worth came up to congratulate him. He put an arm around the boy. 'Nice throw.'

'A nice throw, indeed!' Theodora Castlewood added, smiling widely.

'Thank you.' B.J. seemed slightly embarrassed by the praise.

'Congratulations.' Amelia bowed slightly. 'You are truly the superior stone skipper and worthy of your prize.'

B.J. smiled. 'You are kind to say so.'

'You've met Lady Amesbury?' Mr Worth acknowledged Amelia with a nod. 'This is my sister's ward.'

'Yes, Winifred introduced us.' Maybe that's why the boy had an unfamiliar lilt in his voice. He might have been from another country, adopted by the family.

'And her sister, Miss Scott.' Mr Worth only slightly stumbled over the name, and Amelia thought it was a positive first step in repairing the damage between them.

Miss Castlewood greeted Margaret graciously. 'I adore your dress.'

'Thank you,' said Madge. 'Mrs Addington made me wear it.'

'She has good taste,' murmured Captain Fitz, and the couple became enmeshed in a private exchange.

'I see congratulations are in order, young man.' Lord Drake stuck out his hand, and the rest of the small group looked on, impressed. It wasn't every day that a boy drew the attention of a would-be duke. Amelia thought it was incredibly thoughtful, and it fit what she knew about Lord Drake from their brief interactions. He went out of his way to do a kindness just as he had when he called upon her at her house.

'Thank you, sir.' B.J. shook his hand, and his face flushed red.

It was apparent to Amelia that the boy was growing uncomfortable with all the attention. Winifred must have realized it as well, for she nodded at a spot several yards away. 'Let's try our luck over there.'

They wandered off, and Mr Worth and Miss Castlewood followed, Miss Walters several steps behind.

'It's good to see you again, Lady Amesbury,' said Lord Drake. 'Are you enjoying the afternoon?'

'I was,' Amelia answered. 'Until I lost.'

He chuckled at the joke. 'I was never good at sports. I couldn't reach the other side of the lake if I had the best stone in the park.'

She lifted her brows. Not only was he handsome, but he was well built *and* humble. Goodness, she couldn't imagine why he was still unattached.

'I am quite serious.' He made a throwing motion with his left arm. 'Bad shoulder.'

She laughed.

'Better luck next time.' He buttoned the top button of his coat. 'I hope our paths cross again soon.'

Amelia stared at the garment. 'Lord Drake, you are missing a button.'

He glanced down at his coat. 'So I am. Thank you for bringing it to my attention. My housekeeper is brilliant with a needle. Now if I only knew where the button was.'

Amelia knew where his button was. It was in her top dresser drawer. She'd put it there after finding it in the garden the night of Arthur Radcliffe's murder.

TWENTY-FIVE

Dear Lady Agony,

What is the best method for cleaning buttons? The house-keeper and I disagree, and we believe you might provide the answer. Any attempt to settle our quarrel is welcome.

Sincerely,

A Fastidious Butler

Dear A Fastidious Butler,

How do I clean a button? Let me count the ways. There are many, Dear Reader, but none worth a quarrel. My advice is to let the housekeeper keep to her ways and you keep to yours. Because you asked, however, here are instructions for keeping your buttons beautiful.

Buttons should be cleaned by placing them on a board made for that purpose so as not to dirty the article of clothing. Depending on the button color, rub them with a sponge dipped in whitening, rottenstone or plate-powder. Polish with a soft brush to shine.

Yours in Secret,

Lady Agony

Amelia stared at Lord Drake's frockcoat, but she was thinking of more than its exquisite black linen fabric, brown silk lining and smart slits. She was memorizing the remaining tortoiseshell buttons: shiny, round and remarkable. 'An extraordinary thing, but I believe I have your button.'

'Truly?'

'I found a button such as those in my lawn the evening of Margaret's ball.' She pointed to the remaining buttons.

His brow creased. 'How can you be certain?'

'Tortoiseshell isn't something one mistakes – not as fine as that.' She smiled, trying to keep the conversation light, but her heartbeat began to increase. 'I didn't know you had the opportunity to enjoy my lawns that evening. If I remember correctly, you arrived late.'

'I'm habitually late for everything.' He waved away the comment, but Amelia noted the way his eyes darted to the left as if he was searching for an escape. 'Unfortunately, I'm known for the bad habit.'

Rather than sounding offhanded, the comment reinforced the idea that Lord Drake could be the thief. As he said, he was habitually late, which gave him the time and opportunity to commit the crimes. Originally, she believed the thief pocketed the goods and departed early. But in truth, it might have been the other way around. He could've stolen the jewels first and arrived later. After all, her garden gate was left open, which suggested he entered via the back entrance rather than the front. Yet what of his motivation? He was dressed in the finest clothes and latest styles. Money, and a lot of it, was needed to keep up appearances. But for all intents and purposes, his family was well-off. And it wasn't as if he could use the jewelry himself.

The thief had left his mark at Lady Hamsted's concert, and Lord Drake had been in attendance. She glanced down at his footwear. He wore a fine shoe with a shapely toe. It very well could have been he who absconded with the jewel. She couldn't be certain, however, without seeing a print. If she got a little too close to the water's edge, it might do the trick.

She took a sly step backwards as she said, 'I understand the dilemma. If it wasn't for Lady Tabitha, I wouldn't arrive on time for half the events I've committed to.'

The corners of his eyes creased with amusement. 'I imagine she keeps everything running smoothly.'

Another inch backwards as she laughed. 'Like clockwork.'

'I'll be sure to stop by for the button.'

'Please do—' Amelia's heel hit something hard, and although she planned on only getting close to the water, she stumbled, losing her balance. 'Oh my!'

Lord Drake reached for her hands. 'Lady Amesbury!' He caught them, preventing her from spilling backwards.

'Thank you.' She looked down at the mud. Large, narrow, shapely – a footprint identical to the one in Lady Hamsted's lawn stared back at her. Not only did the button match but the footprint did as well. The connections were too many to dismiss. 'It is you. You're the thief who has been terrorizing Mayfair.'

'Excuse me?' He dropped her hands.

She took a step away from the lake. 'Your footprint matches the one made in Lady Hamsted's lawn the day her ruby was stolen, and your button matches the one left in my lawn the night the Amesbury diamond was taken.'

'Mere coincidences, I am sure.' He attempted nonchalance, but Amelia detected a quiver in his statement. It betrayed him more than his words. The scar near his lip twitched a little.

'I am not so sure.'

'The thief in Mayfair has been busy all season.' The amusement fled his face. 'I only arrived the night of your ball.'

She smiled. 'I thought of that too, but you mentioned Lady Applegate's infamous lawn ornamentation. You said it was more garish than last year's. You were here, but no one knew it.'

He looked at the ground, the footprint. His shoulders rounded with what she imagined was a heavy burden. If only he would trust her enough to lighten his load. He was a good man. He had brought back the Amesbury diamond; his call on her had been an excuse to return it. She imagined he sneaked it into Tabitha's room when she'd kept him waiting in the drawing room. 'I know you are a thief, but I also know you are a gentleman. You returned Aunt Tabitha's diamond.' He glanced up, and she caught his eye. 'Thank you. It means a good deal to Lady Tabitha. Her brother gave it to her.'

Her gratitude seemed to open a door in him that he'd kept closed for a long time. She saw him release a breath deep in his chest, and he deflated slowly like a balloon with a tiny hole. 'The night of the ball, when we danced, I knew I'd made a mistake. You were kind to me, not just for my title or house, and so was Lady Tabitha.'

'Is that why you stole from the others?'

'No.' He shook his head. 'I need the money for the repairs on the house in Cornwall. My father's health has taken all our funds, and our home is the only thing that brings him comfort.'

'You are wrong.' Amelia touched his arm. '*You* bring him comfort. I'm certain of it. He would rather have your companionship than every brick in the foundation of an old house.' Seeing his hesitancy, she added, 'Wouldn't you prefer a loved one over all material things?'

His eyes took on the buoyancy of the water. 'Yes.'

'You say that as if you have someone in your life who is that person.'

'A childhood friend from Cornwall.' His lips lifted with a smile. 'I have known him my entire life, and he means a good deal to me.'

Amelia could see that he did. Perhaps he meant everything. And perhaps he was the reason Lord Drake had a reputation for being a rake who refused to commit. He couldn't give his heart to a woman when he'd already given it to a man. 'Then you must know if you had his company, nothing else would matter, even an estate that is the talk of London.'

He nodded slowly. 'It is true.' His eyes flicked at the marquees flooded with people, petals and fruits. 'Are you going to tell them about the thefts?'

'No.' Seeing his surprised expression, she continued. 'But I'd like you to return the jewels to their rightful owners.'

'Rightful? Some of them hardly know the meaning of the word.'

'I can't disagree with you, but all the same, they should go back.'

Lord Drake considered her words for a moment. Then he looked her in the eye and nodded. 'I will. On that, you have my word.'

'Thank you.'

The corner of his mouth kicked up in a smile. 'I'll have to attend the rest of the season's soirees, mind you, but it is a small price to pay for your silence.'

'You will get by somehow.' Amelia returned the smile.

He stuck out his hand. 'I'm glad we met, Lady Amesbury. I'm glad we're friends.'

'I feel the same.'

They shook hands warmly before he walked up the hill. Amelia watched him go, surprised to have caught and released the Mayfair Marauder. Good people did bad things for the right reasons. Who was to say she wouldn't do the same when it came to her family members? If she thought she could ease their suffering, even a little, she would have tried to move heaven or earth. His father took comfort in their home, and Lord Drake had done what he thought was right to keep him there. Rather than fault him, Amelia empathized with his plight, and even admired his actions.

She was almost feeling pleased about the outcome when Simon appeared at her elbow with a peevish question. 'Are you on friendly terms with Lord Drake now?'

'I am,' she said, keeping her gaze neutral. 'He just confessed to being the Mayfair Marauder.'

Simon spun her toward him. 'What?'

'That's right. The Cornwall estate is in disrepair, his father is unwell, and he's done what he's had to, to keep his father at home.' Amelia couldn't completely keep the smugness out of her voice. It felt good to be the one to reveal the information.

'But how did you know?'

She relished telling him the details. 'I found a lost button the night of Margaret's ball. It was in the garden. Remember? I found it before we . . . when you assisted me with my shoe.' She swallowed before continuing. 'I noted a missing button on Lord Drake's coat this afternoon, and it was the same tortoiseshell material as the button on my lawn.' She shrugged. 'When he made a print in the mud and it matched the one on Lady Hamsted's lawn, my theory was confirmed.'

He crossed his arms. 'And you just let him go.'

'He promised to return the jewels.' Amelia frowned. 'He's already returned the Amesbury diamond.'

'You have it all figured out, then.' His shoulders stirred in a way that felt like a test.

She blinked. *Isn't that what I just stated?*

Her confusion must have been palpable, for the next moment, he leaned in so close she thought he'd kiss her again. Instead, he stunned her with the words, 'What if he isn't only the thief but the murderer?'

For the first time in her life, Amelia swooned, and Simon grabbed her arm. Of course Lord Drake could have been the murderer. What had she been thinking? She'd been thinking he was a nice man undergoing a difficult time. But if Arthur Radcliffe had discovered the thefts, he would have blackmailed him with the information. Not to mention Drake's relationship with the man back in Cornwall. If he knew of that . . . she couldn't even imagine what he could do with that information. She closed her eyes. Lord Drake would have a motive to kill him to stop the rumor from spreading.

'Amelia, are you all right?' Simon shook her gently.

She opened her eyes to meet his, which glimmered like green grass in the wind. 'I'm fine. Just obtuse.'

'You're not obtuse.' He squeezed her shoulders before releasing her. 'You are the brightest woman I know. You would have come to the conclusion had I not shown up.'

Ignoring the compliment, she flung her hands in the direction of Lord Drake. 'If he was willing to commit theft to save his estate in Cornwall, imagine what he might be capable of to save his reputation.'

Simon shifted his stance. 'What do you mean?'

'I mean he might do anything to avoid being named a thief.' She was not going to tell Simon about the man in Cornwall. Lord Drake had confided in her as a friend, and even if he was a murderer, he would be the one to decide with whom to share the information. She knew of the additional motivation, and that was most important. 'And recollect that he arrived late to Margaret's ball.'

Simon frowned. 'I remember.'

'His absence gives him an alibi for Radcliffe's murder. That might have been his plan all along – to remove himself from suspicion.'

'By Jove, it does.' His eyes widened with full understanding.

'I told you, you'd work it out soon enough. You're three steps ahead of me.'

She sighed. 'But still a step behind Lord Drake.'

They were silent for a moment, and Amelia's eyes strayed to the water, where Winifred and B.J. skipped stones, and Margaret, Captain Fitz, Mr Worth and Miss Castlewood looked on. Here were two perfectly happy couples who made relationships look easy. Her eyes returned to Simon, thinking their experience had been more difficult. Not their friendship or investigations. Discovering murderers was simple compared to their feelings for one another. He caught her glance and quickly looked away.

Why? What was he afraid of? Now was not the right time, but never would there be a right time. She needed to ask him. If she didn't, she might never. '*They* look happy . . .'

'They do,' he seconded.

'Do you think *we* could be happy?'

His eyes snapped back to hers. 'I think I would make you miserable.'

She was so surprised by his answer that she started.

'I am used to being alone,' clarified Simon. 'At sea, at home. I'm not good with people.'

'You're good with me,' she said gently.

'No, I'm not.' The muscle in his jaw flexed. 'I am the reason you're a widow. If it weren't for me, you would have never met Edgar Amesbury. I had no care for the woman he married, only for my friend. As you stated when we first met, it was selfish of me.'

New understanding dawned like the first day of spring. He blamed himself for her being alone. When they first met, she had accused Simon of being selfish, of not thinking of the woman he told Edgar to find, a woman without knowledge of his position or wealth. But Amelia didn't blame him. If anything, she was appreciative of the advice he'd given Edgar. After all, it had led to some of the best moments of her life.

He cleared his throat, continuing. 'A magnetism, physically, exists between us.'

Wax poetically, please. Goodness, it sounded as if he was explaining a science experiment.

'That's what you're feeling. Nothing more.' He stared at her with serious eyes. 'I am a fool Amelia. You want nothing to do with me.'

'You are a fool – and as dense as mud.'

He flinched but dipped his chin in agreement.

'But not for the reasons you state.' She refrained – just – from stamping on his foot. 'Yes, I am a widow, but I am not alone. Edgar gave me a family, Tabitha and Winifred, and I love them so very much. I wouldn't take back a single, solitary second. Not our meeting, not our fleeting happiness. And I certainly don't blame you for putting the idea in his head. If anything, I'm grateful, in a roundabout way, for what you did. Life doesn't have to be perfect to be good. In fact, I've found it's the imperfections that make it meaningful.'

His face brightened like that of a child on Christmas morning who's discovered an unexpected gift. 'Do you mean that?'

'I don't say things I don't mean.'

His eyes were as blue-green as a bough of a spruce tree, as if a veil had been lifted or an obstruction removed. For the first time, she felt as if he saw her completely. The pity was gone. What remained was relief, acceptance and perhaps even permission. He studied her lips as if he wished to kiss her, to test their physical magnetism, as he called it. She felt her head tilt automatically, even though she knew they could not engage in such an act publicly. He brought his hand to her cheek, brushing his thumb over her lips, and she closed her eyes, relishing his touch. A touch she hadn't been sure she'd ever feel again.

Margaret's voice intercepted the feeling, and Amelia's eyes flew open.

'It is the truth! Don't you believe me?' Madge's voice carried across the water as easily as it did across audiences when she sang. Several people looked in her direction.

'It sounds as if we have a situation on our hands,' Simon murmured.

'If, by situation, you mean Margaret, then yes,' said Amelia through gritted teeth. She was angry at Madge for taking this moment away from them. 'She is one situation in need of controlling.'

He smiled. 'Let us go and try.'

TWENTY-SIX

Dear Lady Agony,

My sister is intolerable. My parents have indulged her since birth, and she does and says whatever she likes. Last week she announced to my friends that I sleep in the buff. Who knows what she will utter this week! What might I do to keep her quiet?

Sincerely,

A Gregarious Problem

Dear A Gregarious Problem,

I sympathize with your situation, but how to fix it? That is the real question. My advice is to switch topics. If that does not work, drop an intimate detail about her – accidentally, of course. Sometimes the only way to fight fire is with fire.

Yours in Secret,

Lady Agony

Amelia and Simon quickly shortened the distance between them and Margaret. Despite her myriad foibles, Madge was never afraid to reveal new ones. By the looks of the conversation, she was showing Benjamin Worth just how bad-tempered she could be. An auburn curl swirled over her forehead, her hands fisted tightly at her waist, and her chin jutted out in challenge. Amelia rolled her eyes. Just as she thought the two had gained common ground, here they were, staking battle lines again.

'I did not say I didn't believe you, Miss Scott. I merely stated a fact.' Mr Worth's tone was aloof, and if one thing irritated Madge, it was dispassion. 'The Metropolitan Police believe something happened at the ball to precipitate Arthur Radcliffe's death. Surely, you're not refuting their involvement.' Amelia prepared herself for a stinging retort from Margaret.

'They're involved, but they're looking at the wrong person. Anybody with two eyes can see that.' Madge surveyed the group as if challenging them to dispute the number of eyes they had.

Despite not wanting to prolong the conversation, Amelia asked her what she meant. If she had a clue to the identity of the murderer, Amelia needed to hear it.

'The murder was premeditated.' Margaret flung up her hands. 'Did you not introduce Mr Radcliffe to me for the very first time that night?' She didn't wait for confirmation. 'Yes, you did. And wasn't the poison put into a little glass bottle *before* the night of the ball? Yes, it was.' She shrugged. 'How could I have planned to murder him if I had not yet met him?'

A very good point, thought Amelia.

'I understand your argument, but someone accused of murder is bound to point the finger elsewhere,' Mr Worth muttered. 'It is always the case, and the police might not find it convincing.'

At the word *murder*, Winifred cocked her head in their direction. B.J. held his stone by his side.

'My sister has been accused of no crime,' Amelia whispered. 'Let us not ruin such a fine day as this one with the unseemly topic. A moment ago, I stated to Lord Bainbridge how happy you look.' She smiled at Miss Castlewood, who wore a rich teal gown that made her plain brown hair and complexion warmer, lovelier. 'Remind me of your nuptials?'

'Less than a week.' Miss Castlewood returned the gesture, seemingly glad to switch topics. 'The banns were announced the first of this month.'

'And will you take a honeymoon afterwards?' Amelia asked.

Theodora Castlewood's smile reached her eyes. 'Oh, yes. We are taking a fine European holiday. I've never seen Italy, and now I'll have the chance.'

Benjamin Worth looked adoringly at his fiancée. 'You deserve it, dear.'

'As do you, friend,' Captain Fitz added. 'No man served his country better.'

'Except you.' Mr Worth patted his friend's shoulder.

A stone splashed the water, and B.J. laughed at his misthrow. He tried again and landed on his rear. In spite of the mud, Miss Castlewood went to him, helping him up and ensuring he was all right. B.J. said he was fine, so she found him another stone, watching as he tossed it across the lake. She clapped when it skipped several times.

'She'll make a fine mother, won't she?' Mr Worth said admiringly.

'The finest,' Captain Fitz agreed.

Amelia smiled. It was hard not to be glad looking upon the children playing, the band making music and the masses of flowers and fruit. And, most importantly, Simon by her side. If she could only find the person who killed Arthur Radcliffe, all would be right in the world.

As if her wish had been spoken out loud, the clouds cleared, and high on the hill stood Lord Drake, waylaid by Lord Morton and Felicity Farnsworth. Here was a chance to ask Lord Drake about the murder of Mr Radcliffe.

From what Amelia could surmise, congratulations were being exchanged. After overhearing Felicity Farnsworth in the park, Amelia could guess, yet Miss Farnsworth's porcelain face was emotionless, a mask of impenetrability. If she married Lord Morton, she would officially be Lady Morton, her goal accomplished. Yet no real affection was guaranteed between the couple. In fact, Lord Morton's attention to Margaret might have affirmed that fact to her. Perhaps it was the reason she displayed no signs of happiness.

Amelia gave Simon's coat a discreet tug, and when she had his attention, she lifted her chin toward the hill.

'Excuse us for a moment,' Simon said to the group.

'Look after Winifred?' Amelia asked Madge.

'Of course.' Madge smiled in Winifred's direction.

'We won't take our eyes off her, my lady.' Captain Fitz gave them a small salute, and they started up the hill, away from the lake.

'The couple must have good news.' Amelia sidestepped a divot in the grass. 'Felicity Farnsworth may get her title yet.'

Simon lifted his dark eyebrows in her direction but said nothing.

After a few steps, Amelia prodded, 'Why do you defend her, after what she did to you?'

'I said nothing in her defense.'

Amelia stopped, needing to clear this up once and for all. There could be no question between them left unanswered. Not if they were to go forward, which was her most secret desire. 'Did she not have a relationship with a friend of yours during your engagement?'

He stopped as well. 'Yes.'

'And did you not allow her to beg off when you found out?' she pressed.

'Yes.'

Amelia tossed up her hands. All that she'd heard was true, so why didn't he speak out against her? Did he think it was acceptable for her to seek out Lord Morton for the same reasons?

'What you don't know is that she was very much in love with my friend, who was not an officer but a lieutenant. Her father would not approve of the relationship. He has money, and he thinks it should buy him a title for the family. Knowing the shipmate was a friend of mine, Felicity sought my attention. She figured I would be the aloof husband, away most days, which would give her time with my friend.' He swallowed, perhaps reluctant to keep talking. 'She didn't count on me returning her affection. Indeed, it was a foolish thing for a man like me to do, and my shipmate relented when he found out my feelings.'

She grasped his hand. 'It wasn't foolish.'

'Naïve, then.' He squeezed her hand and let it go. 'The fact remains, she did what she did for love. I could not fault her then, and I still cannot now.'

I can, thought Amelia, but as they continued up the hill, she realized she didn't. She felt empathy for Miss Farnsworth. She had been put in a difficult position by her father. What might a young woman truly in love do to save a relationship? Only now was she realizing the distance one might go to be with another. Because she herself was in love with Simon.

She glanced at him covertly. Yes, she loved him. It wasn't excitement or adventure; it was love. An opening of oneself to another, the sharing of one's deepest thoughts and dreams with someone else. He knew her like no one did, and now, finally, she could say the same of him. That Felicity Farnsworth was the cause of it was the most ironic turn of all.

He caught her looking and smiled. Not a smile of amusement

but one of understanding and mutual respect. Without a word between them, she felt their connection deepen.

By the time they reached the top of the hill, Lord Drake had left. He must've been detained only a moment, for she couldn't see him anywhere near the food or flower marquees.

'Are you looking for someone in particular?' asked Miss Farnsworth as they neared.

'Lord Drake,' Amelia answered. 'I thought I saw him here a moment ago.'

'You did.' Miss Farnsworth nodded. 'He was congratulating us on our future nuptials.'

'But not too distant future, right, my dear?' Lord Morton added with a chuckle. 'Your father is anxious for the marriage to occur, as is mine.'

Felicity smiled. 'Our fathers have made up their minds for it to happen yet this season. Usually, it is the mothers who cannot be deterred.'

'Congratulations,' said Amelia. 'That is wonderful news.'

'Congratulations,' Simon added.

'Thank you,' said Felicity, and Amelia noted real emotion in her words to Simon. Now it was she who was being utilized – for her dowry. It was as Tabitha had suspected: Lord Morton's father had squandered their wealth, and Lord Morton needed money. While the circumstances were different, the feeling had to be much the same as the one Simon felt two years ago. So often was the case in London. People were measured by the money, title or status they could bring to a marriage. Love was, for the most part, for the youthful and inexperienced. Yet Amelia held out hope that exceptions existed, such as Oliver and Kitty. And maybe, one day, she and Simon.

Amelia, who was still scanning the area for Lord Drake, spotted someone else she knew near a towering lemon tree. Someone who couldn't possibly have good news. She sucked in an audible breath. Detective Collings, hell-bent on public retribution, must have made the trek to the Regent's Park for one reason only: to inform her the substance he'd found was arsenic.

TWENTY-SEVEN

Dear Lady Agony,
They say that which does not kill you makes you stronger,
but I do not wish to be stronger. I wish not to know any
more of the hardships of life. Wherever I turn, a friend or
family member is sick or struggling. I know it will sound
selfish, but I would like to run away, even for a minute, to
get away from the problems. Do you think I could?
Sincerely,
Not Stronger Any Longer

Dear Not Stronger Any Longer,
It is not selfish to want health and wellness for yourself
and your family. Everyone wishes for a good life. You need
– nay, require – a respite, time for yourself to rejuvenate.
When you return, even if it is from a quiet walk in the park,
you will be able to handle what life throws at you. Be sure
of it, Dearest Reader. You can do hard things.
Yours in Secret,
Lady Agony

Amelia had a sudden urge to flee, even though she had done nothing wrong. It was physical and overwhelming, and she took two steps in the other direction before she realized she had done so. Simon understood the problem immediately, his eyes reaching the detective in a matter of moments. He excused himself and Amelia with a final word of congratulations to the engaged (if not happy) couple.

Amelia forced herself to breathe. Her family needed her. *Madge* needed her. And while it would be easier to avoid the problem altogether by hiding behind the influence of the Amesbury name or the muscle of Simon Bainbridge, she would not. As she had told her readers on more than one occasion, she could complete difficult tasks.

'To think the man would come here, during a social event, is out of order.' A muscle in Simon's jaw twitched with anger as he stared at Detective Collings, who noted their location and was approaching in a loping walk. His lips were a thin line, anticipating the opportunity to right the imagined wrongs that had been done to him so many years ago.

'His hatred for the Amesburys has no bounds,' Amelia whispered. 'He will come after Margaret with everything he has. I know it.'

'Then I shall come after him.'

Surprised by the vitriol in his tone, Amelia glanced up at him, noting that the amber fleck in his eyes engulfed the normally green irises. She put a hand on his arm. 'Whatever happens, we will manage. Together.'

Their eyes locked for a moment, and the amber flames subsided.

'Lady Amesbury.' Detective Collings, nearly out of breath, took a greedy gulp of air. 'Your lordship.'

'Detective.' Simon crossed his arms, making it clear the intrusion was not a welcome one. 'I cannot imagine why you are here unless it is to find vegetable marrows for your garden.'

Looking stupefied, Detective Collings blinked. 'I don't have a garden.'

'What other reason could you have for interrupting the lady on such a fine afternoon as this?'

'Maybe she hasn't told you.' Detective Collings's small eyes widened eagerly as if he hoped this was the case. 'I found the substance that killed Arthur Radcliffe in her house yesterday, and it is arsenic. The chemist confirmed it just an hour ago.'

'What of it?' asked Simon. 'Arsenic is as common as rain in this city. I don't know a house in town that doesn't need it to keep the rats away.'

Detective Collings held up a finger. 'Not arsenic papers, but a slim bottle, such as might be carried by a lady who wished to quietly poison a suitor.'

'But that doesn't make sense, Detective,' Amelia interjected, remembering Madge's earlier words. 'What you're describing is premeditated murder. My sister only met Mr Radcliffe on the evening of her debut.'

'Hasn't your sister had trouble before, with Charles Atkinson?

And might she not prepare for other unwelcome advances?' Detective Collings didn't wait for her response. He answered the questions himself. 'Most certainly. Margaret Scott is a woman who lives by the adage, "Fool me once, shame on you. Fool me twice, shame on me."'

'On that, we agree, Detective, but refusing to be ill-used does not make her a murderess.' Amelia's nostrils flared with anger. 'It makes her smart. Too smart to be entrapped by the likes of you.'

'We will see about that, your ladyship,' Detective Collings spat back. 'We'll see about that right now.' He looked over her shoulder, and Amelia spun to follow his gaze down the hill, but her sister was gone and so were the captain and Winifred. Kitty and Oliver were there, however. They might have seen where they went.

'Let's not let emotions run away with us,' Simon said to the detective, perhaps trying to appeal to his masculine pride. 'Let us talk to Miss Scott with a rational and clear head.'

With a dip of his chin, Detective Collings pulled down his coat, but it instantly bunched under the armpits again as he strode down the hill. Amelia marched after him, and Simon touched her arm, the weight of his hand steadying her in a way nothing else did. She slowed her pace, or at least quit stomping. It would do no good to be seen chasing after a detective in the Regent's Park.

On the boating lake, the water gurgled, gently pushing a stray sailboat. Kitty and Oliver, engaged in a private conversation, weren't aware of the detective's approach.

'Kitty, have you seen Margaret?' Amelia called from several yards away.

Kitty started. Oliver frowned. Detective Collings waited for a word.

'She left with the captain and Winifred. Miss Scott has never seen the zoo, and Winifred wanted to show her. They started for the Broad Walk a few minutes ago.'

Amelia smiled and said, 'Perfect. Thank you.' But what she was thinking was *Dash it all, Madge!* With all to see here, she'd decided to make the trek to the London Zoological Gardens. For a moment she thought the decision – or the long walk – would

deter Collings. But he immediately took a step toward Chester
Street, and they were forced to follow. It was too much to hope
that he wouldn't go after her.

'They cannot be far,' Detective Collings grumbled. 'I didn't
come all this way to stop now.'

Indeed, with the confirmation of the poison, Collings seemed
to have redoubled his efforts to convict Madge of the crime. With
their breakneck pace, they would come across her sooner or later.
But when they did, what would he do? Question her? Take her
from the park by force? Arrest her?

Questions loomed in Amelia's mind as they turned left and
the path widened. Rows of towering trees surrounded them on
both sides now. Instead of enjoying the shade they provided, as
she usually did, Amelia felt confined, as if walking through a
tunnel she couldn't see the end of.

'Amelia,' said Simon.

She slowed for a moment, almost forgetting Simon was next
to her, too focused was she on Detective Collings, who was
several steps ahead of them, obviously wanting to reach Margaret
first.

'It will be all right.' He put a hand on her shoulder. 'I promise
you.'

'I am glad you think so,' she replied, but his words quieted a
buzz that had started in her head on the shadowy path. He always
knew the way to calm her fears. 'Can you imagine what Aunt
Tabitha would do if she were here?' She shook her head, imag-
ining the horror. 'She'd lock my sister and me in the house for
the rest of the season.'

'Nonsense.' A single beat passed, and he added, 'She'd give
the detective a rap with her cane.'

The image brought a laugh to her lips. Tabitha's canes did
seem to possess physical powers that might have stopped Collings
in his tracks. If she didn't stop him physically, she would stop
him verbally with a cutting remark or slight. When it came to
family, she was just as fierce as Amelia. An attempt to injure
one of her own wouldn't go unchecked.

Just as Amelia felt her mood lighten, it took a terrifying turn
a moment later when she heard her sister's voice cry out.

She gaped at Simon.

He confirmed what she already knew. 'It's Margaret. Come on.'

'Was that—?' But Detective Collings didn't have time to finish his sentence before they raced past him.

Amelia knew her sister was in trouble. Perhaps Winifred was in trouble, too. The thought of them both being injured deepened the sickness in her stomach, and for a second, her knees grew weak with running, and she thought she would double over. She knew the captain had a storied war past, yet she had allowed him to care for her sister and daughter. *Idiot!* According to Mr Worth, the captain had suffered from bouts of melancholia since the end of the Crimean War four years ago. He could have hurt Madge – or Winifred.

Relief flooded through her as she saw Winifred and Captain Fitz run past a flowering shrub not far off the path. At least, they were both safe. 'Captain! Winifred!'

They turned backwards but only for a moment.

'It's your sister,' yelled Captain Fitz. 'She's gone.'

Captain Fitz and Winifred zigzagged around beds of flowers, and Amelia was forced to follow, the colors flying past her in a dizzying array of yellow, red and orange. Simon was beside her, with the detective a few steps behind. Captain Fitz and Winifred disappeared behind a large plane tree, and a cry stuck in Amelia's throat. She was too hoarse to call out, and her breath was coming too fast to make any real noise.

'It's all right.' Simon was calmer and perhaps not as winded as she was. 'He's looking for her, also.'

Amelia wasn't sure she believed him but could do nothing except follow the captain and Winifred into the wooded area, far off the path, beyond the vibrant flower beds. All color was gone, and only the murky cold shade surrounded them. Around they went, circling one tree, only to be assaulted by another, and for a moment, Amelia imagined she was not in the city at all but a forest. It seemed to stretch forever, although reason told her it couldn't. Just as tears started to sting her eyes, Captain Fitz cried out for help. They took a quick turn left, following the sound.

Amelia ran even faster, her legs like jelly by the time she reached Winifred and Captain Fitz, who hovered over a body.

It was Margaret, her eyes closed, her neck marked with red blotches.

'Madge!' In an instant, Amelia was on her knees beside her.

The only response was the quiet rise and fall of Margaret's chest. Relief hit Amelia's core. Her sister was not dead; she was hurt.

Amelia glared up at Captain Fitz. 'What on earth happened here?'

'I did not do anything. On that, I give my word.'

'He's telling the truth,' Winifred added, her blue eyes filling with tears. 'We heard a woodpecker and went in search of it. Miss Scott spotted something beyond the tree line and promised she would be right back. Then we heard her scream. We ran to help her. And now . . .' She gulped back a cry.

'It's all right, dear,' Amelia assured Winifred. 'She is going to be all right.' Amelia looked to Simon to make certain she wasn't lying.

Simon kneeled beside Margaret, examining her face. 'Someone tried to hurt her. You can see finger marks here and here.' He pointed to each side of her neck. 'Thank God we arrived when we did.'

'She *will* be all right?' Amelia asked him.

'Yes, I think so, but she should be seen by a doctor immediately.'

'And what of the person who did this?' Amelia was overcome with emotion, and she held back tears, attempting a brave face for Winifred.

'Simon and I will see to it.' A twitch had begun in Captain Fitz's jaw, and his blue eyes had a darkness in them that Amelia had never noticed, as dark as the bottom of the sea.

'You'll do nothing of the sort.' Detective Collings's shoulders heaved as he took in a deep breath. He'd been several paces behind them and only arrived now. 'No one will be serving up vigilante justice on my watch.'

The emotion Amelia had been holding back turned into rage, and she released Winifred to confront the detective. 'Now do you believe that my sister had nothing to do with the murder of Arthur Radcliffe? Now do you believe someone has set her up for the crime?'

The detective's lips remained frozen, like a dead fish's, as he stared down at Margaret. His face was placid, emotionless. He didn't bend to check her breath or pulse.

'You scoundrel,' Amelia spat. 'You despicable man.'

Simon stood up and put a hand on her arm, but nothing could quell the anger she felt toward the detective, and she continued. 'My sister has been strangled, and you stand there like a guppy with nothing to say. Don't you dare come near me or my family ever again.' She turned toward Captain Fitz. 'Help Simon get her to our carriage. We are going home. Now.'

The men did as she asked, each taking one side of her sister.

'This isn't over, Lady Amesbury,' said Detective Collings.

'No, it isn't.' Amelia's answer was immediate and harsh. 'You have failed at your job, Detective, and there will be repercussions.' Amelia took Winifred's hand, leaving Detective Collings open-mouthed. Then she started toward the entrance at Chester Road, thankful that they wouldn't have to maneuver past the crowds at the marquees. She would find who did this, but right now, her sister needed her, and nothing else mattered – not the detective, or the assailant, or the thousands of people in the park. She would make certain Margaret Ann was safe if it was the last thing she did.

And if the murderer had any say in the matter, it might just well be.

TWENTY-EIGHT

Dear Lady Agony,

It's my experience that very few people know how to react to a concussion of the brain, sometimes called stunning. By the time the surgeon is called, much time has been wasted or, worse, spent wrongly. Would you summarize the symptoms and instructions so that others may learn and avoid making the condition worse? Thank you.

Sincerely,
Experienced Housekeeper

Dear Experienced Housekeeper,

Your letter complies with modern advice, and I welcome repeating it in my column:

Symptoms of concussions include cold skin, weak pulse, insensibility, weak breathing, larger or smaller pupils and the inability to move or speak. To treat the patient, place him or her on a warm bed and call for the surgeon. Do nothing else for four to six hours. If the surgeon has not come and a fever ensues, shave the patient's head and apply half an ounce of sal-ammoniac, two teaspoons of vinegar and two tablespoons of gin or whiskey in half a pint of water. Apply two tablespoons of the mixture every four hours.

Yours in Secret,
Lady Agony

A t home, Amelia looked on as their family physician examined Margaret. Her breathing, though shallow at first, was gaining ground, and some of the redness had decreased around her neck. So why hadn't she awoken? Amelia asked the doctor.

Dr Gibson was an older gentleman with a soft white beard and patient eyes, and he looked at Amelia with considerable empathy. 'I don't want to alarm you, Lady Amesbury, but your sister has a second injury.' His hand hovered over Margaret's head. 'She has a bump on the back of her head. I surmise that, and not the act of strangulation, has caused her deep sleep. I'd wager the man hardly had his hands on her before you reached her, thank heavens.'

Amelia's lips parted in surprise.

'What is the prognosis?' asked Aunt Tabitha, who was standing sentry at the bedstead. Her voice, which was always stronger than one expected, was now laced with concern.

The doctor had deep, kind wrinkles, and they showed as his lips turned up in a smile. 'She will be fine, my lady. Just fine.'

Amelia heard Tabitha release a breath, and she herself sighed in relief. Margaret was going to be all right. If the doctor said so, she knew it must be true. Dr Gibson had tended to Edgar when he was ill and had been with them through the worst days. When nothing else was to be done, he'd made Edgar as comfortable as possible, easing Edgar's pain and their minds considerably. There was no one else's advice that she trusted more. 'Thank you.'

Dr Gibson shifted in his seat as if he was not comfortable with praise. 'Yes. Well. Rest is the best thing for her. It will help her heal.' He found his bag by his chair, returning his stethoscope before zipping it. 'Before you know it, she'll be awake and talking again. But until then, let her sleep.' He stood with his bag. 'Call on me as soon as she wakes.'

'We will,' said Amelia. 'I promise.'

'Please join us for tea.' Tabitha opened Margaret's door. 'It has been too long since we had the pleasure of your company.'

'Thank you. I would like that.'

Tabitha nodded in her direction.

'I want to stay here a while longer, Aunt.' Amelia tried a smile. 'I'll get something to eat a little later.' But even as she said the words, she knew she wasn't hungry and probably wouldn't eat a morsel until her sister woke up. Her eyes didn't stray from her sister's bed, where Margaret's chest rose and fell with the regularity of a sleeper having sweet dreams. Amelia prayed she was.

Sometime later, Jones knocked on the door.

'I'm fine,' Amelia assured him. 'Truly.'

'I'm glad, my lady, but it's Lord Drake. He's here to see you.' He frowned. 'He mentioned a button you found in the garden. I put him in the drawing room.'

'Oh . . . right.' It seemed a lifetime ago that they had spoken about the button, and she had to summon the memory like a light in the fog. Not only had they spoken of the missing fastener, but they'd also spoken of the Mayfair thefts. He'd admitted to committing them, and Simon suggested he might also have committed the murder of Arthur Radcliffe. She sat up straighter with the recollection. If that was true, he could be the person who'd put her sister in peril. After all, he'd left moments before her sister's injury. He could have been lying in wait and attacked her.

And then showed up here to retrieve his button? She shook her head, wishing the fog away.

'Shall I tell him you are indisposed?' asked Jones.

'No, I'll be right there. Find Lettie, please. I need her to stay with Margaret.'

'Of course, my lady.'

Jones returned a few minutes later with her trusted lady's maid. Amelia instructed Lettie to stay by Margaret's side until she returned, no exceptions. 'Do not leave her alone.'

Lettie ruffled, offense in her voice. 'I never would.'

'I know it.' Amelia patted her shoulder as she passed by her on the way to retrieve the button.

When Amelia reached the drawing room, Lord Drake greeted her as a friend. The scar near his lips deepened as he smiled his infamous smile. 'I hope you don't mind my popping in for the button. I knew if I did not stop immediately, I'd forget.' His light-brown eyes landed on her frown, and the smile dropped from his lips. 'What is the matter? Have I interrupted something?'

Amelia passed by him, sizing him up as a spectator might a conjurer's bag of tricks, for Lord Drake was magic. He had style, he had charisma and he had an age-old title – a trifecta that might mislead any person in London. Amelia was determined not to be any person.

She pulled the tortoiseshell button from her pocket, examining the rich color in the light. It, like the man himself, had two sides: one the distinguished lord and the other thief in the night.

'I apologize if I have interrupted,' he added with a puzzled expression. 'The butler might have told me.'

'My sister was attacked in the park.' Amelia's voice was even grittier than she imagined, and Lord Drake took a sharp intake of air at either the tone or her words. 'She is still unconscious.'

'What? Why?' He took a step forward. 'I am sorry.'

'I do not know the reason – yet.' She turned the button over in her hand. 'I can only surmise it has something to do with Arthur Radcliffe's death. She has been tied up with the business since the beginning.' She lifted her eyes to his. 'As have you.'

His brown eyes grew wide, allowing in more light, their caramel color shining through. 'I was there that night. That is all.'

'That is *all*?' she pressed.

'I stole the diamond. I returned it.' He shook his head. 'Surely you don't believe I had something to do with your sister's accident?' When she didn't respond, he continued. 'Think of it. I could not take the family jewel after I met you. How could I take your darling sister?'

'You couldn't.' She felt the truth in his words more than she heard it. He enjoyed her company, and their connection was a rarity for him. He wouldn't hurt her sister. 'I'm afraid this situation is driving me mad.' She clasped the bridge of her nose, where a headache had started. 'Did you know Mr Radcliffe?'

'I knew of Radcliffe, which is why I stayed away from him.' Lord Drake's statement dipped as if Radcliffe might still be alive and overhear what he was saying. 'If he ever found out about the thefts – well, you can imagine. He was the backbone of the London rumor mill. No one was immune from his allegations. I have a feeling he profited from them somehow. Perhaps in status.'

It was as her sister had said all along, and it was timely to hear Lord Drake repeat it more succinctly. Mr Radcliffe used his information for power and influence. Everyone had said so, just not in so many words. One person, however, was determined to put a stop to his antics once and for all. But if it wasn't Lord Drake, who was it? 'He knew my sister had quarreled with a man in Mells. She accidentally broke his arm.' When Lord Drake's brows lifted in question, she continued to explain. 'The man tried to kiss her, and she had a visceral reaction.' She indicated the scar on his lip. 'Perhaps not unlike the one you experienced when the tavern wench was in peril.'

He clucked his tongue. 'This scar? I got it from a slip on the ice when I was a child.' He leaned in. 'Just don't tell the ladies.'

For the first time in what felt like forever, Amelia laughed out loud. Mr Radcliffe wasn't the only secret keeper in London, but Lord Drake's secret was safe with her. 'I won't. I promise.' She pressed the button into his hand.

He clasped her fingers for a moment. 'If I can do anything at all for your sister, you need only ask.'

'Thank you. I appreciate it.'

They shared a smile before she walked him down the stairs and to the front door. After bidding him goodbye, she returned upstairs, standing in the hallway and listening to the clinking of the teacups in the drawing room. She didn't need to partake to know how wonderful the experience was. Taking any meal with Tabitha was always a delight, and from the sound of the doctor's voice, this one was no different. Amelia could hear the smile on his lips.

'I'm glad to hear Lady Winifred enjoyed the exhibit, despite Miss Scott's trouble.'

'I believe Mr Worth's nephew helped considerably,' said Tabitha. 'From what I understand, she and the boy skipped stones on the water most of the day. Neither was interested in fruits or vegetables, and Amelia, as you can see, had her hands full.'

'B.J. Worth,' the doctor stated. 'I met him last week. A fine boy in need of the smallpox vaccine.'

'Imagine waiting until his age to take the vaccine,' Tabitha huffed. Smallpox had hit London hard in the late 1830s, which led to free vaccines in the 1840s, and eventually compulsory vaccination in the first four months of life in 1853.

'He only moved here recently.' The doctor paused, perhaps trying to recall where he was from and failing. 'What's important is he has the vaccine now. I believe they depart for Italy quite soon.'

That's right, thought Amelia, continuing toward the stairs. *Benjamin Worth is taking his fiancée on a European vacation after the wedding.*

Amelia paused. But his nephew wouldn't go with him.

Would he?

She stepped into the drawing room. 'Excuse the interruption, but I couldn't help but overhear your conversation on my return trip upstairs.' Ignoring Tabitha's sidelong glance, she looked to Dr Gibson. 'Did you say B.J. Worth will be traveling with his uncle and his uncle's new wife on their honeymoon?'

'Quite.' Dr Gibson set down his fork. 'Although now that I hear you say it out loud, it does seem odd.'

'Most things that come out of Amelia's mouth sound odd,' mumbled Tabitha.

Ignoring Tabitha, Amelia continued. 'Did he say why they are taking the boy?'

'No.' The doctor's fuzzy eyebrows lifted. 'I did not think to ask. I assumed his brother was away or it was a family affair.'

'I imagine the brother and wife are traveling with them.' Tabitha paused, glass in hand. 'Not everything is a mystery to be solved, Amelia. Many families travel together on the wedding tour, to visit family members who cannot attend the ceremony.'

What Tabitha said was true – newlyweds did sometimes travel with family members – but something rang false. More and more, couples used the time to foster the new relationship. Even so, why would Benjamin Worth, and not the boy's adopted father or mother, take him to see the doctor?

'Amelia!' called Lettie.

Amelia started at the sound of her Christian name, stunned by Lettie's use of it.

'Your sister. She's awake!'

In an instant, Amelia was on the stairs, taking two at a time. Madge was awake! She was going to be all right. The relief she experienced was like no other, and she felt as Atlas might have if the world had been lifted from his shoulders for a single moment. Her little sister would be alive to make more music and mischief; both sounded equally glorious to her ears. Her heart trilled with gratitude as she turned the corner, and by the time she entered Madge's room, tears moistened the corners of her eyes.

Amelia expected Madge to be sitting up in her bed, demanding a drink or dinner. Sadly, she was doing neither. Her light-brown eyelashes were fluttering, finding their way open. A furrow crossed her brow, and Amelia wondered if she was recollecting a memory of the horrific event.

Amelia immediately went to her side and grasped her hand. 'It's me, Madge. Amelia. I'm right beside you, and all is well. You're at my home, in your bed.'

The furrow smoothed, and Madge released a breath through her nose.

It was the best sound in the world. Amelia squeezed her hand.

Madge's eyelashes fluttered open, her pupils large and unfocused. They went to the ceiling, then the window and then found Amelia's face. They grew smaller, the hazel iris growing larger as she focused.

Amelia could only smile, so happy was she to see her sister regain consciousness.

Dr Gibson entered the room, a little out of breath. 'Miss Scott.' He glanced at Amelia. 'May I?'

Amelia, reluctant to relinquish her sister's hand, acceded to the doctor's request. 'Of course.'

The doctor peered into Margaret's eyes one at a time, saying, 'Good. Good.' He patted her arm. 'I'm glad to see you're awake so soon. It bodes well for your recovery.'

'I'm afraid it takes more than a rap on the head to keep a Scott woman down,' Amelia said, and when she did, Margaret's eyes flew to hers. Amelia winced at her own stupidity. The last words Madge needed to hear were *rap on the head.*

'How *is* your head, dear?' asked Dr Gibson. 'Does it hurt?'

Margaret ignored the question, still staring at Amelia. 'I . . . the culprit. I know.' She licked her lips.

Amelia reached for the glass of water on the nightstand. 'She needs something to drink.' The doctor stepped out of the way to let her pass. 'Here, Madge. Take a small sip, if you please.'

Madge took a drink and closed her eyes. 'Thank you.' Her voice was stronger, and her eyes looked more normal when they reopened. 'I know the fiend who did this.'

They were the words Amelia had been hoping for, the name of the man from whom she could seek retribution. The murderer. 'Who?'

'Benjamin Worth.'

TWENTY-NINE

Dear Lady Agony,
What is the cure for stammering? I heard of it once but
have since forgotten. Could you find it for me?
Sincerely,
Stammering Seraphina

Dear Stammering Seraphina,
Reading aloud for two hours a day, with teeth closed, is
the recommendation for stuttering. Continue for at least
three months to see improvement. Please write back and let
me know of your progress.
Yours in Secret,
Lady Agony

'**B**e . . . Ben . . . Mr . . . Benjamin Worth!' Amelia stuttered. It made sense, perfect sense. Benjamin Worth had been certain of Mr Radcliffe's demise because he'd been the one to administer the poison. He knew he hadn't fainted; he knew he was going to die and proceeded to remove him from the supper room post-haste. Furthermore, Mr Worth returned to accuse Margaret of the crime, a crime he himself had committed. Now he'd struck for a second time. But why, and why now? They weren't questions she needed answers to – yet. All she needed to know was that he was the one who'd hurt her sister, and he would pay for his actions. 'I knew he was using misdirection to confuse the police about his own vile actions.'

'Indeed!' Aunt Tabitha interjected. 'The detective will hear about this.' She snatched a piece of notepaper from Margaret's bureau. 'Justice will be served.'

'Let us not assault Miss Scott with these notions right now.' Dr Gibson's placid face remained calm as he once again glanced at his patient. 'She needs her rest, and I'm afraid exerting her at this time is not good for her health.'

'I feel fine, sir.' Margaret closed her eyes. 'It is only my head that aches.'

'And it will ache still more if you tax yourself.' The doctor tutted. 'These fine ladies know all there is to know, and there's nothing more to be done about it. You can rest now.'

'Umm. Rest.' Margaret yawned.

Tabitha scratched off a note to the detective and gave it to Mr Jones.

'The doctor is right, Madge,' agreed Amelia. 'You must rest to regain your strength.' Amelia had no intention of resting, however. She, like Tabitha, planned on apprehending Benjamin Worth immediately, before he could escape justice – or London.

Simon and Captain Fitz had returned to the Regent's Park to look for clues to the criminal's identity, and with any luck, they'd discovered it was Mr Worth. Heaven knew Captain Fitz was determined enough, although when he found out it was his friend, he would be devastated. Mr Worth had spoken of the captain's mood changes after the Crimean War, but perhaps it had been Mr Worth who had the problem all along. Maybe Mr Radcliffe had said something that made Worth snap. Or maybe Margaret had.

Simon and Captain Fitz would be along any moment to check on Margaret's progress. If they hadn't discovered the culprit, she would tell them herself. Then they would deal with him. She refused to rely on the detective or his skewed view of justice.

A small snore escaped Margaret's lips, and the doctor nodded with satisfaction. 'There now. Let her rest.'

'Shall we finish our tea?' asked Tabitha.

'I'd be remiss not to taste one of those strawberry tartlets.' The doctor chuckled.

Amelia waited until they were gone and then turned to Lettie. 'I'm not going to leave the matter to the dim-witted Detective Collings,' she whispered. 'When the marquis arrives, I'm telling him the news.'

Lettie nodded. 'And then what, my lady?'

'We will take action ourselves.'

But Simon didn't arrive, nor did Captain Fitz. Amelia waited a full hour beside her snoring sister, her nerves as tight as a bowstring. When she heard the tea things being taken away, she could wait no longer. For all she knew, Benjamin Worth had already fled London. What's more, the detective would arrive any minute if he answered Tabitha's note, which he most likely would. *I don't know of a man or woman who would dare keep her waiting.* And she'd dashed it off an hour ago.

Yet Amelia and the detective had not parted ways amicably at the park. He promised to find out the truth behind her sister's injury, but she believed him as much as she did a street seller promising the lowest prices. He might see Tabitha's note as a demand from the high and mighty Amesburys, whom he despised. If so, he'd make them wait until tomorrow.

It was a chance she couldn't take.

Amelia left Madge in Lettie's capable hands, pausing only to secure her parasol and her favorite footman, Bailey. Not only was he capable (he could take whatever Mr Worth dished out), but he was discreet. He'd kept her secret about Petticoat Lane. She knew she could trust him now.

Mr Worth lived on Newman Street, a fact she'd gained when she perused the guest list for thieves. Amelia pointed her coachman in that direction. The afternoon had grown overcast, the clouds sheets of silver as the black evening sky waited to succumb the light. The city remained free of fog, and for that Amelia was thankful. It was hard enough to confront a murderer, let alone confront him in the thick London haze, where one could disappear as easily as a fish into the sea. Although she kept watch for signs of Mr Worth, she was certain he'd disappeared as soon as he committed the violence against her sister. The exhibition was over, and there would be no reason for him to linger in the streets after making an attempt on Margaret's life.

Oxford Street was bustling, with most stores open until eight o'clock or later. Shoppers bustled to and fro with packages, while carriages and hansom cabs clogged the street waiting for them.

Amelia's carriage was waiting to cross. And waiting and waiting. Amelia tapped her toe impatiently. If Mr Worth had returned home, she was giving him plenty of time to pack a valise and escape. Then again, if he thought he'd killed Margaret, he might not be in a hurry to leave. He might believe his identity was secured by her death.

As they approached the thoroughfare at a snail's pace, a snatch

of a dress caught her attention. It was the distinctive teal Theodora
Castlewood had been wearing at the park, and against the steel-
gray sky, it was as bright as a starling's feather. There was no
mistaking its owner.

The dress disappeared into the chemist shop Harley & Son,
and Amelia indicated to her driver to halt. It took him several
moments to maneuver to a stop on the busy street, and Amelia
walked as quickly as she could to catch up with Miss Castlewood
without drawing attention to herself. She wished to speak to her
discreetly, to warn her about the danger she might be in. If Mr
Worth murdered Mr Radcliffe and nearly strangled Madge, who
knows what he would do to Theodora Castlewood once they
were married. It was better she knew what she was getting into.

Yet they had seemed so happy. He'd even remarked that she
would make a wonderful mother. Obviously, he planned to have
children, and after three years in the Crimean War, he deserved
peace and happiness. She might have empathized with his
violence against the terrible Mr Radcliffe. If only he hadn't hurt
Margaret . . .

But he had.

Amelia set her shoulders and trudged toward Harley & Son,
noting the brightly colored bottles against the gray day. Blue,
orange, red, green – they were filled with tinctures and powders.
Past the front window stood shelves and shelves of dried herbs
and flowers, tea leaves, unknown liquids and salves. Below them
were rows of small drawers, perhaps filled with important
formulas.

Amelia pulled open the door with the intent of walking directly
to Miss Castlewood and informing her of her fiancé's crimes,
but she paused when she saw Miss Castlewood talking to the
druggist near a pill dispenser, a nice-looking man in his thirties.
Perhaps he was the 'Son' mentioned on the signage. Amelia
stopped altogether when she saw Miss Castlewood toss back her
head in a coquettish laugh. Amelia ducked behind a particularly
tall display case, pretending to read the labels on the bottles
overhead.

She peeked around the corner. *Goodness!* It couldn't be that
Miss Castlewood was betraying her betrothed. Amelia couldn't
reconcile the idea with the woman. She was kind, considerate –

plain, even. The last person to dally with another's feelings. She'd apologized for Mr Worth's behavior in her ballroom when she could have easily stayed away. She'd done the right, albeit hard, thing. Why would she choose deception now? She loved Mr Worth. She wouldn't betray him. Would she?

If she had, it would certainly be fodder for blackmail, and Mr Radcliffe had used the ancient art to his benefit. It might be the motivation for his murder, which, until now, had evaded Amelia.

Miss Castlewood tilted her head in Amelia's direction, and Amelia stared at the selection of alcohol to avoid detection. She had no idea it could cure so many ailments – cough, headache, nerves, sleeplessness.

'Haven't you heard?' said a low voice. 'Alcohol is no pastime for a lady.'

Amelia didn't have to look to know it was Simon beside her.

'Lettie told me the news. You should have waited for me.'

She turned to him. 'I waited an hour. How much longer was I to wait? And if Lettie told you, why aren't you seeking out Mr Worth right now?'

'I am.'

Amelia squinted as if doing so would make her understand his statement better. He was not seeking out Mr Worth. He was standing with her at the chemist's shop.

Simon waggled his eyebrows in the direction of the druggist.

'Miss Castlewood?' she asked without looking.

He shook his head.

She turned around. It was indeed Miss Castlewood. The woman was still dallying with the druggist.

Simon moved her a step to the left.

Why, it was Benjamin Worth! Here in the store. Could he not see what his fiancée was doing? And right before his very eyes. How painful. And yet . . . he didn't seem to mind. In fact, he didn't seem to notice her.

How odd. He must have. No one could mistake her in that teal dress. Mr Worth looked left and right before leaning over the counter. Amelia automatically took a step forward.

Simon put a hand on her arm. 'Wait. Let us see what he does.'

What he did was snatch a page out of the ledger.

'The poison register,' she hissed. Since the 1851 Sale of Arsenic Regulation Act, the register had to be signed by persons who purchased arsenic. The act also required a coloring agent to be added to the poison so that it wouldn't be confused with flour or sugar. But it was more of a suggestion than a requirement. Druggists and grocers sold it all the time without adding color. To a would-be-poisoner like Benjamin Worth, color or not, the poison would work just the same.

'I'll deal with Worth,' whispered Simon. 'You see about Miss Castlewood. She might be stunned to learn of her fiancé's actions.'

Amelia had taken a step in Miss Castlewood's direction when Benjamin Worth turned and noted Simon's approach. Mr Worth had shoved the sheet in his coat pocket, and it bulged slightly. He dropped a casual smile and stepped left. When Simon did the same, he stepped right. Then he broke into a run, perhaps seeing it as his last option to flee with the damning evidence.

Not today, Villain.

Amelia stuck out her parasol, and Mr Worth tripped, taking with him a basket of dried rosehips. He lay face down on the wood floor, sprinkled with flowers, a fitting end to the season.

'Benjamin!' shrieked Miss Castlewood.

Simon turned him over, pinning an arm across his chest when he reached for his pocket. 'It's no use, Worth. We saw what you did.'

'Please, let us talk outside,' said Mr Worth in between haggard breaths.

'I see no reason for not speaking of your misdeeds here and now.' Amelia snatched the log out of his pocket, unfolding and scanning it for his name. Thomas, Andrew, Katherine, Victoria— She stopped. She looked at him, seeing him for who he was for perhaps the first time. 'On second thoughts, let us remove ourselves from the store.'

'What?' asked Simon unbelievingly. 'Why?'

The druggist, shocked by the disturbance, or perhaps shaken out of his flirtation, shuffled forward.

Amelia put the sheet behind her back.

'May I help you?' The druggist was a tall man, and when he bent down to pick up the spilled basket of rosehips, Amelia noticed a shiny bald spot on the top of his head that reflected her image.

Still staring at Amelia, Simon gave Mr Worth a hand up. 'Excuse us. We apologize for the inconvenience. Mr Worth tripped on . . .' He looked around.

'My parasol,' supplied Amelia, tapping its tip on the floor. 'So sorry. We will take our leave now. Miss Castlewood?'

Theodora Castlewood stared at Mr Worth, and he dipped his chin. Amelia noted the quiver in it, realizing fully, as he did, what this meant for the couple.

Amelia linked her arm with Miss Castlewood's, and they stepped outside.

Simon, his hand cuffed around Mr Worth's bicep, held his grip tight. 'Why the change of location, Amelia? Why couldn't we allow the police to apprehend him then and there?'

'This.' Amelia unfolded the register for him to see.

On the list of names was *Theodora Castlewood*.

THIRTY

Dear Lady Agony,

It's hard to conceive that you are concerned about crime. In my experience, women rarely bother themselves with fears outside the home. I think your efforts would be best spent there – in the house. It's where all women belong.

Sincerely,

A Man About London

Dear A Man About London,

Although I do not owe you an explanation, your dull statement necessitates one. Crime affects not only the city but its inhabitants – our friends, our families, our neighbors. What happens in our city happens in our houses. To feign otherwise is ignorant or obtuse. Which one are you?

Yours in Secret,

Lady Agony

'You poisoned Arthur Radcliffe.' Amelia blinked at Miss Castlewood. 'It was Mr Worth who saw you and covered up the deed.'

'Not very well, it would appear.' Mr Worth swallowed.

Miss Castlewood gave him a fleeting smile. 'You did a fine job. It was I who bungled the deed.'

'No, the murder was a success, Miss Castlewood.' Amelia put the paper into her pocket before someone took the opportunity to snatch it out of her hand. 'After all, Mr Radcliffe is as dead as a doornail. And some might say the world is a better place because of it.'

Surprise caught in Mr Worth's throat.

'But I cannot applaud your efforts,' continued Amelia. 'You sought to detract attention from Miss Castlewood by placing the blame on my sister, and it has caused our family much pain.'

'When Radcliffe lost consciousness at the party, I had to put the blame somewhere.' Mr Worth's words came out with a rush of air, and a bead of sweat trickled down his curly hairline. 'His brother is a physician. I knew he would find the death suspicious, and I was right. It was only a matter of time before the surgeon applied the Marsh test and found arsenic.'

Miss Castlewood's words came out just as quickly, both of them trying to excuse the other's behavior. It would have been sweet if the deed weren't so sinister. 'I thought the ball was the perfect place to administer the poison. So many there secretly despised him. So many suspects.'

'But you leaned into one suspect. Margaret Scott.' Simon glared at Benjamin Worth. 'Why her?'

'It had to be a woman,' Mr Worth explained. 'I understood Theodora poisoned him, and there would be an investigation. I confronted her, and she gave me the vial, which obviously belonged to a woman. I hatched a plan, discarding it within plain sight.'

Amelia remembered the container. The vial was violet with a gold fastener. Of course it belonged to a woman.

'And Miss Scott had fought so passionately with him on the dance floor. Everyone had seen. When word got out, I thought it would be the easiest thing.'

'Easiest for you!' accused Amelia. 'What of my sister? Did you think of anyone besides yourself and your betrothed?'

'We assumed she wouldn't be punished.' Miss Castlewood blinked back tears. 'You are Lady Amesbury, heir to a distinguished family and fortune. I never dreamed the police would take it as far as they have.'

Nor would they have if the detective hadn't held a secret grudge against my deceased husband. But only Amelia and her family were privy to his motivation.

'Theodora is telling the truth. She wasn't thinking of herself.' Benjamin Worth's gaze hooked on something in the distant sky. 'Neither was I.'

Amelia felt a connection click in her brain. 'You were thinking of your son.'

'Excuse me?' By the confused look in his eye, Simon did not follow the connection. 'Mr Worth doesn't have a son.'

'B.J. is not his nephew.' Amelia caught him up. 'He's his son, from the war. I imagine the B stands for Benjamin?'

Benjamin Worth nodded. 'I met his mother in Crimea in 1853. She died only recently. Until then, I had no idea our relationship had led to a child. When my brother took B.J. in for me, the boy had a cough, and Jonathan Radcliffe treated him. Not long after, Radcliffe discussed the case with his brother and made the connection. We went to a new doctor, but the trouble remained.' Mr Worth smoothed his frizzy hair and returned his hat to his head. 'Radcliffe pestered me ceaselessly. He said Miss Castlewood would never agree to the marriage when she found out. When I told him she was aware of the situation, it vexed him considerably. He was intent on telling her parents. He wouldn't stop until he gained *something* from the information.'

'I still don't understand why Mr Radcliffe did what he did.' Frustrated, or perhaps angry, Simon shoved his hands in his trouser pockets. 'Blackmail, I mean. He didn't need the money, as far as I could see, and he was popular with the social set.'

'It wasn't popularity; it was extortion.' Miss Castlewood tipped her head thoughtfully, focusing on the word. 'He used information to get what he wanted.'

'But what did he want?' asked Simon.

'Isn't it obvious?' Amelia supplied. 'Arthur Radcliffe wanted entrance into the most exclusive ballrooms in Mayfair, and he got it, not as an inconsequential would-be baron, but as the proprietor of the most powerful secrets in London. The people in his debt would do anything to appease him. Think of it. Lady Hamsted's brother had a gambling habit; Radcliffe must have been privy to the information for her to request an invitation for him to my ball that evening. It's mind-boggling, when you think of it, how one event led to another.' She thought of Felicity Farnsworth and her upcoming nuptials to the bankrupt nephew. Lady Hamsted had it planned all along. No wonder she was irate when Lord Morton became infatuated with her sister. Had he continued with his flirtation, it would have ruined her design to restore her brother's family and their wealth.

'I wanted none of it,' whispered Miss Castlewood. 'Only love. And a family. I couldn't bear to see Benjamin bow to his commands. And our son would, too – eventually. We'd live under his thumb – all of us. B.J. didn't deserve that. No one did.'

'How did you administer the poison?' Amelia needed confirmation of the act.

'I told Mr Radcliffe I decided I didn't want the rout cake that had been passed around after the third dance. In actuality, I had dosed it with arsenic.' Miss Castlewood's tone was dispassionate, detached. She had performed the action, but it had nothing to do with her personally. 'Knowing my wish to fit into my wedding gown, which had already been sized, he took care of the problem by eating it like a gentleman.'

Of course! Miss Castlewood's refusal of cake during her call might have suggested the idea earlier. Amelia remembered Mr Radcliffe holding two cakes at the ball. At the time, she took it as a sign of him moving past the argument with her sister. She had been happy he was indulging in the festivity's fare. Now she understood it was the method of murder.

'That's when I knew.' Mr Worth's voice was barely above a whisper. 'She'd given me several cakes to eat this season when she thought she'd overindulged. But that night, she said she saw almonds, and knowing my sensitivity, turned to Radcliffe.'

'There were no nuts in those cakes,' Amelia said.

'I know.' He swallowed. 'Theodora only meant to lessen my load, Lady Amesbury. Not hurt you or your sister.'

'Except you did.' Amelia responded with acrimony. 'My sister is bedridden right now because of your actions.'

'That's my fault, too, Lady Amesbury,' confessed Miss Castlewood. 'Miss Scott realized the murder was premeditated. You heard her yourself near the lake with the children. She must have been pondering it when she came upon us on the walk. She asked if the 'pretty bottle' in your plant belonged to me.' She cleared her throat. 'I'm embarrassed to say we tussled – your sister is a very physical person – and Benjamin tore us apart. That is when she fell to the ground. She hit her head, but we knew she would be safe when the captain arrived. We left before you could discover us.'

'You're right, Miss Castlewood. It *is* your fault, as is the death of Mr Radcliffe.' Amelia noted the approach of Detective Collings in the distance. By his side was an angry Captain Fitz. 'You will have to answer for your actions.' She turned to Miss Castlewood with more empathy than she thought she possessed. 'For my part,

I will ensure the detective knows of Radcliffe's deplorable actions. How he used women and children to get the prestige he craved. Whether or not it will make a difference, I am unsure.' Now that the Amesburys weren't involved, Amelia might be surprised to find the detective had a heart after all. She hoped so. 'What I am sure of is that you have done a good deed by confessing the crime.' She smiled. 'A lie can only lead to more lies. But the truth,' she looked at Simon, 'can lead to the greatest of things.'

EPILOGUE

Dear Readers,

I am happy to inform you that I've found out the Mayfair Marauder, and he has returned the stolen jewels to their rightful owners. Some of you might be upset that he is not in Ludgate or worse. But who of us has not acted desperately in desperate times? If any exists, you are welcome to throw the first stone. Dear Reader, I will wait.

Yours in Secret,

Lady Agony

The next morning, Amelia was walking along the Serpentine in Hyde Park. Despite all the difficulties, she'd had a glorious summer in this city. She was a different person from the young woman who arrived two years ago, eager and starry-eyed. Life had taught her lessons she hadn't necessarily wanted to learn, but she was wiser because of them.

What she would do with the knowledge, she couldn't say. She hoped she would use it for good. That she would continue to answer letters from her correspondents and assist those in need. At times, she thought she wouldn't. Winifred was growing older, and Amelia could spend every second with her and still yearn for more time.

But always Amelia's thoughts strayed to the adventures she might have if she kept writing. The people she would meet. The difference she might make. This space belonged to her and no one else. Not Aunt Tabitha. Not Winifred. Not even Simon. She did not know if she could give that up.

His name in her thoughts might have summoned him, for Simon appeared around the next bend. He wore a fine suit, a white shirt and no cravat. His green eyes alighted on hers, and she knew he'd been looking for her. The knowledge made the air that filled her lungs a little sweeter. Amelia imagined it smelled of lavender, rich and heady, although there was none in sight.

'Amelia.'

Her name was a prayer in his mouth, and she answered in kind. 'Simon.'

'I wanted to talk to you, in private.'

'Yes.' A mute swan swam by, its white feathers marking the pause in conversation.

A frown crossed his forehead. 'Your sister?'

'Is better,' answered Amelia. 'Awake and talking – and talking and talking.'

'Glad to hear it.' Simon smiled and lifted one eyebrow. 'Not actually *hear* it, mind you, but I am glad she is doing well.'

Amelia chuckled. He knew all there was to know about her, and she did not have to explain. Being alone with him was like that. Like finding what she had been searching for all along.

'The other day.' He swallowed. 'After the library.' He pulled on his shirt collar although he wore nothing around his neck. 'This is incredible, isn't it? I've sailed seas. Ordered men to fight. Watched them die. And I cannot express my feelings.'

'Actually, it makes perfect sense.'

'To you.' He quit tugging on his shirt and stared into her eyes. 'Which is why I must say how much you mean to me.'

She inhaled a breath.

He held out a hand as if she was going to interrupt him.

She wasn't.

'I know you are Edgar's widow, and I know you are the Amesbury matriarch now. You are responsible for Edgar's niece and his aunt.'

Well, his niece at any rate.

'But I also know that I care for you more than I have cared for any woman, and yes, I do mean *any*. I cannot describe how I feel, except to say I do not feel complete without you near me. I am always wondering about you, wishing.' He looked at her pointedly. 'You occupy my every thought, Amelia. If you were a witch, I'd suspect you of witchcraft.'

She smiled.

'But despite what your male correspondents might write about you, you are no witch, so I must deal with these feelings of mine. They are new, and you must be patient. I am not accustomed to being vulnerable.'

'Love may make you vulnerable, Simon, but it may also make you strong.' She watched the amber flame in his iris alight on the fact. 'It has the power to make you do things you thought you could not do. Or, in Miss Castlewood's case, things you should not do.'

'Such wisdom.' He touched her chin. 'I admire your brain as much as your heart.'

'I admire you, too.' Her whisper was thick with emotion. 'I have since the first moment we met.'

'You are quicker than I to recognize your feelings. I am envious.'

She chuckled. 'I have more practice with them.'

'Where might I find such a teacher?' He leaned closer.

'Close your eyes, and you'll find out.'

Then his lips were upon hers. They were warm, chasing away the chill of the day and the unknown of the future. What mattered was here and now. This wonderful, mad life. With Simon, she could navigate whatever the world handed her.

So it was as her mother had said all along. It wasn't so much what happened to you in life as who you had beside you when it did. Simon was her person, and if his kiss was any indication, she was his. Amelia relished the thought, looking forward to many happy days, with letters in her post and Simon at her side.

ACKNOWLEDGMENTS

Whenever I start a new book, I'm always amazed at the breadth of knowledge early agony aunts possessed and the authority with which they shared it. From word origins to human origins, agony aunts answered questions both curious and sundry. In this installment of the Lady of Letters series, I dug deeply into the agony column annals to share more of the practical advice given on health, beauty, and parties. I hope you enjoyed the tidbits.

Thank you to Severn House and Victoria Britton for giving me the opportunity to continue a series I love with my whole heart. Thank you also to my agent, Amanda Jain, for championing the series. Many thanks to copy editor Katherine Laidler for your meticulous proofreading. Thank you once again to my dear friend Amy Cecil Holm for reading an early draft of this novel. Your feedback is priceless! Also priceless are readers and reviewers who send or post kind words. They are more appreciated than you know. A very special thank you to reviewer Colleen Cameron, who has supported my work for many years. It has been a joy to connect with you. Thank you to all my friends and family members who encourage me and lift me up, especially the Engberg clan – aka the Love Family. (You know who you are.) Finally, thank you to my daughters, Madeline and Maisie, who are growing up faster than I'd like, and to my husband, Quintin. I hope the next thirty years are as happy as the last!